The Skeleton Rides a Horse

and Other Stories

The Skeleton Rides a Horse

and Other Stories

By Toni L.P. Kelner

(also writing as Leigh Perry)

Introduction
by Dana Cameron and Charlaine Harris

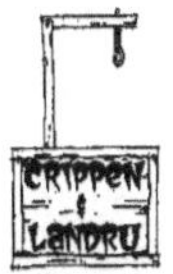

Crippen & Landru Publishers
Cincinnati, Ohio
2024

For information contact:
Crippen & Landru, Publishers
P. O. Box 532057
Cincinnati, OH 45253 USA

Web: www.crippenlandru.com
E-mail: Info@crippenlandru.com
ISBN (softcover): 978-1-936363-86-5
ISBN (clothbound): 978-1-936363-85-8

First Edition: July 2024

10 9 8 7 6 5 4 3 2 1

Table of Contents

Dedication

To the editors who originally published these stories:

Marie Gerules and Margo Power; Carole Nelson Douglas; Jeffrey Marks; Skye Alexander, Kate Flora, and Susan Oleksiw; Linda Landrigan; Janet Hutchings; Bill Crider; Charlaine Harris and Ginjer Buchanan; and Heather Graham.

Introduction

Toni L.P. Kelner's voice as a writer is unmistakable. Her work is immediately recognizable, but her ingenious skill in story-telling, her understanding of what makes a mystery work, and her imaginative twists, turns of phrase, and clue-laying are hallmarks of her talent. Toni takes topics dear to her heart, delves into them, and shows us why she's fascinated by them. And why we should be fascinated, too.

The same qualities that make Toni a great short story writer also make her an excellent editor. She has an unerring sense of where a story goes wrong and where it goes gloriously right.

Toni once described her writing wheelhouse as "worlds within worlds." Though she doesn't write literal locked room mysteries (though she could, and they'd be great), she sets many of her stories in groups set off from the rest of society. Isolated teens, carnies and circus folk, pirates, fandoms, small towns, and unique magical beings populate her stories. Toni looks at these isolated groups with a magnifying glass. In her stories, she reveals the intrigues and politics the larger world never sees—or shouldn't, if all goes well. Since these are crime stories, things seldom go well. Those communities often need to rely on their own to achieve justice.

Despite her cozy settings—especially in the stories set in the South—things aren't always as they seem, or as the characters would have us believe. There's a deep vein of cold-blooded callousness in the killers' motives that may take the reader by surprise—but shouldn't. No group, no setting, no world-within-a-world is free of the darker emotions. Toni's craft ensures that the tone is even and that the perpetrator is always cleverly hidden–yet all the clues are there, if the reader is up to the challenge.

This collection includes every sort of mystery: rifts within genetic families (a curiously distant mother in "Rage Warehouse—Ire Proof" and a renegade daughter in "Nasty") and chosen families (the itinerant entertainers of "Where Does a Herd of Elephants Go?" and "Sleeping with the Plush") make it clear that there's no smooth sailing when it comes to the ties that bind. The consequences of these rifts can be both funny and terrifying.

When the mysteries do take place in the heart of a settled community, it's because the local institutions have had time to see—or hide—all of the secrets of their citizens. A sleazy bar ("Now Hiring Nasty Girlz"), a family-style restaurant ("Kids Today"), the local bowling alley ("Bell, Book, and Candlepin"), and the corner store ("Murchison Solves a Mystery") all have their dark sides: visible, not so visible, and sometimes with a touch of magic.

There are even courtroom dramas, but far from the ordinary lawyers-in-smart-suits fare you might imagine. Toni takes us to unlikely settings, one aboard a pirate ship ("Skull and Cross-Examinations") and one set among outdated high school traditions ("Kangaroo Court").

Finally, there are the mysteries we suspect are closest to Toni's heart: those set in the world of popular culture fandoms ("Security Blanket" and "The Skeleton Rides a Horse"). Cult classics, especially old TV shows and movies, provide a unique set of characters, motives, and methods of concealment, and Toni's delight in creating these worlds is manifest.

That's Toni. Or Leigh. Or whatever name you give her. She's a damn fine writer, and she's funny.

And terrifying.

Dana Cameron
Charlaine Harris
February 2024

Murchison Solves
a Mystery

I am Abram Murchison, and even though I'm not like those detectives on TV, one time I solved a mystery, a real–life mystery without commercials interrupting.

Yes, Murchison the grocer, who is now Murchison the convenience store owner, though it's the same store I opened over forty-five years ago when I came to North Carolina to serve the Jewish community. I was the only one in Raleigh who sold kosher groceries in 1958, and I may be the only one now. Of course, no one keeps kosher these days.

When I first started, I didn't sell anything but kosher foods. As time went on and North Carolina State University across the street got bigger, I added snacks and soft drinks for the students. Pretty soon the things for the students filled more shelves than the kosher groceries. Things don't always end up the way they start.

Like this mystery I solved. I don't notice that it's a mystery when it starts. Even now, I don't know when it started. It didn't start when William first came into my store, because it was almost over by then. And it didn't start when I heard about Slotkin dying, because I saw no mystery in that. The man had cancer for a year when he died. Maybe I have to go all the way back to when Slotkin married Gloria, who was quite a dish, and found out that she didn't want an old–fashioned doctor for a husband, making house calls with a black bag and "How's the back, Murchison?"

Let's say that the mystery started that afternoon when I was stocking shelves. It's Friday afternoon and it's kosher items I'm stocking, so when my son, David, comes in to run the store so I can go to temple, and he's got two friends with him carrying a pizza box, I give him the look my father used to give me. "What's that you've got?"

He gives me the look I used to give my father. "It's a pizza, Pop."

"Of course it's a pizza. You think I thought it was Kentucky Fried Chicken in that box? What's on the pizza?"

"Sausage and pepperoni," one of the boys says.

"Sausage and pepperoni?" I say.

"With extra cheese," the fellow adds. "Would you like a slice?"

I raise my eyebrows at David. "You're going to be eating this pizza? With sausage and pepperoni? And extra cheese."

"It's just a pizza, Pop."

"Just a pizza. Just a sausage and pepperoni pizza with extra cheese. Couldn't you get a shellfish on it? If it had a shellfish on it, it would break every law of kosher I know. You know it's Passover."

"Fine, it's Passover. I won't eat any of the pizza, if that's what you want."

"That's what I want." I turn to finish putting matzo on the shelf, but I'm not so old that I don't hear David mumbling. "What's that you said?"

He says, "I think it's nuts to worry about sausage and pepperoni. What difference does it make?"

"It makes the difference between being kosher and not being kosher, that's the difference it makes."

"You don't keep kosher."

I nod as I put up the last box. "I do at Passover. I don't think it hurts so much to be kosher once a year." This seems reasonable to me, but David doesn't think so.

"What about those?" he says, pointing at the shelf of candy by the register.

"What about them?"

"Easter bunnies?"

"Chocolate is kosher."

"Pop!"

"I sell them, I don't eat them. You think I don't know that not everybody is Jewish?" I turn to David's friend who told me about the extra cheese. "You're not Jewish, are you?"

"No, sir," he said. "I'm Catholic."

"Catholic, that's good. You can eat chocolate Easter bunnies if you want, and sausage and pepperoni, too." Then I remember something. "Isn't it Lent?"

He nodded, then remembered what it was I remembered, that Catholics aren't supposed to eat meat on Fridays during Lent. He hands the pizza box to the third boy.

"You're not Catholic, then?" I say to that boy.

"No, sir. I'm Baptist."

"That's good. You can eat anything, so long as you don't enjoy it."

"Pop!"

"What?"

"You're missing the point!"

"What point am I missing?"

"That this stuff about Lent and keeping kosher is ridiculous."

I hold up one finger. "You don't show disrespect for other people's religion. If your friend doesn't want to eat meat on Fridays, you respect that."

"Fine, I respect that, but what about keeping kosher? Why should I keep kosher one time a year, and not the rest?"

"There's not keeping kosher, and then there's not keeping kosher."

"That doesn't make any sense."

I shrug my shoulders. "Of course it doesn't make sense. It's religion. If it made sense, it wouldn't be religion." He wants to argue with me, but the door to the shop opens then and my old friend Nathaniel Slotkin walks in. "Slotkin, where have you been keeping yourself? Come tell my son the difference between not keeping kosher at Passover and not keeping kosher."

Slotkin just smiles. "Hello Murchison, David."

"Hi, Dr. Slotkin," David says. Then he introduces his friends, the Catholic and the Baptist, which he didn't bother to do for me, but then I'm just his father. Slotkin is a big shot doctor, going all over the world to take hearts and livers out of one person and put them into another. You would think that my knowing this man would impress my son, but nothing impresses my son.

"Dr. Slotkin, you don't keep kosher, do you?" David asks.

"Not anymore," he says, and David looks at me as if to say I-told-you-so. But then Slotkin adds, "Only at Passover," so I give David his I-told-you-so right back.

Slotkin pulls a Diet Coke out of the cooler and a box of matzo off of the shelf, and he puts the exact change on the counter, just like always. "How's the back, Murchison?" he asks.

"About the same," I say. "No better, but no worse. And you?"

"Fine."

I know he's not telling the truth, because everybody knows he's got cancer of the pancreas, which is the worst kind you can get. He's always been a good-looking man, not so much weight on him like I've got, but now he looks like he isn't eating and his color isn't so good. I know he's not telling me the truth, but he knows I know, so we don't need to say anything else. "And Mrs. Slotkin? She's doing well?"

"She's fine."

This time I know he's telling the truth, because Gloria Slotkin is fine so long as she gets what she wants. Which is most of the time. Like when she wanted Slotkin to marry her and when she wanted him to quit his private practice and work at Rex Hospital and when she wanted him to be on the board of directors there and then chairman of the board. She wanted him to be such a great doctor that he wouldn't have time to see patients anymore, so of course she's fine. "Tell her she should stop in some time."

"I'll tell her."

It's another lie, because Gloria would rather have her hair go back to its natural color than to come into my store, but that's all right. I'm waiting for him to ask about Mrs. Murchison, like he usually does, but he doesn't. He just stares into space for a while, long enough that David and his friends lose interest and start talking among themselves. Finally I say, "Is there something wrong?"

He shakes himself a little. "Sorry, I was just thinking about going to the hospital tonight."

"You're feeling ill?" I ask.

"No, it's not me."

"You're seeing patients again? I've been thinking that my back isn't doing so well as I thought it was."

"No, he's not my patient. This is a young fellow whose been working with Patel and me. A research assistant."

"An accident? Or he's fallen ill?"

Slotkin just shakes his head. "He's ill, but that's not why he's in the hospital. He tried to kill himself last night."

"How old is this man?"

"Twenty–seven."

My father always told me that youth is wasted on the young, but it wasn't until I got older that I knew what he meant. "Why would a twenty-seven-year-old do such a thing?"

"He's got pancreatic cancer."

"In pain?" I ask.

"Some," Slotkin admits, "but it's in the early stages, yet. His doctor wants to treat it with chemotherapy and radiation, but he won't let him. He said he's going to try to kill himself again as soon as they let him out of the hospital."

"Just like that?"

"Just like that."

I consider it for a moment. "What about his family? Can't they talk him out of it?"

"He's an orphan, nothing closer than a second cousin."

"No wife? No girlfriend?"

Slotkin shakes his head.

"What about his work? Isn't this project enough for him to live for?"

Slotkin shrugged. "Patel tried that, but he knows we're just getting started. It's going to be years before we perfect the techniques, and he knows he'd never live to see it."

I think of something else. "He's not Catholic then."

"He says he's an agnostic," Slotkin says.

I never had much use for agnostics. An atheist, he's made a decision. An agnostic can't make up his mind.

Then David says, "What's wrong with suicide?"

"What's wrong?" I say. "God gives you life. It's your duty to enjoy it."

"What's the point of living in pain?"

"You think I don't know pain? You think being on my feet twelve hours a day is a constant joy?"

"Come on, Pop, you know what I mean. He's dying anyway."

"Every day since my mother bore me I'm dying."

"Besides," Slotkin says, "with treatment he could be comfortable for a long time. With the research going on in the field, there could be a cure tomorrow. And there's always the chance of remission."

"Sure. Maybe."

"There are miracles in the labs and hospitals everyday. New treatments, drugs, and transplants… We can replace almost every organ in the body now. Give us a few years, and we'll be able to put all new parts on an old chassis. If you could just see some of the things my friend Patel and I have seen."

"Maybe you should see if you can transplant some sense into this boy's head," I say.

"I didn't know you followed my work, Murchison."

"What work? You can transplant sense?"

Before Slotkin can say anything, David says, "He's talking about brain transplants, Pop. That's the project he and Dr. Patel are working on. I read about it." Then, he puts respect in his voice when he says to Slotkin, "Are you really going to try it on humans?"

"Someday, maybe. Right now we're just working with animals."

"So tell me," I say, "when you transplant a brain, does the mind go with it or does it stay with the body?"

"Mind, brain, it's the same thing," David says.

"Why is it two words, if it's the same thing?" I ask him.

"It's the same thing, isn't it, Dr. Slotkin?" David asks.

"I don't know, David. Too soon to tell."

"What about the soul?" the Catholic boy asks, which is an intelligent question, not like my son's.

"I don't know that either," Slotkin says.

I snort and start adding up the receipts. "Who needs to move a brain around? Now if you could transplant me a new back, then you could make some money."

David rolls his eyes, but Slotkin grins and pats me on the shoulder. "There are more things in heaven and earth, Horatio, than are dreamt of in your philosophy."

He leaves, and I call after him, "Tell Mrs. Slotkin not to be a stranger. And quit calling me Horatio."

David gives me a funny look. "He wasn't calling you Horatio, Pop. That's a quote from Shakespeare."

"You think I don't know that? Can't a man make a joke sometime? I read *Macbeth* before you were born."

If this was a TV mystery, the next part would be finding a body with all kinds of clues scattered around, but not in this mystery. All I see is a sealed coffin because about a month later, Slotkin put a gun in his mouth and fired, and no undertaker could do anything with that.

I do see Slotkin's wife, Gloria, at the funeral, looking sad like she should, but my wife said the dress she was wearing cost more money than we get in our store in a month. By me, it looked good, but I don't think it makes her look younger, certainly not as young as the man holding her hand at the funeral.

Slotkin's partner Ravi Patel is there, too, and I want to ask him about that research assistant, but it doesn't seem like a good time. I wonder if there really was a research assistant, or if Slotkin was just talking about somebody else so he could talk about himself, the way people will.

David goes to the funeral, and when we get home, he says, "Pop, I don't understand. I thought Dr. Slotkin didn't believe in suicide."

"What's not to believe? People kill themselves every day."

"You know what I mean."

"I know what you mean, but I don't know why Slotkin killed himself. I thought you would understand, the way you were talking that day."

"I thought so, too," he said softly, "but I don't."

I put my arm around him, which he won't let me do very often anymore, and say things to him in Yiddish. He doesn't know exactly what it is I'm saying, but he knows what I mean.

Even with my not understanding why Slotkin would kill himself, I still don't know it's a mystery. When Mr. Everett comes in to the store a week after the funeral to buy a Coca-Cola and a pack of peanut butter crackers and starts talking like it's a mystery, I don't listen to him.

Of course Mr. Everett doesn't say what he's thinking at first. People from the South never do. First we talk about business, which doesn't take long because he sells fuel oil and not many people buy fuel oil in the spring. Then he asks me how the Mets look this year.

Every year he asks me about the Mets and the Yankees like I just left New York, like I wasn't here when the university was just a place to teach boys how to milk cows faster, and before the Varsity Theater became a McDonald's. Why he thinks I want to go back to New York and all that crime, I don't know, but I just say that I hear they've got a new pitcher.

Then he asks what me what I think about Slotkin.

"What's to think? He had cancer, and he killed himself."

"I didn't think you folks believed in suicide."

I know the folks he means are us Jews. "When a person decides to kill himself, he doesn't go to a rabbi first."

"So you think it was suicide?"

"What else would I think?"

Mr. Everett looks around as if there were somebody else in the store who could hear him. "Murder?"

I snort at this. "And who would want Slotkin dead?"

"Maybe that wife of his. I hear she never gave the man an hour's peace. Always wanting more money."

"And she's going to get it with him dead?"

"Insurance," he says, like it means something. "I hear he had himself a big, fat policy, and now she gets every bit of it."

For a minute I think about it, but then I shake my head. "The paper said Slotkin was alone in the house. Only his fingerprints were on the gun, and he left a note saying the pain was more than he could bear. How can it be murder?"

He says, "You can pay off an awful lot of cops with that much insurance money."

Bribing police I cannot believe, but it makes me think again about Slotkin killing himself, and how it feels wrong somehow. Still, I don't know it's a mystery and another couple of weeks go by. I don't know how these TV detectives figure so much out in an hour. Me, it takes longer.

In June, I meet William. Only I don't know his name at first. I just know that a nice-looking young man a little older than David comes into the store and goes right to the cooler. He reaches for the low-calorie drinks, then reaches again and comes out with a Coke, the one that hasn't changed but now they call classic. He lays the right amount of change on the counter, even though they aren't marked. I put the money in the register, and watch him. He's drinking that Coke like it's the best thing since women. Then he sees me looking.

"Can I get you something else?" I ask, thinking maybe he wants a box of the men's protections I keep behind the counter and is too embarrassed to ask. You get that near the university.

"No, thank you. Sir." The 'sir' he adds after a second, like he isn't used to saying it. Not that any young person is these days.

Some women come in then and I keep busy ringing up and passing the time of day. Still, I watch this young man out of the corner of my eye. He walks around looking at packages, every once in a while reaching out to run his fingers over something. Not just touching the way people do while making up their minds, but caressing it. I wonder if he's a shoplifter maybe.

The young fellow stays until after the women leave, then brings up a dirty magazine. I think this is why he waited, that he didn't want to buy it with so many women there.

That fellow starts coming in regular. At first it's just business, but he's friendly and we start to pass the time of day. He's a polite young man, and we talk quite a bit. His name is William Hughs. He says he had a job, but now he's on medical leave because of cancer. Sometimes I see his hand shake and know he's hurting, but he always smiles.

He's a good boy, but there's something funny about him. The way he laughs, the things he laughs at, they don't seem right for someone his age. Like maybe a man would have to be my age to know that they were funny. One time we were talking about his sickness, and the treatments, and I told him, "William, it's like my mother used to say. 'Cancer, schmancer. As long as you've got your health.'" David told me later it was in bad taste, but William laughed.

Then sometimes he acts like he's a lot younger. One time David asked him if he had heard about the Genesis reunion, and William thought he meant like in the Bible, not the musical group coming to town for a concert.

Always William looks at the store like it's the first time he's seen it, and it's a treat. A couple of times I see him around town looking at everything like that. And the way he looks at women. Like a boy in a candy store.

Things go like this until the summer comes to an end, and he comes in one afternoon when David is in the store. He comes straight to the register, not even getting a Coke first. "Murchison! I mean Mr. Murchison! Have I got news for you!"

"Hello, William. What news have you got?"

"I'm in remission! I got the results back today. My cancer's in remission!"

He thrusts his hand at me to shake, and David pats him on the back. I even give him his Coke on the house, it's such good news. We talk a while, and he says he's thinking about going back to work. David asks him what it is he does, and he says he used to work for Dr. Patel.

"Dr. Ravi Patel?" I say. "Then you must have known my good friend Slotkin."

William nods, but he looks kind of funny. I want to hit myself for being such a fool, asking about a man who killed himself over cancer when this boy has cancer. So I give him another Coke to change the subject.

He drinks it down, then he's off. He's got a date with the receptionist from his doctor's office, and David winks at him and tells him not to do anything he wouldn't do.

After a while I leave David in charge and go home to watch wrestling. Only I can't keep my mind on the wrestlers, not even the lady wrestlers in their skimpy clothes.

While I'm looking at TV, finally I realize that William is the research assistant Slotkin told me about all those months ago, the one who was going to kill himself because of cancer. Only William didn't kill himself. Slotkin did. Slotkin, a man who talked about what a terrible waste that would be.

Then William starts coming into the store. He's got cancer, but he looks at life like it's God's gift. Which it is, but how many of us remember that?

These two men, one young who wants to die and one old who wants to live, and they both work with Dr. Patel, a man who knows how to transplant parts of the body. What had Slotkin said? That soon they would be able to put all new parts on an old chassis.

I remember how it was when I was young, how everything smelled and tasted and looked. And I think of William with his date, probably doing what young men and women have always wanted to do but weren't allowed to do in mine and Slotkin's day.

Then I think about how it felt not to have the responsibilities I have now, my wife and my son. For a second, I think I would like it that way. Then I look at my wife, who's fallen asleep because she only watches wrestling because I want to. And I remember David not eating sausage and pepperoni pizza because I don't want him to, and I know that he's a good boy, kosher or not. Them I would not give up, not even for youth.

But if my wife was a Gloria Slotkin, and I didn't have a son… Maybe then I would trade, even with the cancer. In a young body to enjoy what time remained, who would care if there was a little pain thrown into the bargain?

Now I know there's a mystery, and I have part of the answer, but not all. I don't sleep much that night, because I am thinking of how I will find out the answer I need.

The next day, William comes in a little before lunchtime, looking tired. I don't think he slept much either, and David snickers about it. Then I send him back to straighten up the storeroom.

William gets his Coke and pays for it, exact change like always.

"William," I say, "have you told Dr. Patel about your good news?"

He looks a little uncomfortable, but he nods.

"He must have been glad to hear it. It's important research he is doing, and I know he can use your help."

"I'm not sure I'll be going back to work with him."

"No? I thought it would be quite an opportunity for a young man. Slotkin and I used to talk about this research, about transplanting brains from one body to another."

Now he won't meet my eyes, and he looks at his watch like he's got an appointment to rush off to.

"There's something I've been wondering about," I say, "and I would like to hear what you think."

Again he looks at his watch. "I really need to get going."

"Stay a minute, make an old man happy. You've got plenty of time."

He stays, but he isn't standing like a young man anymore.

I say, "I know Dr. Patel can't try his transplants on humans, because there are all kinds of laws and rules to stop him. But suppose he knows a young man named Mr. Smith and an old man named Mr. Jones, and they want to switch the brain of Mr. Smith into the body of Mr. Jones, and vice versa."

William is looking at me closely.

I go on. "Now suppose Mr. Smith, who is in Mr. Jones's body, is found dead. It looks like suicide—maybe it is suicide. Who is dead, Mr. Jones or Mr. Smith?"

"Smith," William says, without hesitating.

"Would you think that Mr. Smith really killed himself?"

"Abram!" William says, using my first name, which he had never used before. "You don't think I'd—" He stops himself. A couple of seconds later, he says, "I'd think he killed himself, but not with the gun."

"Then how did he kill himself?"

"Suppose that both Smith and Jones have cancer, and they're both dying from it."

"Then why would they do this transplant?"

"Because they're both in a lot of pain, and they want to die. The transplant is experimental, and they don't really think it will work. They think that they're going to die on the operating table."

"Both of them think this?"

William nods.

"Then why not both use a gun?"

"Jones can't. He's Jewish, and it would be a serious offense to God."

"What about Mr. Smith?"

William halfway smiles. "He's agnostic, so he doesn't think it's a sin, but he's not sure."

"So what happens?"

"Patel performs the transplant, and Smith dies during the operation."

"In Mr. Jones's body?"

"Yes. Then Patel fakes the suicide, just like he, Smith, and Jones planned beforehand."

"What about Mr. Jones?"

"He wakes up in Smith's body. Somehow, the operation worked. He wouldn't have thought it possible, but it worked."

"And?"

"And he's got time to himself for the first time in years. The cancer is still there, but it's not so bad that he can't enjoy himself. He expects to have six months, maybe a year. It's enough."

I nod. "That's a good answer. You're a smart young man."

But William didn't look any happier. "Can I ask you a question? It's something I just realized. What if the cancer in Smith's body goes into remission?"

"Then Mr. Jones gets more than six months to a year," I say. "Maybe a whole lifetime."

"Shouldn't that life have been Smith's? Has Jones cheated him out of it? Isn't that the same thing as murder?"

I take a long time to think about this, because it's something I hadn't thought about before. "Hasn't Mr. Smith tried to kill himself before?"

"Yes."

"So he's not likely to change his mind. He's prepared to die."

"That's what Jones believes."

I think some more, and William fidgets like young men will. "I hear that remission is a funny thing. Nobody knows when it will happen."

"That's true."

"But I've heard that sometimes it happens when the person really wants to live. Mind over body, is how I understand it."

William nods slowly.

"And when this brain was transplanted, the mind came with it. This is what my son tells me."

He keeps nodding.

"Then it seems to me that since Mr. Smith did not want to live, if he had stayed in the body he would have died in it. There would have been no remission. He has lost nothing that he hadn't already lost." I shrug. "I'm not an educated man, so I don't know what the law books or the Talmud would say, but I don't think it was murder."

Neither of us says anything for a long time, then William takes a deep, deep breath. "Thank you," he says.

I just nod. David comes from out back and says, "William, are you still here? Pop will talk your ear off if you're not careful."

"I was just leaving," William says.

"Wait," I say, and I pull a nice babka off of the shelf and hand it to him. He just grins, puts the correct change on the counter, and leaves.

"I didn't know he was Jewish," David says.

I just shrug, and say, "Are you hungry? It's time for lunch."

"You want me to go get us something?"

"I thought maybe a pizza from down the street."

"Sure. What do you want on it?"

"How about sausage and pepperoni?"

He just looks at me. "I thought you said—"

"It's just a pizza. Besides, Yom Kippur is the week after next, and what good is a day of atonement if you don't have anything to atone for?"

David grins, and starts out the door.

"Don't forget the extra cheese!" I call after him.

That's all there is to the mystery I solve. It's not like on TV. I don't tell anyone, and things go on the same. William still comes in to talk. He decides not to be a research assistant anymore, and starts classes at the university. He wants to be a doctor.

That's all there is, except some days, when no one else is in the store, William asks me, "How's the back, Murchison?"

Afterword

I don't always remember where I got the idea for a story, but I vividly remember the starting point for "Murchison Solves a Mystery." I was living in Charlotte, North Carolina, and my father and I were on the way to meet my mother at the hospital. (Don't worry—she was a nurse, not a patient.) After parking, we walked past a reserved parking place for Dr. Slotkin, and for some reason the name got stuck in my head. I started imagining a conversation with Dr. Slotkin and who would be talking to him. So, as with many of my stories, it started with a character.

The bit about a Catholic, and a Jew, and a Baptist eating a sausage and pepperoni pizza on a Friday during Lent? That happened to me, only it was at Pizzeria Regina in Boston's North End. I still eat their pizza regularly.

Where Does a Herd
of Elephants Go?

"Which one was it?" I asked, looking at the four elephants grazing in the paddock.

"That one," Deputy Sweeney said, pointing.

"Hermia?" I said. "That is Hermia, isn't it?"

Crabby, the handler who'd worked with my father, spat and said, "Of course that's Hermia, you stupid townie. But she didn't do it."

I wanted to believe him, just like I wanted to believe that Pop was still alive. How could he have been trampled by one of his own elephants? He'd loved them nearly as much as he'd loved me, and knew them better. There was no way he could have made the kind of mistake that would have gotten him killed.

But here I was at Fox's Old-Fashioned Circus while Pop's body was in the tiny North Carolina town's morgue. "You're sure it was Hermia?"

"We found her next to your father's body, May," said Chris Fox, the show owner. "There was blood all over her feet."

At Deputy Sweeney's firm suggestion, I'd forgone viewing Pop's body since Crabby had already made the formal identification. Sweeney had danced around it the way only a Southerner can, but I knew Hermia must have had a lot more than blood on her feet.

"Why do elephants have round, flat feet?" I said.

"I beg your pardon?" Fox said.

"It's an elephant joke. Pop gave me a book of them one year for my birthday. Why do elephants have round, flat feet?" None of the others answered, so I answered myself. "To walk on lily pads."

No doubt they all thought I was nuts, or maybe just grief-stricken. In addition to Sweeney, Fox, and Crabby, there was Mr. Waterson, who owned the lot where the show was set up, and Madame Cassandra. It was Cassie who put her arm around me, but I didn't respond. It wasn't that I didn't appreciate the gesture, especially when she must have been hurting, too, but I just couldn't tear my eyes away from the girls.

I was surprised they hadn't hobbled Hermia and staked her, but the only ones who would have known to do that were Crabby and Pop; obviously Crabby was in no mood to help. So they were relying on a member of the big-top crew to watch and make sure she didn't go rogue.

Not that it looked likely, as the girls blithely scratched up dirt with their feet and used their trunks to toss it onto their backs to keep flies away.

In traditional circus lingo, elephants are called bulls, even though most circus elephants are female, but Pop called them his girls, or, if he was talking with me, his other girls. Maybe I should have been jealous, but I loved them, too, and waited impatiently for the rare visits my mother allowed so I could see them again. There was imperious Titania, the leader of the small herd; flirty and mischievous Juliet, who would toss hay at people when they walked by if they didn't stop to say hello; loving Portia, who cuddled as much as an elephant can cuddle; and docile Hermia, who never seemed bothered by the one-night stands, long road trips, and horrible weather a circus elephant lives with.

Like many elephant men, Pop supplemented his paycheck by giving elephant rides, and Hermia was the one he always used. He trusted her not to move too quickly and scare the kids or run off with them on her back, because her temperament was as even as her pace. What could have happened?

I asked the one person left who should know. "Crabby, has Hermia been sick? Did that abscessed tooth come back?" Pop always doctored the elephants himself, saying that the vets in the small towns where the show played wouldn't have the first idea of how to help his girls. All I could think of was that he'd accidentally hurt her, and she lost control. It only takes a second to get hurt when you're dealing with something as big as an elephant.

"Does she look sick? Even you should be able to tell that she's healthy as a horse—you can see it by looking at her. I don't care what this townie cop says—she didn't kill Leo! I was in my camper all night. I'd have heard if she'd gone after him."

Unless he was drunk again. It was early afternoon, but his breath was already enough to make me high. No doubt he'd been mourning Pop in his own way. Crabby had been with him since before I was born, and he loved the elephants nearly as much as Pop had.

Deputy Sweeney sounded apologetic as he said, "The injuries were consistent with trampling, and none of the other elephants had any blood on their feet. It had to be Hermia."

"I know that elephant better than I know myself," Crabby said. "She wouldn't do it. If you kill her, I'll—"

"Kill her?" I said. "Who said anything about killing her?"

Deputy Sweeney looked uncomfortable. "I'm sorry, but I thought you understood that we'd have to destroy the elephant. It's town law."

"You have a law about elephants?" I said in disbelief.

Sweeney colored slightly. "No, ma'am. The law was written for dogs, but it's been applied to cougars, snakes, and so on. This is the first time anybody here was killed by an elephant."

"What are you going to do?" Crabby demanded. "Electrocute her? Poison? They hanged an elephant once, you know."

"Actually, we're still researching the most humane method. The chief has been in contact with the state zoo at Asheboro."

Crabby's face was dark red, and his fists clenched. "She didn't do it!" he said again, sputtering in his indignation. Then he glared at me and said, "Your father would never have let anybody hurt one of the girls."

"But Pop's not here," I said evenly.

Crabby looked over at Hermia again, and stumbled away, muttering about townies. I knew he was going back to his drinking, but for once, I didn't blame him.

"Y'all aren't going to do it on my land, are you?" Waterson asked, looking a little sick. "I'd never have asked you people here if I'd known this was going to happen. I just wanted a little publicity for the antique fair."

Fox went into action, still as smooth as he'd ever been as ringmaster. "I assure you, Mr. Waterson, there's no way to predict an incident like this. Mr. Solano knew the risks, and he was a careful man, but there's no guarantee when working with wild animals. Though elephants look friendly, they are at heart creatures of the veldt." With Fox laying it on so thick, I figured he must want to book the lot again next season.

"Should we cancel tonight's show?" Waterson asked.

Fox looked shocked. "Never! That's the last thing Leo Solano would have wanted. Like all circus people, 'The show must go on' was the creed he lived by. To disappoint the children who've been dreaming of tonight's show would be an insult to his memory."

I heard a tiny snort from Cassie, and turned to see the twinkle in her eye. I wanted to laugh, too, thinking of how Pop would have reacted to Fox's spiel. Then I suddenly wanted to cry.

As always, Cassie knew what I was feeling. She said, "Gentlemen, if you'll excuse us, there's things May needs to attend to."

"Of course," Mr. Fox said. "May, later this afternoon, we should meet and discuss your plans for the elephants. Other than Hermia, of course."

"Oh, right." How could I have forgotten that I was going to have to make arrangements for the girls?

"Later," Cassie said firmly, and pulled me toward her trailer, with its ruffled curtains and shiny exterior. The inside was just as pristine, everything as neatly arranged as a pocket sewing kit. On a shelf over the couch were the crystal ball and tarot cards Cassie used to make her living before taking over the ticket booth. Some people still called her Madame Cassandra, but these days she preferred Cassie.

"Sit," she said, pushing me toward the couch. Then she conjured up a mug of hot coffee with two sugars and put it into my hand. If I hadn't lifted it to my lips, she'd probably have done that for me, too.

"It will get better, May," she said.

I nodded, knowing she was right, even if it didn't feel that way. "How about you? I mean, you and Pop were… You two were very close."

"We were lovers, sugar. This is 1998. You can say it out loud."

I smiled sheepishly. "Sorry."

"Anyway, I'm doing all right." She reached over and touched my hand. "May, I meant to tell you about Leo myself, but Fox had the phone tied up. I'm sorry you had to hear about it from a stranger."

"It's okay, Cassie. Deputy Sweeney was very kind." Not only had he broken the news to me as gently as possible, but he'd picked me up at the nearest airport and brought me to town.

"Good. He seems pretty nice, for a townie. Did Fox tell you about the memorial service?"

I shook my head.

"We were planning a little something to honor Leo tonight. If you don't mind, that is."

"Of course I don't mind." I'd be taking his body back to Massachusetts, but of course the people from the show wouldn't be able to attend a funeral up there. This way, they'd have a chance to say good-bye. "That's just what Pop would have wanted."

"I think so, too." She paused. "Does your mother know?"

"I called her as soon as I heard. She said she'd tell Gram and Papa." Pop's parents had never liked him being in the circus. Neither had Mom—that's why they'd divorced. I suspected the three of them had wagged their heads over Pop not heeding their warnings all those years ago, but even they couldn't have guessed that he'd end up this way. "Cassie, how did it happen?"

"Sugar, you know as much as I do. Crabby came out of his camper to take a leak late last night, and saw Hermia messing with something on the ground. He went to see what it was, and once he realized it was Leo, he let out a yell that woke the whole lot up. By the time I got there, he had his arms around your father, blubbering like a baby. Crabby has his faults, but he loved Leo."

"I know." Despite Crabby's personality and lack of hygiene, he was devoted to Pop and the girls. In fact, they were apparently the only ones he cared about. He had little use for the rest of the circus people, and none at all for me or any other townie.

"Anyway, we called the police, and they called you. That's all there is."

I wasn't sure if I had the right to ask the next question, but I couldn't help myself. "Have you consulted the crystal?" I didn't know if it was because of all the years she'd been a fortune-teller or from something inborn, but Cassie did seem to know things she had no other way of knowing.

"You know I don't call on the departed, sugar. Leo is gone—there's nothing we can do to bring him back."

"I don't mean that. I mean, have you tried to find out more about what happened?"

She looked at me as searchingly as she did the crystal. "You don't think Hermia did it?"

"No. I mean, yes, I guess I do, but there must have been some reason. You know how Hermia is. Something must have spooked her or…." She was still looking at me. "I just want to know why."

"People die, May. There isn't always a reason."

But she was reaching behind me for the crystal as she spoke, and she held it out in front of her. Fortune-tellers on television have elaborate pedestals for their crystals, but Cassie prefers holding the ball herself.

I stayed quiet as she stared into it, her brow slightly furrowed. Then she sniffed several times. A moment later, she shook herself all over and put the crystal back on the shelf.

"What did you see?"

"Not much," she admitted. "It was dark last night. New moon. But I smelled something."

"The elephants?" They do have a pungent smell, but I loved it, just as Pop had. Even the dung isn't bad when you get used to it.

She shook her head. "Not that. It was marijuana."

"Pop didn't smoke pot, did he?"

"Not that I ever saw, but that's all I got—the smell of pot. Most likely I smelled some when we found Leo last night, but didn't notice it until now."

Cassie never claimed to have any special powers. She said the crystal was just a way to focus her thoughts, and that her tarot readings depended more on the body language of the customer than on which cards she laid out on the table. Whatever it was, she was right more often than not.

"Maybe Pop caught somebody getting high and trying to bother the girls," I speculated. "Or maybe somebody thought it would be funny to give some to the girls." I'd met people who thought it was funny to get a dog stoned. Why not an elephant?

She shrugged her shoulders.

I finished the last of my coffee. "I suppose I better go on over to Pop's trailer and start sorting. And I've got to decide what to do with the girls."

"Don't rush yourself, May. You've had that long flight down from Boston, and there's the memorial service tonight. No matter what Fox says, there'll be time to make up your mind tomorrow. Go for a walk, take some time to think. Check out the antique fair—they've got some nice things."

"Maybe you're right," I said noncommittally, meaning to get to work anyway, but once I gave her a quick hug and went outside, my feet led me away from Pop's trailer almost of their own accord.

I spent the next hour or so wandering through the outdoor antique fair. I didn't know if the circus had helped drum up business or not, but there were plenty of people out there, enough that I had to concentrate on not running into anybody. I didn't have any room left to brood about Pop.

I'd stopped to look at a display of brightly colored, iridescent dishes, wondering if Mom would like one of them, when I saw a whole shelf full of elephants. There were china and onyx figurines, brass ashtrays with elephants dancing around the edge, an umbrella with an elephant for a handle, lacquered boxes with designs of elephants on the lid, and right in the middle, a porcelain circus elephant with a bright red plume. My first thought was that Pop would love them. My second was to remember.

"Damn, I'm sorry," a voice said.

I turned and recognized Mr. Waterson. He started grabbing elephants and shoving them into a box. "I shouldn't have left these out, under the circumstances."

"Don't worry about it," I said. "Pop loved elephant stuff. If he could have, he'd have bought every piece he saw." Pop started giving me elephants the day I was born, much to Mom's dismay.

He stopped, not sure if he should keep putting pieces away or if he should return them to the shelf. So I reached inside and pulled out the circus statue and placed it back in front.

"Your father was here yesterday, as a matter of fact," Waterson said. "He mentioned that he might come back to get that one for his daughter. I guess that's you."

I nodded. "It's a nice one."

He picked it up, looked at it for a second, then pushed it at me. "Here, take it."

"No, I couldn't."

"I insist. I feel responsible for what happened. After all, I arranged for the circus to come here."

Looking at his face, I relented. It would make him feel better, and the fact that Pop had wanted it for me meant something. "Thank you."

"It's the least I can do."

A woman came over then to ask about an umbrella stand she'd seen the day before, and I used that as an excuse to leave. Cassie had been right about my needing a break, but I really did have to start taking care of Pop's business.

There were more people out and about on the circus lot, performers rehearsing, animal handlers cleaning out pens and cages, concessionaires making sure they had plenty of popcorn, and workmen toting equipment in all directions. This time I didn't stop to look at the elephants, just went straight to Pop's trailer. Deputy Sweeney had given me the key they'd found in Pop's pocket, and since nobody had been inside since they found him, everything was just the way Pop had left it. In other words, the place was a mess.

One corner of the living room was filled with a pile of harnesses waiting to be mended, and another was stacked high with magazines, books, circus programs, and yellowing newspaper articles about elephants. The coffee table was covered with files and antiseptics for taking care of the girls' nails, and the kitchen counter was piled with bottles of the concoctions Pop used to supplement their diet. Pop lived with the elephants. He only slept in the trailer. And with Cassie around, he didn't always do that. I wasn't looking forward to going through it all.

First things first, I decided, which meant the girls' food. Elephants go through roughly a hundred pounds of feed at day, not counting peanuts, so I needed to make sure there was enough on hand to keep them satisfied until I decided what I was going to do with them. Fortunately, Pop had always been meticulous about keeping supplies on hand. I found his ledger in the kitchen drawer, and ran my finger down the rows until I saw that he'd just bought hay, fruit, and vegetables two days before, and a load of timothy the day after that. That should hold them a while.

I closed the ledger and was putting it back in the drawer when an envelope slipped out. Inside, I found two hundred dollars, which surprised me. Pop didn't like to keep cash on hand. A drifter had joined the show a few years back, and stayed just long enough to find out where everybody kept their money. Then he robbed them during a matinee. That's when Pop got an ATM card and started paying for everything with checks.

I started to slide the money back into the envelope, but I thought I smelled something. I held a twenty to my nose and inhaled deeply. Marijuana.

Maybe Pop had started smoking pot, no matter what Cassie thought. Naturally, he'd want cash to pay his dealer. That could even explain his death. A stoned elephant handler was an accident waiting to happen. It made more sense than anything else I'd thought of, but knowing Pop, it didn't make any sense at all. Even though I'd never seen him smoke, on those rare occasions when he'd drunk more than he should have, he knew to stay away from the girls. Why would he start smoking now, and then break his own rule by going around the girls while high?

I briefly considered calling Deputy Sweeney to see if they'd found any signs of marijuana on Pop, but decided it wasn't something I wanted to ask a stranger. Maybe I could talk to Crabby later. He should know, and he might be convinced to tell me.

I put the money and ledger away, and spent the rest of the afternoon going through the trailer, filling four garbage bags with the trash nobody could possibly want. I found a box for the things I thought Crabby could use, another for keepsakes for Cassie, and a third for things I wanted to take home for myself, including the circus elephant statue Waterson had given me. That still left an enormous amount of elephant harnesses, medicine, and assorted stuff, but I decided that I could include it when I found somebody to take in the girls.

That's how I tried to think of it, like I was putting them up for adoption rather than selling them, but mostly, I worried about them. Fox would want them for the rest of the season, of course. What was a circus without elephants? Large parts of the show, especially the opening and closing spectacles, were designed with them in mind. What I didn't know was whether he'd want to buy them or just lease them. If I had to sell them to somebody else, would I be able to keep them together? Titania was used to being in charge—what would happen if I had to sell her to a show with another boss elephant? How could I be sure that the new owner would care for them properly?

My last Christmas gift to Pop had been a book about an elephant named Modoc. This one man had handled her, but then moved on to another circus or something. Years later, he found her in dreadful shape from being mistreated. I couldn't bear the thought of that happening to the girls.

Was there some way I could get them to Massachusetts? Obviously I couldn't afford to keep them myself, much as I wanted to. Marketing pays well, but not that well, though it might have been worth going into debt just to see my mother's face if I showed up with them. Still, there were zoos nearby, and at least I'd be able to see them once in a while. Of course, it would cost a fortune to transport them, even if I found someplace. Besides, they were happy in the circus. Would they like living in a zoo?

Then there was Crabby to think about. What would happen to him? Though he was wonderful with the girls, he wasn't personable or completely reliable when it came to working hours. Pop himself had paid him, not Fox, so I didn't know if he even had a job anymore. Or if he could get another one.

And I kept worrying about Hermia. I just couldn't be angry at her. No matter what had happened, I didn't believe she meant to hurt Pop. None of the elephants had ever hurt him, not on purpose anyway. True, Titania had gotten in a snit once because Pop gave her stale hay, and knocked him over, but that was different—she'd only used a fraction of her strength. It had to have been some sort of accident, no matter what the police thought, and it didn't seem right that Hermia had to die, too.

At least Pop was going to get a funeral and a memorial service. The best poor Hermia would get was a quick death. I didn't know what would happen to her then. I remembered Pop telling me about a so-called elephant man who'd put down an elephant who'd gotten too old to perform, then butchered her, selling her head to be put on somebody's wall, her hide to make boots, and her body for meat. Pop said he'd have ground her tusks for an aphrodisiac and made her feet into umbrella stands if he could have gotten away with it. The whole idea sickened me.

I was nearly in tears when I heard a tap on the door, and Cassie stepped in, her arms full of paper bags. "Don't just sit there," she said. "Take something before I drop it!"

Whatever she was carrying smelled wonderful, and I realized I hadn't eaten since that bagel on the plane. I didn't know whether it was just luck or something else that brought Cassie to me just then, but I was happy to join her in an enormous meal of pulled–pork barbecue, hush puppies, cole slaw, and syrupy iced tea. After we ate, I tried to get her advice for what I should do about Crabby and the girls, but she kept telling me that everything would be clearer in the morning. Then she'd tell me another hilarious story about Pop or one of his terrible elephant jokes, like why elephants have trunks and how do you make an elephant float. I'd heard them all before, but maybe she'd spiked the iced tea, because I laughed so hard I forgot to worry.

I realized later that Cassie must have gotten a replacement at the ticket booth so she could be with me, because we talked right through the night's show, hardly noticing the music and distant applause. I hadn't wanted to go to the show anyway. Seeing the girls go through their routine without Pop would have upset me, and I wasn't sure if it would bother me more to see Hermia in the act or to know she was wondering why she'd been left out.

About the time the townies were heading for their houses, Cassie told me to get ready for the memorial service. I'd left my suitcase at her trailer, so we went over there to change. She wouldn't let me put on the dress I'd brought, because she said it would be too formal. Instead I wore a pair of khakis and a white blouse, while she wore one of the vivid caftans she liked.

Mr. Fox had said we'd be gathering in the main tent, and when we stepped inside, I saw men pulling chairs from the grandstand seats to arrange them in the center ring. I had to grin. Like most circus folks, Pop had a thing for the center ring. What better place to say good-bye to him?

It looked like everybody from the show was there: performers, animal trainers, concessionaires, even the kitchen crew. As Cassie had warned me, people were wearing everything from their costumes to blue jeans to shorts and T-shirts. Deputy Sweeney had come, and Mr. Waterson was there, too, looking uncomfortable and overdressed in a black suit. The only one I didn't see was Crabby. I'd have to ask Cassie if we should check on him later.

Fox got things started, and I have to admit he did a nice job. Sure, he made it sound like Pop had been a cross between Gunther Gebel-Williams, Gandhi, and Ozzie Nelson, but as far as I was concerned, he had been. Fox even had a handful of telegrams from other elephant men, including Gebel-Williams and the legendary Woodcock family. There were plenty of tears, probably more than there'd be at Pop's funeral, especially when Cassie spoke about him. Pop would have been proud.

One of the clowns was eulogizing Pop when there was a commotion from the side entrance to the tent. It was Crabby, and the girls were walking behind him, trunk to tail. Seeing the surprised faces, he shouted, "They deserve to be here, damn it!" The man who'd been left to watch them was following, looking helpless. Which he was, really. Like Pop always said, "Where does a herd of elephants go? Wherever they want."

This being a circus, people might have accepted the tribute the way Crabby meant it if he hadn't brought Hermia, too. There was dead silence when we saw her, and everybody stared as she came toward us. For the first time since I'd known her, she looked menacing. Then the whole line stopped, with Titania in front just a few yards from us.

In a determinedly calm voice, Deputy Sweeney said, "Sir, I think you should take the elephants back to their paddock."

"Why? Are you going to kill all of them?" Crabby was crying so hard I didn't know how he could see, and he stumbled over his own feet. Titania, sensing the tension in the air, trumpeted loudly, and a couple of people started to edge toward the other entrance. "They won't hurt you! They wouldn't hurt anybody!" Crabby sobbed.

Normally, he was right, but the situation was anything but normal. All of the girls were showing signs of nervousness, and I was afraid someone would panic and run, which would only make things worse. Crabby was leaning up against one of Titania's front legs, barely able to stay upright.

I carefully stood up, and started walking toward Titania with deliberate steps. A couple of hands grabbed at my sleeve, and I heard Deputy Sweeney say something, but I ignored them all. My attention was on the boss elephant.

Despite the myth, elephants do forget, but their memories are as good as the average human's, so I thought Titania would remember me. Whether she'd follow my orders was another question. Pop had taught me that the best way to approach an elephant you're not sure of is from the left rear, so I walked past Titania, making sure to stay out of trunk range.

Watching to see how she was going to react, I moved closer to her. When she didn't move, I got close enough to slap her on the shoulder, letting her know I was there. Still no reaction, so I got closer still and patted her on the back of her ear, her favorite place for attention. She seemed to relax a bit.

Crabby was still leaning against her, holding the bull hook. Pop never used the hook much, preferring to use his voice, but I knew I'd feel better if I had something in my hand. All I had to do was convince Crabby to give it to me. I said, "It's okay, Crabby. They've paid their respects—it's time for them to go to bed. I'm not going to let anybody hurt them."

He didn't hand me the bull hook, but when I reached for it, he didn't fight me.

Feeling a little more confident, I said, "Titania! Turn."

Titania looked at me. I'd never given her orders without Pop there to back me up, so she wasn't sure if I had any authority over her or not.

I used the hook to tug at her leg. "Come on, lady. Turn." Elephants can move quickly, but most times, they don't. I had endless seconds to wait until she finally started turning and heading back the way she came.

I had to use the hook to get Juliet and Portia going, too, but Hermia was perfectly willing to follow along. I stayed with them, moving back and forth along the line to make sure they stayed together until we reached the paddock. Once each one filed inside, I carefully closed the gate behind them. Later on, they'd need to be hobbled in the menagerie tent for the night, but the paddock would keep them contained for the time being.

Then I took a breath, inhaling the scent of elephant and feeling a little like I'd been drinking with Crabby. At that moment, I knew exactly why Pop had wanted to spend his life with elephants.

Deputy Sweeney must have been following, because he was suddenly there. "Are you all right?"

All I could do is nod.

"Ms. Solano, I've never seen anything like that. You could have been killed."

I had been as scared as I'd ever been in my life, but no elephant handler likes to admit that she's afraid of her own elephants, so I said, "I've known these elephants since I was a little girl. All they need is a strong hand, and they'll do just what they're told. Hermia doesn't even need that—she'll follow anybody."

That's when it struck me, and the buzz from handling the girls melted away. Hermia really would follow almost anybody. "Deputy, what if somebody murdered my father, maybe drugged him or shot him or hit him with something. Then he led Hermia back and forth over the body. Wouldn't that make it look like she'd killed him?"

He shook his head. "No, ma'am. There were no drugs in your father's system, and the coroner couldn't find any injuries that aren't consistent with an elephant's foot."

I looked over at the girls' feet. There's nothing to compare with an elephant's foot, in size or shape. Except another elephant's foot, of course. That's when I figured out how Pop had been killed, and from that, it was easy to guess who had done it.

By now, most of the other people from the tent were gathered around. Fox was trying to soothe Mr. Waterson, probably still worried about next season. I pointed at them. "He did it! He killed my father!"

Fox just looked surprised, but Waterson went white as a sheet and jerked into a run. Before I could say anything, I heard Cassie yell, "Hey, rube!" That's the traditional circus cry for help, and Waterson didn't get a dozen yards away before he was dragged back by a trapeze catcher and a concessionaire.

"Ms. Solano, would you care to explain that?" Deputy Sweeney said, using the same careful tone he had with Crabby.

"He used an elephant–foot umbrella stand to either kill Pop or knock him out, and then got Hermia to trample the body. Search his store, and I'll bet you'll find it. They used to be popular, but you only find them in antique stores now."

"She's crazy," Waterson sputtered. "I sold that stand yesterday."

"Prove it!" I snapped.

"Ma'am, he doesn't have to prove anything. We do. Why would he have killed your father?"

Crabby was standing nearby, looking dumbfounded. "Crabby," I said, "was Pop selling Waterson elephant dung?"

"Yeah. He said he wanted it for fertilizer."

"That's right. For fertilizing marijuana," I said. That's why the money in Pop's ledger had smelled of it.

"Sweeney, you're not going to believe this old drunk, are you?" Waterson said.

But Sweeney was looking intrigued. "The fact is, there's been rumors that somebody around here has been shipping out a lot of weed, but we haven't been able to pin down who it was. Waterson, you don't mind if we search your land, do you?"

Waterson slumped in the arms of the men holding him.

I said, "I bet Pop figured out what you were using the fertilizer for, and told you he wouldn't sell you any more."

"I was afraid he'd tell the police," Waterson said. "I'd have lost everything—the DEA could have taken the land, my house. This land's been in my family for generations. I had to keep him quiet."

That's when I saw red. Pop had died because of a few worthless acres of dirt? If I'd been Titania, I'd have trumpeted and charged at him. "Do you really think Pop gave a damn about your little pot patch?" I said in as scathing a tone as I could manage. "No offense, Deputy, but Pop wouldn't have wasted a dime to call you. All he wanted was to stay out of it." I gave Waterson a moment to realize that he'd destroyed himself. Then I said, "Only a townie would be that stupid."

***

I expected to have to testify, but a plea bargain preempted the trial. In return for the names of his distributors, Waterson pleaded guilty and avoided the death penalty. That was good enough for me. But I swear, if Hermia had been put to death before we found out that Waterson was guilty, I'd have done everything I could to make sure he followed her to the grave.

As for the girls, all four of them are still with Fox's Old–Fashioned Circus, being looked after by Crabby and doing fine. I'm there to make sure they stay that way. Mom said I was crazy to waste a college education and that I was too old to run away to the circus, but she finally resigned herself to the fact that I'm Pop's daughter. She even promised to come see the show when we get closer to Massachusetts.

Of course, Cassie had known all along that I was going to stay. I asked her if it was the cards or the crystal, but she said it was nothing more mystical than the expression on my face when I looked at the elephants.

It's not much of a joke, but do you know why the marketing director joined the circus? Because she liked working for peanuts.

Afterword

When I heard Carole Nelson Douglas was editing an anthology of animal detective stories, I pitched an elephant mystery without the first idea of what I was going to write. Fortunately I'd read a fair amount about circuses and elephants over the years, including *I Love You Honey, But the Season's Over* by Connie Clausen; *Modoc: The True Story of the Greatest Elephant That Ever Lived* by Ralph Helfer; and *One Hundred and One Elephant Jokes* by Robert Blake. In addition to the elephant jokes, I learned that elephant dung really is excellent fertilizer. I named my protagonist May because circus seasons traditionally start on May 1, and a new performer or backlot worker is known as a First of May.

Security Blanket

Living through a science fiction convention is incredibly intense. In less than forty-eight hours, from Friday evening to Sunday afternoon, you can experience everything in fast-forward: friendship, romance, rivalry, hatred.

In my case, I went from admiring Pinky, to being embarrassed by him, to disliking him, to mourning him, to solving his murder.

***

Naturally Pinky saw the situation before anybody else. He moved to intercept even as he used his walkie-talkie to alert me. "Regina, we have a toucher—repeat, a toucher—moving in on Masters. Older female, blue sweatshirt, white hair."

I buzzed the rest of the available redshirts, but though we immediately headed in that direction, the room was filled with fans hoping to catch a glimpse of someone famous. By the time Andi, Donna, Elliot, and I made our way through, Pinky had blocked the toucher's access to her goal: the guest of honor, William Masters, who'd played the recurring role of Bane, good-guy werewolf on the TV show *Werewolf Hunter*.

In a polite-but-firm voice, Pinky said, "I'm sorry, but other fans are talking with Mr. Masters right now. If you'll show me your ticket, I'll let you know when you'll have an opportunity to speak with him."

"I just want to give him a quick hug and kiss." The silver-haired woman looked more like Bane's grandmother than one of his fans, but you really can't judge fans by their appearances. "I know he won't mind."

"Mr. Masters himself requested that there be no unauthorized touching," Pinky replied. "The rules were included in your registration packet." He reached into his belt pouch. "I've got a copy here, as well, if you've lost yours."

"I don't need your damned rules," the woman spat, destroying the illusion of grandmotherhood. "I paid my money, and I came a long way to meet Bane, and that's what I'm going to do."

Pinky said, "You'll get your chance to meet Mr. Masters when it's your turn, but there will be no touching. May I see your ticket?"

"I've lost it," the woman said unconvincingly.

I'd have bet my favorite *Werewolf Hunter* T-shirt that the woman had never even seen a ticket, let alone paid the extra fee for a personal meeting with Bane. Still, as head of security, I had to play nice, so I asked, "Is there a problem?"

Pinky actually kept a straight face as he said, "This lady lost her ticket for her meeting with Mr. Masters."

"I'm sure we can take care of that." The woman's face brightened, but only until I turned to Andi and said, "Can you take this lady out to registration and see about getting her a replacement ticket?"

"Sure thing, Regina." The woman was trying to come up with another lie as Andi escorted her out, but I knew she'd be kept out of the way until the meet-and-greet ended. Fortunately, Bane hadn't even noticed the uproar and continued speaking to one of the legitimate ticket-holders in that Australian accent fans found so irresistible.

I let Elliot and Donna go back to working the room and said, "Good catch, Pinky."

"I shouldn't have had to catch anyone," he retorted. "There should never be a ticketed event in the middle of a meet-and-greet. You can't do decent crowd control this way."

"I know," I said, annoyed. "Ted said there wasn't enough in the budget for a separate room." Ted, the chairman of the convention, had refused most of my requests.

"If you can't afford decent security, you shouldn't put on a convention."

Again he was stating the obvious, and I ran my fingers through my bangs in exasperation. "We've only got half an hour to go. Maybe we'll make it through without any more problems."

"If Shannon pays attention, that is. I saw that toucher a mile away—she should have, too."

I turned to look at Shannon, who was serving as Bane's personal attendant. Rather than keeping an eye on the people nearby, she was staring at him in rapt attention. "Starstruck?"

"Big time."

Security crew members, known as redshirts, were supposed to maintain objectivity, not stare in adoration at the guest of honor. But it was hard sometimes—we were fans, too. I'd purposely kept my own distance from Bane because I was such an admirer. "It happens," I said.

Pinky grunted, and I knew what he was thinking. It had never happened to him, and never would. Even as we talked, his eyes were constantly moving, watching for trouble. He didn't look that formidable—he was plump with glasses and thinning hair—but his devotion made him a much sought-after security team member at conventions up and down the east coast. I'd been delighted when I found out he was willing to work at FullMoon, a small convention for fans of *Werewolf Hunter*, especially since I was taking my first stab at running security. By rights, he should have been in charge, not me, but he'd said he'd rather not. At the time, I'd thought that meant he had confidence in my abilities. Now I wasn't so sure.

"Did you realize Shannon was so inexperienced?" Pinky asked.

"She's not inexperienced," I objected. "Ted says she's worked plenty of conventions in the midwest."

"Ted says? When you've worked as many conventions as I have, you learn to check out your team members yourself."

"You're probably right," I admitted. It was something else I'd have to remember for the next convention, assuming that I didn't screw up so badly this weekend that I never got another chance. "I'll keep an eye on her."

"Does she have an exit strategy?"

"A what?"

He assumed a pained expression. "A strategy for getting the subject—that's Masters—out of the room expeditiously."

Everybody else called the actor by his character's name, which Masters himself encouraged, but Pinky insisted on using his real name. "I'm sure Shannon has a plan," I said. "She's worked as a personal attendant before."

Just then, an exuberant fan grabbed Bane by the neck and loudly kissed him, while Shannon watched in a blend of horror and envy.

"Maybe you should go see—" Pinky was gone before I could finish. "And I didn't even get a chance to thank him," I mumbled to myself.

"Did he say when he's going to destroy the Death Star?" asked Elliot, who'd appeared at my elbow.

"You mean Pinky?"

"Who else but fandom's answer to the Pinkertons?"

"He's helping Shannon with her exit strategy. I can't believe I forgot to check on her exit strategy."

"I can't believe you just said 'exit strategy.' Look, Regina, that guy may think he's the Terminator crossed with a Klingon warrior, but the rest of us are just volunteers with walkie-talkies, doing the best we can. And you're doing fine."

"Then how come I nearly let that toucher get through?"

"Nearly only counts in horseshoes and hand grenades. By the time Granny Goodness gets away from registration, Bane will be back in his suite drinking Fosters."

"Granny Goodness?"

"The toucher."

Security people tend to attach nicknames to troublemakers. This one came from the DC comic book universe. Granny Goodness, like our toucher, was not nearly so nice as she appeared.

Just then, I noticed a flurry of activity in one corner of the ballroom. It was probably nothing, but it was best not to take chances. "Can you check that out?"

"You're the boss," he said with a mock salute, and sauntered off. Unlike Shannon, I knew Elliot could handle anything that came up. We'd worked together before, and though I didn't know him as well as I wanted to, I had hopes. Of course, even if he was interested, it would have to wait until after the convention.

True to his word, Pinky had Bane out the door at the stroke of ten, confounding the hopeful fans lingering in hopes of personal interaction. Shannon was left behind, too, though I wasn't sure if it was on purpose or because she couldn't keep up. Either way, Pinky was right. It was only Friday night, and Bane had a slew of events scheduled for the weekend. Shannon just wasn't up to being his personal attendant.

The rest of the redshirts and I waited until the room cleared out, with most people heading either for a marathon showing of the first season of *Werewolf Hunter* or to their rooms to get some sleep. I checked in with the other redshirts distributed around the hotel, and was relieved to hear that everything was calm. I sent most of them off-duty, which left me and Elliot as the only ones active. Elliot had volunteered to stay on call for the night, and I figured I'd be on call until the last fans dragged themselves out of the hotel Sunday evening. Pinky, of course, said he'd keep his walkie-talkie on, too, even though he was doing his overnight on Saturday.

After that, I was almost done for the day. I still had to stop by Bane's room to make sure he had everything he needed. This was annoying for two reasons. First, to ensure Bane's security, he'd been given a suite that was only accessible by going outside and up a steep flight of stairs, so it was completely out of the way. And second, it was a waste of time anyway because Bane wasn't alone. He and a happy crowd were noisily partying. As I'm sure Pinky would have told me, the location of Bane's room should have been kept a secret, but I suspected Ted the con-chair, who was in the thick of it, had been less than discreet. I noted resentfully that he didn't even have his walkie-talkie with him.

Shannon was at the party, too, sitting as close as possible to Bane, and laughing too hard at everything the actor said. Not that she was the only one. Bane was known for being the kind of wolf that didn't need a full moon to bring out his animal side, and there were several other women there hoping to be chosen for the night. Bane waved me over when I saw him, but I just smiled and shook my head. I'd spoken to the man earlier, and tripped over my tongue so badly that I wasn't inclined to repeat the experience. Drinking an extra-large Australian beer wasn't likely to help.

On the way to my much less plush room, I walked down the corridor designated for room parties, and made sure the hosts knew to keep noise down, avoid serving beer to minors, and refrain from recreating famous chase scenes from *Werewolf Hunter* in the hallways. Lastly, I checked in with the hotel's night security man to let him know things seemed under control.

Then I went to bed.

***

The first thing I did the next day was meet with my team over donuts and coffee in the control room, the function room reserved for convention business. We were all wearing our uniforms—jeans and blood-red shirts with white bulls' eyes on the front and the word SECURITY on the back. The shirts were easy to spot, and I'd been told it was a good color to set off my dark hair and eyes. I wondered if Elliot agreed.

We reviewed the day's schedule, which included morning panel discussions with writers and artists connected with *Werewolf Hunter*, autograph sessions for those writers and artists, an afternoon talk by Bane that we expected the whole convention to attend, more panels, and a werewolf-themed costume contest that was likely to be our biggest headache. Ongoing were the art show, video room, dealers' room, and hospitality suite where Bane would meet with the rest of the people who'd bought private tickets.

I was dreading the next part, so I kept my eyes on my clipboard as I said, "I've got some assignment changes. Shannon, I'm switching you to morning panels and autographs. Float between the panel rooms, and keep the lines moving in autographs. Pinky, you'll be with Bane."

I paused, waiting for an outburst, then looked at Shannon. She was nodding, maybe a bit annoyed, but there wasn't a tantrum in sight. Pinky just looked smug. I breathed a sigh of relief. "Okay, people, get out there and keep things secure." They headed for their first assignments, leaving only me and Elliot, who had the morning off in return for his being on call overnight.

"Good call," he said.

"I'm surprised Shannon didn't make a fuss."

"Didn't you hear what happened last night?"

"What now?" I asked, sure that I'd let something slip.

"You know there was a party in Bane's room, right? Well, Shannon practically threw herself at the guy, but when the party ended, Bane invited a different girl to spend the night with him."

"Ouch. So that's why she was willing to switch. At least we won't have that problem with Pinky. Unless… Elliot, Pinky's not gay, is he?"

"Who can tell? The only one who shares his bed is his walkie-talkie. I hear he even puts it into a plastic bag so he can take it into the shower with him."

***

Though the morning had started out well, the lull didn't last long. A wannabe writer showed up at the first autograph session with a stack of copies of her manuscript, intending to shanghai as many authors as possible into reading her *Werewolf Hunter* novel and then forward it to their agents and editors. It wasn't an unusual situation, and Shannon should have been able to handle it. Unfortunately, she wasn't where she was supposed to be. It was Andi, who was stationed in the dealers' room, who heard the commotion and buzzed me.

By the time I got there, the aspiring writer and Marilynn Byerly, well-known author of *Werewolf Hunter* novelizations, were having a shouting match in the middle of the room, lobbing phrases like "incompetent amateur" and "sleazy hack" at one another. Plus the signing lines were in disarray, with people pushing and shoving their way to the front. I yelled, "Linus in the signing room!" into my walkie-talkie—that was the code word that meant that all available redshirts should blanket the room with security.

Needless to say, Shannon showed up late, after the rest of us had things back in order. Wanda Wannabe had been sent off with a warning that she'd be ejected from the convention if she approached any more authors with her manuscript, and Ms. Byerly had been soothed with a Coke and the promise of a good seat at Bane's talk. As for the lines, Pinky had people queued up like Catholic schoolchildren, and I'd been both too busy and too embarrassed to see how he'd managed it.

Shannon didn't even have the good grace to look winded. "What's up?" she said.

"Where the hell were you?"

"I had to go to the bathroom. I was only gone a minute."

"Then how come I've been here for ten minutes, and the people here said there was nobody here when the session started twenty minutes ago? Why didn't you tell somebody you were going to the bathroom? That's what your walkie-talkie is for. And why didn't you come when I called the Linus?"

"I left my walkie-talkie in here."

I was furious. Not only had she been away from her post and out of contact, but she'd left an expensive, rented walkie-talkie unattended. If I'd had anybody to replace her with, I'd have fired her, but the convention was too far along to scrape up another volunteer. "Then since you've had your break, I don't want you to leave this room again until one."

"What about the panels?"

"I'll take care of them."

"What about Bane's talk? I want to work that."

I just glared at her, then turned to see Pinky shaking his head in disgust. I wasn't sure if it was at Shannon, me, or both of us.

***

The next disaster was right before Bane's talk. It was scheduled for after one-thirty, which meant that most of the fans were skipping lunch so they could line up for good seats. While they waited under the watchful eyes of most of the redshirts, Bane was enjoying a private lunch with a few privileged members of the convention staff. Naturally, the invitation list for that lunch had caused more dissension than almost anything else during convention planning. I'd stayed out of it. Just being in the same room as Bane got me flustered—I could only imagine what would have happened if I'd tried to eat in front of him.

Through my careful planning, Elliot and I both had the lunch hour free, and were headed for the hotel restaurant when we saw Pinky being confronted outside the door where the VIP lunch was being held.

"Should we give him a hand?" Elliot asked.

"He hasn't called for backup," I said.

"I know, but that's the woman Bane took to bed last night."

The woman in question was blonde, buxom, and swearing like a sailor. Since she'd been Bane's Friday night conquest, I mentally tagged her Girl Friday.

Elliot and I joined them, and I asked, "Anything wrong?"

"Nothing I can't handle," Pinky replied, keeping his security guard face firmly in place.

The woman appealed to me. "I'm supposed to go in there to meet Bane for lunch, but this fascist won't let me in."

"It's by invitation only," Pinky said, "and she's not on the list."

"Bane didn't know me when the list was made," the woman argued, "but when I asked him to meet me for lunch today, he said I could come if I wanted to." Presumably realizing that wasn't the most enthusiastic invitation, she bolstered her authority with, "It was early this morning— when we got up—so he probably forgot to add my name."

More likely he didn't remember her name, I thought to myself. "Pinky, have you checked with Bane?"

He gave me a look. "There's no need to disturb Mr. Masters."

Since I knew there were twenty people already in there, I didn't think one more would hurt, especially since it was a buffet. "I'll go ask him." But Pinky continued to block the door.

"Don't bother. Mr. Masters informed me that he doesn't want to spend any further time with this woman."

"You're lying!" Girl Friday shrieked. "Bane would never say that."

Pinky just stared at her.

"You're lying," she said again, her voice cracking. Then her face crumpled, and she ran off down the hallway, sobbing like a woman betrayed by her idol.

"Geez, Pinky," Elliot said. "Do you think you could have said something to make her feel worse?"

"I wouldn't have said it if Regina hadn't interfered."

"Regina is head of security," Elliot snapped. "Doing her job is hardly interfering."

"Regina assigned me to Mr. Masters, and I'm meeting my obligations the best way I know how. If she wants me to step aside…"

They both looked at me, finally acknowledging that I was right there, even though I wished I weren't. "No, Pinky, you keep doing what you're doing."

He nodded, mollified, and I started toward the restaurant, with Elliot close behind.

"Who does he think he is?" Elliot wanted to know. "Why are you putting up with him?"

"Because he knows what he's doing," I said, leaving unsaid the thought that maybe I didn't.

***

The rest of the afternoon went reasonably smoothly. We had to defuse a couple of arguments over seats at Bane's talk, but the talk itself was a big success. The afternoon's panels went fine, too, and a gap in programming at dinnertime meant we redshirts could meet for pizza. Except for Pinky, of course, who was maintaining watch over his subject, and Shannon, who'd announced that she was in the costume contest and wouldn't be helping with security for the night. By the time we'd eaten and planned the evening's coverage, it was time for the masquerade.

***

The first part of the costume contest went fine. Of course, getting the contestants into the right order was the masquerade staff's headache, not ours, while the tech crew was in charge of setup, lights, and sound. All we had to do was make sure nobody snuck into the ballroom early and resolve the inevitable arguments over seats. After that, we got to relax and enjoy the show.

Though I wasn't all that happy with her, I loyally cheered for Shannon, who was dressed as a woods-dwelling sprite who'd lured Bane to her tree in Season Two. Or rather, undressed, because sprites wear fur bikinis with boots. At least Shannon could carry off the skimpy outfit, unlike some of the other contestants.

Once the procession of werewolves, werewolf hunters, miscellaneous lycanthropes, and other *Werewolf Hunter* characters had paraded across the stage, the judges retired to deliberate while a band came on stage to perform "Werewolves of London," "Bad Moon Rising," and other appropriate songs.

All the judges were supposed to go to the control room, which had been emptied for that purpose, but after they left, Pinky buzzed me on the walkie-talkie.

"Regina? Pinky, in the main corridor with Mr. Masters, en route to his suite. He prefers to deliberate on his own, and will join the other judges later."

"He's going to get a beer, isn't he?" I said.

I could hear laughter when Pinky keyed his walkie-talkie, and realized Bane had heard me. "Affirmative," Pinky said dryly. In the background, I heard Bane say, "After looking at that lot, I deserve it!"

Feeling like a complete idiot, I asked, "Do you need backup?"

"Negative. The halls are clear."

"Good enough. Call me if you change locations."

"Roger."

Then I checked with Elliot, who'd accompanied the other judges.

Since they hadn't expected much input from Bane, they were perfectly willing to carry on without him.

The band was followed by a demonstration of sword fighting, but despite the display, the crowd was fidgety. There was a constant flow of people going to the bathroom, or to grab a Coke from a machine, or just deciding they'd rather party now and find out who the winners were the next day.

I knew the contestants had to be sweating bullets. Competition is always fierce, but the stakes this time were higher than usual. At the con's closing event, Bane was going to act out a scene from the opening episode of *Werewolf Hunter*'s next season, and he'd promised to pick one of the contest winners to perform with him.

About twenty-five minutes into the wait, my walkie-talkie buzzed again. "Regina, this is Pinky, outside Bane's room."

"Go ahead, Pinky."

There was no response.

"Pinky?"

There was a burst of noise, which I later decided was from the button of the walkie-talkie hitting something, and a horrific yell.

"Pinky!"

Now there was nothing.

"Linus! Outside Bane's room!" I barked into my walkie-talkie. Then I ran as fast as I could, not knowing or caring who I ran into. Elliot, who was closer to Bane's room, beat me there, and was at the bottom of the stairs leading toward the suite. When he heard me coming, he turned to stop me.

"There's nothing you can do, Regina."

Elliot was six-foot-something to my five-foot-four, but I pushed him out of the way just the same, and saw Pinky's body at the foot of the stairs. I'd thought our shirts were blood red until I saw real blood staining his. His walkie-talkie lay on the sidewalk next to him.

"There's no pulse," said Elliot, who was an EMT in real life. "He must have fallen just the right way to break his neck."

More like the wrong way, I thought.

Shannon padded up behind me, still wearing her fur bikini and boots. The other redshirts came on her heels. "Andi," I said, "get hotel security. Donna, call the cops."

Bane stood at the top of the stairs, looking down at Pinky, swearing fluently. I wondered what the fans would have thought if they'd heard him, because for the first time all weekend, he'd dropped his Aussie accent.

***

The hotel's security man got to the scene first, and, ignoring Elliot's protests that Pinky was dead, insisted on checking himself, getting bloody in the process. Ted showed up, too, but just dithered uselessly.

Eventually the cops arrived, followed by a doctor to examine Pinky's body and take it away. The police were visibly tense at first, but then got more relaxed, and I realized that they'd decided Pinky's death was an accident. But it didn't seem right to me.

Pinky had buzzed me to tell me he was on his way to Bane's room, and presumably he'd gotten there without incident. So why had he buzzed me later? Why would he have been heading down the stairs? I mentioned my questions to the cops, but they figured he was going to get a drink or take a break, and was going to let me know. They didn't understand that Pinky would never have left Bane's door unattended, and didn't think there was anything odd about him buzzing me just before he fell—one officer even suggested that he might not have fallen if he hadn't been using the walkie-talkie.

Bane was no help. "I should have let the bloke come into the room," he said apologetically, the accent back in place, "but I was fagged out and wanted a minute alone. He didn't seem to mind."

"Did you hear anything?" I asked.

He shook his head. "Not a sound. I was in the WC at first, and I had music playing. Poor bastard. Has he got any family or anything? I'd like to pay my respects."

"I don't know," I said. "I only met him yesterday. There wasn't really time to get acquainted." But that wasn't true. One of the best things about a convention was the way you could go from stranger to close friend in just a weekend. But Pinky had been all business. Not to mention the fact that he'd intimidated the heck out of me, and annoyed me even more.

"Bruce," one of the cops said, Pinky's wallet in his hand. "His first name was Bruce."

I hadn't even known that.

***

The cops didn't stay long, and looking at my horrified team, I realized I had to get them moving again. "Elliot, will you take Bane for the rest of the weekend?"

He nodded.

"Good. Ted, what's the status on the masquerade?"

"The judges are ready, but maybe we should cancel."

"No, Pinky would want us to go ahead."

"You've got to be joking," Bane said.

I glared at him. "Haven't you ever heard 'The show must go on'?"

"Yeah, but—" He stopped. "Right. Let's do it. But I want to say something about Pinky afterward."

"Good idea," I said. I turned to the rest of my team. "Okay, the crowd is going to be restless. Our job is to keep things running as smoothly as possible. Andi, you and Donna roam the halls, make sure nobody's been taking advantage of our absence. Everybody else will work the masquerade with me."

"Shouldn't I go back backstage?" Shannon asked hesitantly. "I mean, I'm still in the contest. That's where I was when you called the Linus."

I stifled a sigh. Clearly her job in security was secondary to a chance to act out a scene with Bane. At least she'd responded to the Linus. "Fine, we'll handle it."

As I'd expected, most of the fans were milling around, spreading stories that had nothing to do with what had really happened. I heard half a dozen people who claimed to know the real story: everything from a drug bust to an orgy to a government crackdown to alien infiltration. We tried to reassure them and got people back into their seats as fast as possible. Once we had them situated, we brought in the judges, including Bane, and got the show on the road.

The judges dutifully announced the winners, including Shannon, who got an award for "Most Daring" for her scraps of fur. The way she rubbed against Bane when she accepted her ribbon made it plain she hoped to supplant Girl Friday.

Once the awards were over with, Bane solemnly announced what had happened to Pinky, and said some kind words about him. I saw plenty of tears, but I also heard speculation about whether or not the death had really been an accident. I tried to tell myself that the idea was ridiculous, but it sounded all too believable.

It wasn't just the oddness of Pinky's death, it was the faces around me. Granny Goodness actually looked glad when she realized that Pinky was the one who'd kept her away from Bane during the meet-and-greet. Wanda Wannabe was there with a satchel, and I'd have bet dollars to donuts that she had a copy of her manuscript with her, hoping to corner a writer in the bathroom. Then I saw Girl Friday, bawling loudly where Bane could see. As he left the stage, he took pity on her and let her sob on his shoulder. That wouldn't have happened if Pinky had still been alive.

I'd heard that when somebody's been a cop for long enough, everybody starts to look guilty. Now I understood what they meant, because suddenly it seemed as if anybody in that room could have pushed Pinky down those stairs. If it hadn't been for the walkie-talkie in my hand, offering me instant aid from the rest of the redshirts, I think I'd have run screaming from the room. No wonder Pinky had been so attached to his. For one morbid moment, I considered suggesting that the walkie-talkie be buried with him, which led to the even more morbid idea of him sending me a message from the grave.

Then something occurred to me, almost as if Pinky had sent me one last message.

***

Though the plan had been for Bane to choose the person who'd be acting out the scene with him at the end of the costume contest, under the circumstances, it had been forgotten, and I heard people muttering about it. That gave me the idea about what to do next.

I buzzed Elliot, and told him to take Bane someplace where I could talk to him privately. Then I buzzed Ted, and told him to announce that Bane would be picking somebody momentarily. Both of them sounded taken aback, but they didn't argue.

Leaving the rest of my team to keep watch, I went backstage, which was mostly empty now that the masquerade was over. I was happy to see that Elliot had managed to detach Girl Friday, so he was the only one who heard me tell Bane what I had in mind. For once, I forgot that Bane was a celebrity and the most handsome man I'd ever met. From that point on, he was just another member of my team. I told him what I wanted, and why, and made it plain that I expected him to agree. He did.

I buzzed Ted again, told him Bane was ready, and listened as he told the same to the waiting throng. There was a hush when Bane stepped on stage, and I could practically hear fingers crossing.

"I know the timing is awkward," Bane said in that delectable accent, "but a lot of people have come a long way to hear tomorrow's program, and it's fair dinkum that Pinky wouldn't have wanted them to be disappointed."

There were enthusiastic sounds of approval.

"Now I'm hoping one particular sheila will be willing to share the stage with me." Now there were shrieks, giggles, and more than one shout along the lines of "Pick me!" Bane, who was an actor after all, paused dramatically. Then he named his choice. "Come on up here, luv."

There was a delighted shout, and scattered applause as Bane's leading lady accepted his invitation. From the catcalls that followed, I think there was physical contact between them, too.

Still playing to the audience, Bane said, "Of course, we're going to need to rehearse, and tomorrow morning is pretty well booked. Do you think you can spare me some time now to go over the scene? We could work in my room."

There were even louder catcalls, and I didn't need to hear the woman's answer to know she'd agreed. That was my cue to get in position and make the last arrangements.

I'd told Elliot not to rush, so I had plenty of time to get to Bane's room. Too much, in fact, because I had time to reconsider what I was doing. Twice I reached for my walkie-talkie, ready to call the whole thing off, but then the door opened, and Elliot escorted Bane in. Along with Shannon.

She was nestled under the actor's arm, looking at him so lustfully that it took a while for her to notice I was there, long enough for Elliot to close and lock the door. When I'd told Elliot he didn't have to stay, he'd insisted strongly enough to make me think it was more than professional loyalty, but it was the wrong time to think of that.

Finally Shannon saw me. "Hey, Regina. Did you hear? Bane picked me. I guess I'm not going to be able to help out with security tomorrow." She actually giggled.

"That's okay," I said. "I don't want you on the team anymore anyway."

"Hey, I know I haven't been at my best, but—"

I forced a laugh. "No, I think this was your best."

"Now, now," Bane said soothingly, "I'm sure Shannon's been trying."

"Then how did that woman nearly get past her at the meet-and-greet? And you never saw the mess she made in the signing room."

"That wasn't my fault!" she protested.

"Maybe not, but you didn't show up to help, either."

"I told you I didn't hear the call."

"That's right, you forgot your walkie-talkie, didn't you?" I said with a sneer. "Where'd you leave it this time—there sure as hell isn't anyplace to put it in that getup."

"You know I'm not on call tonight," she said defiantly. "It's locked up in my room!"

"Then how did you hear the Linus when Pinky fell down the stairs?" I asked.

She went white. "What?"

"For once, you were where you were supposed to be—you got there faster than Andi. So how did you know there was a Linus?"

"Someone told me."

"Who? I'll buzz whoever it was right now to confirm."

"I… I don't have to tell you anything."

She was right, of course. I wasn't a cop, and I wasn't going to beat it out of her. Fortunately I didn't have to, because Bane took her in his arms, and looked at her with those indescribably blue eyes, and said, "You didn't mean to kill him, did you, luv?"

"No," she whispered. "I mean, it wasn't me."

He gave her the smile that had melted the heart of the werewolf hunter herself, not to mention countless fans. "Of course it was, but you didn't mean for him to get hurt. Just tell me what happened."

I was almost afraid to breathe. If she hung tough, I didn't think there was anything else we could do. But she was a fan, through and through. She'd killed to get close to Bane—she couldn't lie to him. As long as she basked in his attention, Elliot and I might as well not have existed.

"I didn't mean to," she said in a tiny voice. "I only came up here to talk to you about using me in your scene, but Pinky wouldn't let me come in. He said he knew I was lying about working security. He found out which conventions I'd said I'd worked at, and he actually called to check up on me. Can you believe that?"

Bane shook his head in shared dismay.

"I've worked at other conventions, honest I have, but I was just a gopher, and I knew a gopher wouldn't get to see you up close. I just had to meet you."

He nodded understandingly.

"Then Regina got mad at me, and you and that other girl—"

"She meant nothing to me," Bane said convincingly, both because he was an actor and because it was true.

"I know, but Regina had already given you to Pinky, and I knew tonight might be my last chance to talk to you. That's all I wanted. But Pinky said I was a phony, and that you wouldn't want to waste time with me. He was going to buzz Regina to tell her about me. So I knocked that damned walkie-talkie out of his hand. It fell down the stairs, and when he reached for it, he lost his balance and fell. I tried to grab him, really I did. I didn't push him."

Bane nodded again, but I'm not sure if she saw it, because she'd looked away from him at last, either from shame or guilt. "Then what happened?" he prompted.

"I meant to get back to the masquerade, but I saw all the redshirts coming, and knew Regina must have called a Linus. Since I couldn't get back without them seeing me, I acted as if I'd come with them." She looked at him imploringly. "You believe me, don't you?"

I didn't give him a chance to answer. "What he believes doesn't matter nearly as much as what the cops believe."

"Bane would never turn me in," she snarled. "It's your word against ours."

"Don't be so sure of that," Bane said, stepping back from her.

"Besides," I said, "we're not the only ones who heard you." I held up my walkie-talkie so she could see that I was holding the button down. Every redshirt had heard her confession, and they all heard me say, "Linus outside Bane's room." Then I put down the walkie-talkie to say, "Elliot, call the cops."

"You're the boss," he replied.

"Damn straight I am."

Afterword

Though I've attended many science fiction conventions, and hope to attend many more, I have never worked security for one. To write this story I spoke with an experienced convention security volunteer who shared her stories of pushy fans and hard-partying guests, and Regina is named for her. I doubt anybody missed this, but just in case, the fictional TV show *Werewolf Hunter* is my homage to *Buffy the Vampire Slayer* and Bane is a version of Spike. However, I've been told by people in a position to know that James Masters, who played Spike, is a lovely gentleman who is nothing like my character, so that part is all made up.

Sleeping with the Plush

If I had a dollar bill for every time I've slept with the plush, by now I'd be sleeping in the finest motor home ever made. Another man might put that kind of money into the bank or a house, but not me. I'm a carny, through and through, and have been for over forty years, ever since I slept with the plush for the first time one early summer night back in '67. It wasn't the sleeping that changed me, of course. It was the murder.

***

Not that I was anticipating my life's work that night, mind you. I was too busy being steamed.

"Kid, there's not a carny on this lot who hasn't slept with the plush one time or another," Squeezebox Sam said as she spread a sheet over the pile of stuffed plush bears, snakes, turtles, and poodles she'd carefully arranged on the canvas floor of the duck pond tent. "Anybody who says different is lying."

"Yeah? Then why did Gary laugh his ass off when he heard about it?"

"Because Gary is an asshole. Don't you know what everybody calls him?"

"What?"

"We call him Gary."

"That's his name, isn't it?"

"Have you ever met a carny—a real carny—without a nickname?"

Now that she mentioned it, Gary was the only one on the lot who didn't go by a nickname, except Brownie Fenton's wife and his daughter Lorinda, and nobody could deny that the owner's wife and kid were real carnies.

"We don't waste nicknames on people unless we think they're going to stick around," Squeezebox said. "Next time Gary gives you any shit, ask him how long it took to clean the barf off the Octopus after letting a townie ride when his face was puke green."

Though I was glad to store that fact up for later appreciation, I still felt like a jerk. "He's rolling in the dough now, and he's not even that good an agent. I can build a tip better than he can—if Brownie would give me a decent alibi joint like the swinger or the nail store, I'd bring in twice what Gary does. But no, he's got to give me the damned duck pond." I kicked at the stainless steel "pond" in disgust.

"Kid, Brownie Fenton has been with it since before you were born. He knows what he's doing. Every agent starts with the hanky panks—when you're good enough, he'll move you up to an alibi. Now quit kicking the pond, unless you want it to start leaking. If you think sleeping on plush is bad, try sleeping on wet plush!" She tossed a worn blue blanket onto the bed she'd made. "Now give that a try and tell me it isn't a whole lot better than spending your money on the bunk house or a motel."

I gingerly lowered myself onto the pile of stuffed animals and wiggled around a little. "It's not so bad," I had to admit. "Thanks, Squeezebox— I owe you one."

"Damned straight you do, and you're going to owe me another one come tomorrow. When you bring me back my sheet and blanket, I'm going to teach you a few tricks that'll put some cash in your grouch bag."

"Yeah, sure," I said, not feeling particularly grateful as the stout woman headed out. What did she know about being an agent anyway? She and her partner, Junebug, had themselves a sweet setup, selling lemonade and foot-long hot dogs to the townies at their grab joint, and their Coachman trailer was as big as some apartments. She didn't have to shout "Everybody's a winner," all night long, trying to get lot lice to lift ducks, and she sure as hell wasn't going to be sleeping with the plush anytime soon.

Was it my fault that my first time on the job was the night of that podunk town's Little League championship, meaning that everybody with kids was at the damned game? Even the best agent couldn't get a grown man, or even a teenager, to plunk down a quarter to look at a duck's ass to see if it had a winning number. All I had was kiddie prizes, so there was no percentage in it for anybody else.

It would have been a different story if I'd been on the cat rack or the swinger, or Gary's buckets joint, where marks paid to toss balls into gaffed baskets. But from the look Brownie had given me after seeing my take, I'd be herding ducks and handing out Taiwanese paper bird whistles to rube kids until my hair turned gray. To add insult to injury, Brownie's daughter Lorinda had been with him when he collected the money, and though she stayed behind to talk with me for a minute, that went south when Gary came over to ask if she'd go out to eat with him. Even though the look she gave me said she'd rather go with me, there was no way I could make a counter offer with an empty grouch bag. So off she went with Gary, leaving me with the damned stuffed snakes.

I'd known the duck pond was going to be hard work, but I hadn't thought it would be that hard. Like every other townie turned carny, I'd started out as a ride boy, making chump change that barely paid for my meals and a bed in the bunk house, which was nothing but a dingy trailer fitted out with pallets. Early on, Squeezebox Sam had pointed me toward the games, telling me that was where the real money was, but it had taken me a solid month to talk Brownie into giving me a chance, and he probably wouldn't have done it then if Lorinda hadn't pushed him. So there I was, a game agent at last, and I was sleeping with the plush. I had half a mind to pack up in the morning and hitch a ride back home. At least when I worked at the factory, I'd had a real bed to sleep in.

Then again, back home there'd been no Lorinda or anybody who kissed anywhere near as good as she did. The thing was, she'd been with it since she was born. She wasn't going to want to give up show business to live over my parents' garage. That meant I had to stick it out, but with Gary in the picture, maybe I was wasting my time with her, too. I was trying to work it all out when I heard the voices.

"Are you sure this is the place?" some jerk said. I didn't recognize the voice, so I knew it was a townie.

"Of course I'm sure," another townie jerk said. "Right under the duck pond tent. There's the oak tree we leaned the shovels against."

"Are you sure? I thought it was that tree over there."

"I'm telling you it was this here oak tree. They pitched the tent right over the spot where we buried him."

Buried him? I'd been about to yell at them to shut their yaps, but I didn't so much as breathe loud after that.

Jerk number two went on, "We've got nothing to worry about. Nobody's going to find him."

"What if they find him when they pull out those tent stakes?"

"Don't be an idiot! Those stakes aren't in more than a few inches—we dug that hole a good six feet deep. Now let's get gone before somebody wants to know what we're doing here."

I couldn't hear any footsteps on the mixture of dust and hay that covered the lot, but I could hear voices getting lower and lower, and I thought I heard the distant sound of a car starting up a few minutes later. Still, I was in no hurry to make any noise for a good while after. Instead, I considered the situation, and it seemed to me that I could do one of three things.

One, I could find a pay phone and call the local cops, but considering the facts that I'd drunk a beer or two before facing Brownie with my pitiful take, and that I'd bummed a couple more afterward so I wouldn't think too hard about what Lorinda was doing with Gary, I didn't think they'd be inclined to listen, especially since I couldn't describe the men I'd heard talking, and I didn't even know who'd been killed.

Two, I could go roust Brownie out of his bed, but between the beers and my humiliating performance earlier, he probably wouldn't believe me either. It was more likely that he'd rip me a new one for disturbing him, and I'd have to tell him off. Then he'd probably chase me off the lot, possibly for good, but definitely long enough to ruin my chances with Lorinda.

Or three, I could go to sleep.

It didn't take me long to settle on that one.

I got up early the next day, meaning that I was awake before noon, and maybe it was the humiliation of sleeping with the plush or my jealousy at seeing Lorinda go off with Gary, but I woke up determined to turn over a new leaf.

One thing I hadn't changed my mind about was doing anything about the killers I'd overheard. Truth was, once it was daylight, I started wondering if I hadn't dreamt the whole thing. When I was eating bacon and eggs at the cook shack, I did ask if anybody had seen anybody wandering about after closing time, but other than Handsome Harry claiming that two townie women had snuck into his trailer for a night of humping and thumping, nobody had. And he was likely lying anyway.

No, my plan that day was to make myself into the best damned agent I could be, and if Brownie wanted me to work the duck pond, I was going to work it so hard, every child who stepped onto the lot would grab ducks like they were gold. So when I took that sheet and blanket back to Squeezebox Sam, I told her I was going to take her up on her offer to teach me how to be an agent.

And teach me she did. By the time she was done, I knew how to tell which townies had money in their pockets and which ones had less than I did. I knew when to charm the ladies, when to bully the men, and when to shut the hell up. I didn't know it all, not by any means, but I had what I needed to start.

It was Friday, which meant we opened up the show at four, and by three-thirty, I was ready. The flash plush was hung on the sides of the tent to lure in the kiddies and hidden away in boxes was the slum—the rubber worms, Chinese handcuffs, and plastic basketballs they actually won most of the time. I'd changed the water in the pond, shined up the ducks, and souped up the hydraulic pump that stirred the water so that those ducks were swimming like Esther Williams. I had a smile on my face that was one part Santa Claus and one part every kid's grandfather. When Brownie came by on his preopening inspection, I stood up straight and looked him right in the eye. Hell, I damned near saluted.

Brownie just grunted. Gary, who was tagging along for some reason, grunted too.

I didn't care, because Lorinda was right behind them, and she gave me a smile that didn't have a thing to do with Santa Claus, though I sure wanted some under my Christmas tree.

A couple of minutes later, Brownie came over the loudspeaker to announce that the show was open. The crowd started rolling in, and I started pushing ducks. I smiled, I grinned, I cajoled. I did Donald and Daffy Duck imitations that had the kids laughing so hard they wet their pants, and flirted with the ugliest mothers I'd ever seen, just to get more quarters in my money apron. Damn, I was good.

But even Donald Duck can't convince a townie to keep his kid up too far past bedtime, so around eight-thirty I handed out the evening's last teddy bear to a kid who was so tired he didn't even fuss when his mama and daddy told him it was time to go home.

"Can we come again tomorrow?" the kid wanted to know.

"No, the carnival has to leave," Mama told him.

I thought about letting her know we'd be there through Sunday, but didn't think Daddy would want his kid whining all weekend long, so I let it slide.

"Will it be back?" the kid asked, still angling for another visit.

"Maybe next summer," Mama said.

"Well, they won't be coming back here," Daddy said. "By next May, there'll be houses right where we're standing. They're breaking ground on a new development the month after next."

Mama shot him a look that would have shriveled me up for a week, and I could see Junior was starting to think about crying.

"My boss is already looking for a new place to set up next year," I put in quickly, "so you be sure and come see me. Maybe you'll win that giant Snoopy."

Junior looked satisfied, Mama looked happy, and Daddy looked at me to make sure I was talking to his kid and not his wife. Then they headed off, leaving me with nothing better to do than stare gloomily at the agents who were bringing in money from grown-ups hand over fist, even if their call wasn't half as good as mine. They didn't have to wreck their throats talking like a cartoon character, either. The sensible thing would have been for me to lower the awnings and lash them to the tent frame for the night, but Brownie had a strict rule about sloughing a joint until he officially shut down the show, so I was stuck there, hoping Lorinda would come by.

At least I was flush enough to be sure I wasn't going to have to sleep with the plush again, but thinking about that got me to thinking about what I'd heard about a buried body the night before. If what that townie daddy had said was true, and if there really was a stiff under the lot, it was going to get covered up with houses and streets and such before too long. In fact, they might get lucky and find the body while digging somebody's basement, so it would come out all right without me or the show getting involved.

Unless…

Say they did dig up that body in a month or two. I was guessing those townies hadn't planted him too long ago, or they wouldn't still be worrying about him, but by then, how would anybody be able to tell if the poor sap had been dead six months or six weeks? These days, they probably have some way to get it down to the hour, but back then, not even a big city had that kind of know-how, let alone a nothing town in the middle of nowhere. A place like that was lucky if they had a cop who could tell the body was dead.

But even the dumbest sheriff would eventually figure out the body was no longer breathing, and he'd be bound to start wondering how the poor sap had ended up there. If he was like every other sheriff in the country, I'd bet my last duck pond quarter that he'd try to find an outsider to blame it on, and it wouldn't take him long to remember that Fenton's Family Festival had been set up on that lot. Sure as shooting, he'd start issuing warrants and calling other cops so he could track us down and drag us back to cause all kinds of commotion. Whether or not it came down on me personally, it wouldn't be good for the show.

I knew I was in over my head, so I held onto my patience with my fingernails, but as soon as Brownie gave the signal, my tent was tied up tighter than a preacher's wife's knees, and I was on my way to find Squeezebox again.

Squeezebox was having a smoke outside the grab joint, and I could see Junebug inside washing up.

"Squeezebox," I said, "I need some advice."

"Didn't I give you plenty of free advice today? You ought to know enough about being an agent now to make a fortune, marry the boss's daughter, and run this show. Which is what you're after, isn't it?"

"This is something different." I explained the situation, ending with, "What do you think? Should I tell Brownie? Will he believe me?"

"Damned right you should tell him—if he doesn't check it out, he's a fool, and Brownie's no fool. But I'll go with you to talk to him, just in case." Then she added, "Don't thank me. I'd do nigh onto anything to get out of cleaning up. Let's go before Junebug realizes I've had time to smoke a whole pack."

We headed for the show's backyard, where those who could afford trailers set them up, but there was no answer to our knock at Brownie's Airstream. That was unusual. Even if Brownie was still out collecting, Mrs. Fenton usually stayed in the trailer to handle paperwork. Rather than try to chase him around the lot, we sat on the step to wait, and before too long, up strutted Gary, trying to look like a big shot. He was too skinny to do it right.

"Where have you been?" he asked me. "I went by the duck pond to get your take, but when you weren't there, I figured either you'd snuck out with it or there wasn't anything to give me." He laughed as if he'd said something funny.

"I was just looking for Brownie to give it to him," I lied. Fact was, I'd forgotten all about the money, what with the corpse and all, and I was still wearing my apron filled with quarters. "Have you seen him?"

"Haven't you heard? Brownie's in-laws live two towns over, so he took Lorinda and the missus to visit them. I'm in charge until they get back."

"Brownie left the show over the weekend?" I said.

"The old lady had been nagging him about it for a couple of weeks, and I guess Lorinda started in on him, too, so he finally said he'd do it, just to shut them up. He knows I can handle things here. He's even put me in charge of getting us to the next stand—he'll meet us there." Gary puffed himself up further, but when we didn't look impressed, he snapped, "Did you make any money or not?"

I handed over my take, then watched him trying to look unimpressed as he counted it. "Not bad," he finally said. "For a new agent, that is."

"I'd like to see you make that kind of money on the duck pond," Squeezebox said indignantly.

Gary snorted. "What about your take?"

"Junebug will bring Brownie's cut over when he gets back."

"I'm in charge, and I want that money tonight."

"Don't tell me—tell Junebug."

Since Junebug was twice as big as Gary, and three times as mean, I wasn't surprised when all he said was, "All right, but I'm going to have to tell Brownie."

"Call him now, if you want," Squeezebox said.

"No need for that," he said quickly. "Mrs. Fenton said not to phone unless it's an emergency. She doesn't want anybody ruining her weekend with the family. That's why I'm the only one with the number." He looked down his nose at us. "Well? Do you two want anything else?"

I was going to tell him, but I saw Squeezebox shaking her head. "I guess not."

"Then if you'll excuse me, I've got work to do." He marched up into

Brownie's Airstream, his head held so high he banged it on the top of the doorway before he slammed the door behind him.

"What in hell is Brownie thinking, leaving that guy in charge?" I demanded as we headed back for the grab joint.

"Kid, everybody has a blind spot—that idiot is Brownie's. I hear Gary's parents are friends of his, but they had to get out of the business. They sent Gary here so Brownie could show him the ropes."

"That's just great! Do you think we can track Brownie down ourselves?"

"I doubt it—I don't know Mrs. Fenton's maiden name, or which town her folks live in."

"Then what do we do?"

"I guess we wait for Brownie to meet us at the next stand," she said, but I knew she wasn't happy about it.

"By then it might be too late! This is going to come back and bite us on the ass, you know it is. We've got to get it taken care of now. Even if it means dealing with Gary."

"Gary won't do anything."

"He will if you, or maybe Junebug—"

"Gary won't do anything for a pair of bull dykes."

I blinked. I'd kind of known Squeezebox and Junebug weren't just roommates, but nobody had ever said it so plain before. I gave it half a second's thought, and decided it didn't matter to me. "Then I guess we handle it ourselves." I was kind of hoping she'd try to talk me out of it, but she just nodded. "The easiest thing would be to dig up the stiff and move it somewhere else, where nobody would connect it with us."

"Too risky. We don't know the territory, so we don't have a good place to dump him, and we'd have to use a car to even try."

"You've got a car."

"Junebug has a car," she corrected me, "and with my luck, some dumb cop would stop us before we got a mile away. You want to try to explain why we've got a dead man in the trunk? Or tell Junebug why her car is in an impound lot? And that's assuming we could dig it up without being spotted, and for that matter, that we could find it in the first place. It's not like the killers left a treasure map."

That's what gave me the idea, and to understand the idea, you've got to understand townies. I'm not saying townies are dumb, but have you ever wondered why a townie will plunk down a dollar or ten dollars or twenty dollars to try for some cheap piece of plush when he could buy a better toy outright for a whole lot less money? Even when they're sure in their little hearts that our games are rigged, they keep playing, and I'll tell you why. It's because of what every agent says over and over: Win a Prize! Don't earn it, because earning is no fun. Come win something. It's human nature to want to win, even if the prize is slum. So with Squeezebox's help, I came up with a way to make the townies want to win a corpse.

Of course, getting it all arranged took more than just Squeezebox's help. Junebug was in on it, and a couple of ride boys I was friendly with, and some of the other agents. Gary had done a good job of making people dislike him, so we had plenty of people we could ask, but Squeezebox made sure we only got carnies we could trust.

Even with all that help, I had lots to do, both that night and the next day. It took money too, every bit I had, and I had to sign IOU's for the rest—it was my idea, so it only seemed right that I pay the freight. Of course that meant I had to sleep with the plush again, but that didn't bother me. I was too busy worrying about what might go wrong.

The next day, Squeezebox drove me and the ride boys to a printing office, and with a few free-ride tickets, we bribed the printer into making up a stack of posters while we waited. Then the ride boys put posters up all over town, while Squeezebox and I went back to the lot to get things ready there.

Junebug had already found some rope and stakes to mark off a big pen of land just past the back lot where the best rides were, and somebody else had found some extra bunting and strings of lights to add some flash. I hung some more posters around the lot, just to make sure everybody who came to the show got an eyeful.

We were lucky. Gary slept late, probably worn out from throwing his weight around, so he was likely the last person in town to find out about the contest. I was getting a bite at the cook shack when he stormed up, one of the posters in his hand. "What the hell is this about?"

There hadn't been time to make the poster fancy, but the printer had found a picture of a pirate's treasure chest to put over the words:

TREASURE HUNT TODAY
Win $50
at Fenton's Family Festival
$1 Buys a Chance To Dig for a
TREASURE CHEST
FILLED WITH CASH
Starting at 6 PM
Bring Your Own Shovel
Adults Only

I'd thought about not charging, but Squeezebox convinced me that we had to charge something or nobody would believe we'd buried anything. She was the one who said they should bring their own shovels, too, but I added the part about adults only. I didn't want some kid to find the body. Not that Gary appreciated the thought that went into the details—all he cared about was that something was going on that he hadn't been told about.

He waved the poster around, yelling, "Who put these up? Who authorized this contest?"

Nobody answered, even those who knew what was going on. I don't know if it was loyalty to me, dislike of Gary, or just curiosity to see what was going to happen next. Which was for Gary to buttonhole people he suspected might be the ringleaders: Jumps the rides manager, Lulu from the cat rack, and Ugly Bob the drunk who kept the show's generator running. Gary even went after Junebug, which showed how mad he was. Maybe I should have been insulted that he didn't accuse me, but I was just as glad he didn't. When he realized nobody was going to tell him anything, he muttered something about finding out who was behind it if it was the last thing he did, and stomped off.

Of course, we knew he'd be planning to show up at the treasure hunt at six. "You sure you're going to be able to get him out of the way?" I asked Squeezebox.

"Leave it to Junebug," she said. "Brownie always comes by to get a lemonade before opening, and you know Gary won't miss the chance to do the same and get a drink for free. So we're going to add a little something extra to it." I don't know what Junebug put in that lemonade, but when Gary drank it just before opening time, he passed right out. I had a couple of ride boys waiting to lug him to his trailer and tuck him in.

"I'll take over the buckets joint for him," Squeezebox said, "unless you want to give it a try."

I was tempted, but I said, "I'll stick with the ducks—I've got too much on my mind to try something new."

A little while later Squeezebox gave the word to open up, and the townies started streaming in. Half the men I saw were carrying shovels.

I'd thought that as distracted as I was, I'd be useless on the duck pond, but I did pretty well. It being a Saturday helped—there were plenty of kids around—but mostly it was because I was so jazzed that I think I could have talked Brownie Fenton himself into buying a duck. The afternoon flew by, and soon it was five-thirty, and Squeezebox was on the loudspeaker announcing that the treasure hunt would be starting shortly. Most of the crowd started heading that way, so I went ahead and shut down the duck pond so I could hightail it to the treasure hunt pen and start selling tickets. People were handing me dollar bills so quick I couldn't keep track, and it looked as if I might actually make back what I'd spent.

Squeezebox, Junebug, and some of the others came over to get the townies to line up and make sure nobody started digging early. At six o'clock on the nose, Squeezebox handed me the microphone so I could explain the rules.

It was funny. I'd spent all day talking people out of quarters, but now, with what looked like half the men from that town staring at me, I got stage fright. What shook me out of it was when the local sheriff, a tall man with a frown that would curdle milk, walked up.

"Gentlemen, welcome to the Fenton Family Festival Treasure Hunt," I said. "The rules are simple. Buried somewhere in that pen is a treasure chest with fifty dollars in it. All you've got to do is dig it up, and you'll get to take it home, chest and all. In the case of a dispute, your fine sheriff here will decide the winner. Are there any questions?"

There weren't.

"Then good luck!" The game boys pulled down a section of the fence and the men poured in like…well, like townies at a carny.

The sheriff ambled over. "I never saw this gag before. You sure you've got enough men digging to make back that fifty dollars?"

"Maybe not," I said nonchalantly. "The idea was to get people to come to the show. They'll spend enough on rides and games for us to make our money back."

"If you say so," he said doubtfully. "It's a hell of a life you people live."

I had to grin. "Yes, sir, it is a hell of a life."

Ten minutes passed, then another ten. The crowd watching was getting restless, and the diggers were getting suspicious. So was the sheriff. I caught Squeezebox's eye, but all she could so was shrug her shoulders. Another ten minutes went by, and I was starting to sweat. Then I heard the sweetest sound I'd ever heard a townie make—somebody yelled, "Jesus Christ on a crutch!"

"Did you find the chest?" a voice called.

"I found a chest all right, and the arms and head, too. There's a body in here."

We carnies held back as the sheriff ran in and directed the diggers to uncover the rest of the body. In no time, the diggers had him out, a fellow who'd probably looked a lot better before he'd been in the ground so long. I wouldn't have expected the man's own mother to recognize him in that condition, but somebody said, "I know those boots! That's Jackie Barron!"

The plan had worked so well I was having a hard time not laughing out loud, but it got better. One of the townies who hadn't entered the contest turned to the man next to him and said, "I told you that was the oak tree we buried Jackie under."

The other man hissed, "Shut up, you damned fool." Then, when he realized they'd been heard, he shoved the first man, hard, and took off running for the parking lot.

The sheriff shouted for somebody to grab the man who'd spilled the beans, and legged it after the escaping one. I wouldn't have bet on him catching up if I hadn't remembered the microphone in my hand. What I did was the first thing I learned when I joined the carny, which was how to get help. I yelled, "Hey, rube!"

Carnies came from everywhere, tackling the running man before he knew they were there. He punched and kicked for all he was worth, but there were a dozen carnies, and it wasn't hard for the sheriff to get the handcuffs on him. There were plenty of townies willing to drag both prisoners out to the police cruiser, acting as cocky as if they'd caught him, instead of us.

I was feeling a mite cocky myself when the sheriff came back and said, "I'd like a word with you."

"Why don't you ask me your questions, Sheriff?" a familiar voice said. Every bit of my cockiness dripped off of me. Brownie Fenton had brought his family back early.

It's a good thing Brownie didn't give me a chance to speak to the sheriff because I'm not sure I could have managed to get a word out. The sheriff started out suspicious, but I saw firsthand why Brownie was the boss—he turned on the charm and explained away every concern. The sheriff's last question was one I hadn't even thought about. He wanted to know if we were going to finish the contest.

Brownie didn't even hesitate. "Under the circumstances, I think it would be disrespectful to continue. Instead, Fenton's Family Festival is going to present the fifty dollars prize money to the late man's family."

There was a murmur of approval from the townies, until one man said, "What about my dollar? Do I get it back?"

"Certainly," Brownie said, "if you want it. Or you can accept a five-dollar book of ride tickets so you can enjoy the carnival instead." Damned if Lorinda wasn't already holding a stack of tickets. None of those men could resist the combination of free rides and Lorinda's smile, and every one of them took the tickets. It was a smooth move. Giving away rides cost Brownie next to nothing, and the longer the townies stuck around, the more they'd spend on drinks and hot dogs. And since they'd all had their hearts set on winning something that day, they were going to be hitting the games, too. The sheriff looked satisfied as he took his prisoners away.

Next, Brownie took the microphone from me and announced, "Ladies and gentlemen, despite the horrific events, Fenton's Family Festival will meet its obligation to entertain the people of this community." Then he gave the carnies who were still hanging around a meaningful look, and they caught on that it was time for them to get back to work. I wouldn't have minded sneaking back to the duck pond myself, but I didn't get the chance.

Instead, Brownie pulled me over to where none of the townies could hear us, with Squeezebox and Lorinda following. He didn't look mad, exactly, but he didn't look like he was ready to beg me to marry Lorinda and give him a mess of grandkids, either.

"Kid, I want the real story—all of it."

I swallowed hard, and looked over at Squeezebox. She was looking concerned, and I knew my staying with the show depended on what I told Brownie. So I repeated what I'd overheard the killers saying, and explained the choices as I'd seen them.

"Then you went to sleep," he said. "With a dead man underneath you. Didn't they teach you anything about civic responsibility in that wide spot in the road you came from?"

I swallowed again. I hadn't thought about it that way before, but I had to defend myself somehow. "Yes, sir, but the way I understand it, civic responsibility means responsibility to your city. Well, I've never even been in this town before, so it sure as hell isn't my city."

Brownie was still looking at me, poker-faced.

"I mean, townies have all kinds of people looking out for them— police, county cops, state troopers, the National Guard, on up to the FBI and the Marines. If all those yahoos can't keep them from killing each other and burying bodies, what chance do I have? Carnies, on the other hand, don't have anybody but ourselves, and I swear that if I'd heard some townie whispering about a dead carny, I'd have been on him like white on rice." I would have, too, even if it had been Gary who'd been killed. "Besides which, I didn't see any percentage in causing a stink and chasing off business. We'd have had to shut the show down early, which wouldn't have done anybody any good."

"Especially not you."

"True enough," I admitted. "I've got plans, Mr. Fenton, and I'm not going to get anywhere with an empty grouch bag." Deliberately I looked over at Lorinda, who was watching the whole thing, so he'd know what my intentions were.

Brownie kind of grunted, and I still didn't know if he was on my side or not. "Just answer me two questions," he said. "What if somebody had found the treasure chest before they found the body?"

"We never buried any chest."

He nodded, in approval I thought. "Then what would you have done if the killers hadn't lost the body, if they really had buried him under the duck pond?"

"Huh? They did. I dug him up and moved him last night. First of all, I had to be sure he was really there, and once I had him out of the ground, I figured I might as well put him someplace more convenient. I didn't see any reason to move the duck pond if I didn't have to."

Brownie stared at me for a second, then broke out into a belly laugh and clapped me on the shoulder. "Treasure Hunt, maybe you've got a future here after all."

"Treasure Hunt?" I liked the sound of it. Like Squeezebox Sam said, you're not a real carny until you've got a nickname.

Afterword

I enjoy reading about a carnival as much as I do a circus, and this story was directly inspired by *Eyeing the Flash: the Making of a Carnival Con Artist* by Peter Fenton. One of the chapters is titled "Sleeping with the Plush," and I decided that would be an excellent title for a story. Naming my fictional carnival Fenton's Family Festival is a small nod to Mr. Fenton.

The character of Treasure Hunt shows up again in *The Skeleton Haunts a House* (published under my pen name, Leigh Perry), though he is considerably older there. Treasure Hunt's son Brownie appears in that book as well, and also in this book, in "The Skeleton Rides a Horse." It's not at all necessary to know the connections between my fictional worlds, but it tickles me so I keep doing it.

Skull and Cross-Examinations

18 June 1680

Dearest Mother,

I take pen in hand to inform you of the unexpected events that took place during my voyage to Jamaica to begin the career as a lawyer Father so wished me to have. But before I begin in earnest, I must warn you to have your vial of smelling salts near by, should you become overcome by horror at my tale, particularly the murder. Do bear in mind that I survived said events, and of course was not myself murdered, or I would not now be writing this letter. Moreover, the ending is a happy one and speaks well of my expectations. Even Father may admit that I performed adequately, so you may need the smelling salts to counter the shock, should he speak well of me. I admit to feeling not a little pride at the resolution of my first case before the bar, or rather, before the mast.

Are you now fortified? If so, I shall begin. Despite Father's assertions, I did not find sea travel to be invigorating, bracing, or any of the other healthy adjectives he employed before having me escorted up the gangplank of *Fortune's Daughter*. Ironically, any and all of those terms accurately describe my previous life studying at Oxford and dabbling in university theatrics, though I do not think Father agrees.

The voyage was in fact, deadening to the senses. My nose was the first to go. This was a mercy, if truth be told, given the way it was constantly assailed by the odors of unwashed sailors, the tar and other materials of the ship itself, and the livestock brought aboard to provide fresh food. Next, my hearing was attacked by the constant sounds of waves slapping petulantly at the hull, sails flapping in the wind, and the nearly incomprehensible language of the sailors. Though they reputedly speak the King's English, I would be hard-pressed to prove it in court, even if Father himself were sitting on the bench. Finally the sense of sight was dulled, for there was nothing to see. Yes, the sunsets were quite colorful when the weather was fine, but one looked much like the next. When the weather was not fine, there was nothing at all to see.

Fortunately, the one sense that remained perfectly intact was my sense of self-preservation. I had need of it several weeks into our journey, when we were attacked by pirates.

Yes, Mother, pirates. I trust you have made use of your smelling salts by now, perhaps augmented with a strong cup of tea, thoroughly laden with sugar. Either of those nostrums would have served me well when I realized we were under attack, but my only comfort was remembering Shylock's words in *The Merchant of Venice* when he itemizes the hazards of sea travel, specifically mentioning pirates. Had Father given that warning the attention it deserved, I might not have found myself in such dire straits. How unfortunate Father continues to hold a grudge for Shakespeare's jovial suggestion to kill all the lawyers.

I will not spend much time describing the attack, for the attack did not take up much time. When the pirate ship was first spotted, it was flying friendly colors, so the captain was unconcerned as it drew near. Only as they came into firing range was that flag lowered and a more ominous banner raised.

I should explain that a pirate's flag is far more individualized than I had hitherto suspected. Apparently they view them as a coat of arms of sorts, identifying the captain and the depth of his intentions, and the infamous skull and crossbones is but one design. A red flag means… Well, let me say that it is a blessing that our attacker did not fly a red flag. The *Brazen Mermaid*—for that was the name of the attacker—flew a relatively benign black flag emblazoned with a sword thrust into the chest of a skeleton.

By the time the flag was noticed by the sailors aboard the inappropriately named *Fortune's Daughter*, the fight was essentially lost. There was no time to use the small cannon we carried—in fact our sailors barely had time to arm themselves before grappling hooks were tossed onto our deck and the pirates started to board, already primed to attack.

Battle is far noisier than I'd imagined: gunshots and the clashing of swords, punctuated by yells, groans, and vile cursing. I cannot speak of the appearance of those events, because I saw none of them. I did consider joining in, but having neither a weapon nor skill in using same, I relied on the better part of valor and stayed in my cabin with my fellow passenger, Squire Turow, who was as frantically busy as the combatants on deck.

I have not yet mentioned Squire Turow, a stout, self-satisfied gentleman returning to his home in Jamaica. As the only two passengers on board, we'd become better acquainted than perhaps we would have under other circumstances. When I learned that he had a daughter of marriageable age, I had high hopes of continuing and, depending on the charms of the daughter, perhaps deepening the friendship once we arrived in Port Royal. Though Turow is a tedious man, it has long been accepted as truth among my fellows that a young lady's attractions are in inverse proportion to those of her father, and judging by this, Miss Turow must be a rare beauty, nearly as lovely as my dear sister, Kate.

Those plans were far from both our minds that day, as Squire Turow filled a sack with every one of his belongings that might be considered valuable, from a handful of farthings to his snuff box to a rather tasteless necklace intended as a gift for his daughter. Then he concealed the sack in a location he hoped would escape detection by invaders.

I cannot help but add that had I not already known that Squire Turow was not a university man, his choice of hiding places would have confirmed it. No man leaves the gates of Oxford without learning, at the very least, how to conceal one's private effects from his classmates. Turow settled on a marginal site, and by marginal, I mean that it was marginally better than dyeing the sack bright red and placing it in the middle of the room with a placard labeling it TREASURE. As for me, I'd heard tales of the efficiency with which pirates can convince men to reveal the whereabouts of their wealth, and had no wish to experience any demonstrations of that efficiency. So I placed that which I believed worth stealing into my purse, and tucked it into a pocket, easily accessible should it be demanded. Not that there was a great deal to include, of course. Father's decision to limit my funds was unexpectedly fortuitous. Because of the gold trim, I even included the handsome folding case that sister Kate gave me before my departure, much though I disliked the idea of losing it. I did, however, remove the miniatures of you and Kate from its compartments and place them in an inner vest pocket, feeling that a pirate would be uninterested in them. Sadly, I was unable to pry Father's loose.

All too soon, the sounds of battle ended, and a cheer rang out that was patently not from the crew of *Fortune's Daughter*. Squire Turow's florid face went whiter than the sails. Moments later, the door to the cabin burst open. Two of the most frightening specimens I had ever had the misfortune to encounter rushed in, though at first all I saw were the cutlasses they brandished.

The taller man had a horror of black curls waving from beneath the blood-red kerchief tied round his head. "Lay down your arms!" he bellowed. "The ship is taken and you are prisoners of Captain Parker of the *Brazen Mermaid*!"

Having no weapons to lay down, I obeyed the spirit if not the wording of his command by raising my own arms, and Turow did the same.

The other man, a wiry fellow with a yellow kerchief, said, "Hand over your blunt, or it'll be the worse for you."

Though I'd never heard the word used in that manner before, it took no scholarship to recognize the meaning, and I retrieved my pouch of valuables and offered it to the man.

Only then did I notice that the saffron-kerchiefed pirate was missing his left hand. In its place was a club fashioned of wood with bands of steel reinforcing it. The bloodstained wood left no doubt as to how he made use of it.

Unsure of the appropriate way to make the transfer, I tossed it to the other pirate instead, who caught it and tucked it into his belt.

"Now you," the one-handed pirate said to Squire Turow.

"I don't know what you're talking about," Turow said less convincingly than the rawest university player.

Certainly his performance did not impress the black-haired pirate, who stepped forward and raised his cutlass. "You think I won't be able to carve it out of you? You'll be begging for me to take it before I'm even winded!"

"Gardner," the smaller pirate said, "the captain said we was to take prisoners, and kill only if we have to."

"Aye, but he said to find all that was worth finding, too!" the other one snapped. "That's what I aim to do."

Turow assumed a look of obstinate determination, and glared at the pirate, who sheathed his cutlass only long enough to draw a dagger nearly as long.

"For the love of God, Turow," I expostulated. "Give them your gold!"

"Never!"

"Shall I slice off the nose first?" the pirate speculated with an unpleasant gleam in his eye. "Or maybe an ear?"

Turow said nothing, and the pirate paused, whether to draw out his pleasure or to give Turow another chance, I could not say. Then he stepped closer and said, "If that's what you want, you putrid sack of—"

"It's in the dresser," I said. "Wedged behind the bottom drawer."

"You craven!" Turow thundered. "You're no better than they are!"

"Your life is worth more than a bag of gold and trinkets."

"My honor is worth still more," he replied, "but I see that you have none to protect."

While we bickered, the smaller pirate found Turow's bag and tossed it to the other, who looked sorely disappointed as he returned his dagger to its sheath. Then they manhandled us out of the cabin and up onto the deck. The carnage there was horrific, Mother, and in deference to your delicacy, I'll refrain from giving details. I will say that having witnessed the aftereffects of the loss of a hand, the scenes in our university production of *Titus Andronicus* dealing with the amputation of Lavinia's hands were far too circumspect. Then again, perhaps accuracy is not advisable, unless one has the theater's smelling-salts concession.

Turow and I were pushed and prodded toward a huddle of sailors and officers from *Fortune's Daughter* who were being watched over by a trio of armed pirates. Sadly, the captain was not among them. In fact, fully half the crew had gone to their reward.

Once they had rounded up all the survivors, a pirate announced that we were being taken on board the *Brazen Mermaid*. Several gangplanks had been put in place between the two vessels, and we made our precarious way across. Once aboard, we were herded toward the bow of the ship and told to remain there, with a new set of guards on duty.

Meanwhile, back on *Fortune's Daughter*, the pirates were taking everything not nailed down, as well as some items that had previously been quite securely attached. Though there was some gold on board, most of the hold had been filled with foodstuffs and woolens, and it may surprise you, Mother, to find that the pirates were delighted with this commonplace cargo. Even pirates must eat and protect themselves from the elements, not to mention the possibility of trading the ill-gotten goods.

Finally the plunderers had taken everything of value save the boards that made up the ship itself. The gangplanks and ropes connecting the vessels were removed, and we set sail.

The men from *Fortune's Daughter* were much moved by the sight of their ravished vessel, and kept their eyes upon it until it faded from view. Even I was affected, though I had not particularly enjoyed my time aboard. Perhaps it was because I thought it likely I would find my stay on the *Brazen Mermaid* even less congenial.

After no little time, during which we had naught to do but share fears about our probable fate, a tall man with the air of command approached us. Evidently he'd had time to change his garments since the battle, for he was wearing a brocade surcoat, satin breeches, and a handsome tricorne hat topped with an egret feather. Unless he'd been born a gentleman, he was of course breaking every sumptuary law ever written, but he did so with élan.

He was accompanied by a more modestly dressed man carrying a bedraggled quill pen, a bottle of ink, and a document of some sort. Those of the pirate crew not actively involved with sailing the ship circled us, as if to watch a performance.

The first man said, "Gentlemen, I apologize that my duties have kept me from welcoming you aboard. I do so now." He actually made a leg, and quite handsomely, too. "I am Captain Nathaniel Parker, of the *Brazen Mermaid*, and this is Mr. Talman, our quartermaster."

I looked at the man with the pen and paper with interest, having learned that the quartermaster was often more important a personage than the captain, because it was his job to keep track of both provisions and booty. Mr. Talman had the sour face of a provoked Oxford don planted on the body of a brute well able to maintain his place on a pirate ship.

"Now, if you will do me the honor of introducing yourselves…" Parker said.

We prisoners looked at one another. Then the ranking officer stepped up. "First Lieutenant Hart, formerly of the *Fortune's Daughter*."

"A responsible position. Your wife must be very proud."

"I am not yet married."

"A pity. Well, Lieutenant, it happens that our ship is in need of a man of your abilities. Are you willing to to sign our articles, and, in return for a full share, join our crew?"

He drew himself up. "I am not."

"Would you prefer to jump into the sea?"

Hart could only stare.

"You see," Parker said, "those are the only choices. Join the crew, or visit Davy Jones."

There was a long moment, punctuated only by a gesture from Parker which caused his men to step aside, leaving a clear path to the railing.

After swallowing hard, Hart said, "May I read your articles first?"

"Fair enough."

But while Hart made a show of looking over the document, it was clear his decision was already made, and when the quartermaster handed him the pen, he signed and was borne away by the crew with a show of welcome.

The introductions continued, and in each case, Parker made a pretense of small talk before offering the choice he'd made to Lieutenant Hart. Some signed reluctantly, and some willingly, but all but two men signed. One stiffly marched to the railing and threw himself off, with a proud farewell of "God save the King!" Another grabbed for a pistol at a pirate's belt, but he was shot on the spot, and then tossed over the railing as well.

I trust I need not tell you of my trepidation as my own turn approached. Though I was not particularly looking forward to becoming a lawyer, neither did I wish to become a pirate. Even without any useful sailing skills, as a young man in good health, I felt sure I would soon be forced to wear a kerchief of some revolting shade. Then I took note of something. The captain spoke to a sailor, and then said he had no need for a man with his skills. After adding two more men to his crew, he passed by another sailor from the *Fortune's Daughter*, though in that case it was evident the man would probably not last out the night.

Finally, upon reaching the last of the surviving crewmen, he again neglected to issue an invitation.

A thought occurred to me, barely more than a guess, but I resolved to put it to use.

All that remained were Squire Turow and myself, and of course, Turow pushed himself forward.

"And you are?" Parker said, courteously enough.

"I am Squire Turow of Port Royal, and I demand that you release me immediately."

"If I were to do that here, I fear you would drown."

There were appreciative chuckles from the pirates, and sputtering from Turow.

Presumably it was obvious Turow was no use aboard a ship, for Parker turned to me. "And you, sir?"

"William Cunningham," I said. "Formerly of London, and if fate permits, soon to set up practice in Port Royal."

"What would that practice be?"

"I am a lawyer, sir."

If you read this portion to Father, be sure to prepare for the inevitable snort, along with the comment that I have done nothing to earn such a title other than attend classes, and not nearly enough of those. As events played out, I argued my first case before another day had passed. But for now, let me continue my narrative.

"A lawyer," Parker said speculatively.

"Not a skill you need, I suspect."

"Perhaps, perhaps not. Is your wife in Port Royal?"

"No, she is with her parents in London, waiting for me to send for her."

Smelling salts, Mother! I promise you, I have not married without your knowledge or blessing. I lied to the man, intentionally and with forethought. Having noted that the healthy men Parker had passed over had mentioned their wives and children, something the other sailors had not, I was betting my future that it was no coincidence.

Squire Turow stiffened, since I'd made it plain that I hoped to pay my respects to his daughter, but perhaps because he already thought me a cad, for once he kept his mouth shut.

"You are young to be married," Parker said, suspiciously I feared.

"Childhood sweethearts." I could not tell if he believed me, so I added, "I carry her picture with me always, if you'd care to see." I pulled out the miniature of Kate to show him, and after he inspected it, he said only, "A lovely lass." He sounded almost disappointed, though at the time, I could not imagine why.

He stepped back, and addressed the remaining prisoners. "Gentlemen, I'm sure you realize your situation. You are entirely at my mercy." He stopped to let his words sink in. "But I do not kill unnecessarily. Do as you're told, give us no trouble, and at the first opportunity, you'll be left where you can make your way to some town or another. But if you give us grief…" Again he timed his pause for full dramatic impact. "You'll get it back fivefold. Is that understood?"

There were murmurs of assent, but I decided it would do no harm to make my understanding more definite, and in ringing tones, I said, "Perfectly, Captain."

Parker seemed satisfied, and though I heard Turow muttering, "Lickspittle," I ignored him magnanimously. Whether because of my somewhat tenuous claim to a profession or because of my wholly fraudulent claim to a bride, I was alive and not a pirate.

Despite my joy, the rest of that day was the most miserable I have ever spent. First we were stripped down to our skins, while still on deck, to ensure that we'd concealed nothing worth taking. The pirates were not kind in their judgment of our appearance—I even saw one of the former crew members from *Fortune's Daughter* jeering. Once we'd dressed again, we were taken to that part of the ship known as the bilges, and locked into a barred cell. The less said about the conditions, the better, but I will say that there was scarcely enough space for the five men imprisoned there, let alone the vermin in residence.

This, we were told, was where we'd stay until the captain released us.

At first, we were cheerful enough, merely from having survived, and eagerly discussed our circumstances. According to one of the sailors, Parker had been known to release prisoners unharmed in the past. The other sailor pointed out that had Parker killed passengers, they'd never have been heard from again. The first man countered that he could have killed us already, had he been so inclined, but the second opined that he could be saving us for later entertainment. The former shipmates would have come to blows had I not physically restrained them.

Afterward, the two of them were content to glower at one another, ignoring my attempts at conversation. Turow still refused to acknowledge my existence, and the third sailor was barely conscious, and only moaned until some hours later, he died. Nobody came in answer to our calls, so we were left with his body for some time.

I cannot speak for the others, but my feelings were made only worse by the sounds of celebration that rang throughout the ship. The pirate crew was not modest in their victory—there was music, dancing, and undoubtedly feasting and drinking. I suppose it was no wonder that we were neglected for the remainder of that day and night.

Our situation was a little better come morning. First off, a crewman came by with food and drink for us, and it was reasonably generous in portion and quality. Then the poor devil who had died was removed, presumably to be thrown overboard. I'll admit I was so relieved by his absence that I gave little thought to whether or not he would receive a proper send-off.

There seemed to be more commotion on the *Brazen Mermaid* than I was used to aboard *Fortune's Daughter*, but I attributed it to the greater size of the pirate crew and perhaps a lack of formality. It was not until midmorning that I found out that the true cause of the uproar. That was when a crew member came and pounded on the bars. "On your feet for the captain!"

We stood, and a moment later, Captain Parker arrived. "You there," he said to me. "You say you're an experienced lawyer?"

"I am." I realize I've given Father yet another cause for derision, but I was at least a fledgling lawyer, and I have had many experiences. The fact that these two elements of my life were entirely separate was hardly worth mentioning.

"We have need of your services. One of my crew members has been accused of breaking one of the ship's articles, and I hoped you'd be willing to assist."

"In court?" I asked, thinking it most unlikely.

"Not an actual court, no, just here on board. Normally we'd take care of the matter without so much bother, but it seems a shame not to take advantage of your presence and give the crew a bit of a show at the same time."

"I see. What, exactly, would you wish me to do?"

"I was hoping you'd argue his case for him."

"Is he unable to do so himself? That is the usual procedure."

"The accused is a simple man, not much for words. It'd be a mercy if you could speak for him. He's an old shipmate of mine, and I want it handled fair and square, if you're willing."

I hesitated. "Would my other option be the same as you gave the sailors yesterday?"

He smiled, but with more menace than mirth. "Nothing like that. I've given my word that you'll be set free. Of course, the sooner this matter is taken care of, the sooner I'll be able to get you and your comrades to dry land. Unless you're that fond of the accommodations, that is."

Though I would like to pretend my actions were on behalf of my fellow prisoners, it was, in fact, the thought of getting myself off that ship that impelled me to say, "In that I am always willing to speed justice, I accept."

Captain Parker released me, and even ordered a bucket of water for me to perform a sketchy toilet. Turow, of course, had much to say about my decision, especially after I accidentally splashed him.

I was taken to a cabin and told that my "client" would be along directly. You can only imagine my alarm when he arrived, and I saw it was the black-haired giant who'd threatened Turow with such enthusiasm the day before. Even though his hands were manacled, I was most uneasy when the door was closed behind him, leaving us alone.

"Cunningham, that's your name, isn't it?" he asked.

"It is. And you are…?"

"Perry Gardner. I wants to thank you for agreeing to help me. I could tell you were a decent man yesterday. Showing us where your friend's loot were hid was smartly done."

"It seemed the prudent course," I said, surprised by his mild tone.

"Aye, it were that, and saved me no end of trouble. I've no love for torture."

"But… You said…"

He actually broke into a grin. "Fooled you, did I? Funny what a loud voice and a few oaths will do to make a man give up his valuables. And the way Crane acted all nice and concerned? That makes it work even better. The bad looking worse next to the good, as it were."

"You were most convincing."

"Crane was the one to come up with the ploy," the pirate confided. "He used to be an actor before he went on the account."

"On the account?"

"Before he became a pirate."

"I see. I understand you have a case for me to argue."

"That I do. They're saying I done murder."

I nodded, wishing I'd thought to ask Parker exactly which article had been broken before I agreed to help. Then I remembered the pirate captain's smile—it would not have changed my decision.

And so, having accepted the case, it behooved me to treat him as a legitimate client, and one thing I have learned from Father is that a lawyer should never ask a client whether or not he is actually guilty. Seating myself on one of the stools in the room, I gestured him toward the other. "Pray tell me the circumstances that led up to this accusation."

"I can't tell you much," he said, once settled. "I fell asleep topside last night, and when Murbles came across me this morn—"

"Murbles?"

"The first mate. When he saw me, he tossed a bucket of water on me to rouse me. I leapt up, cursing a mite from the surprise, but the man on the deck beside of me didn't stir. We turned him over, and saw it was a man by the name of Biggs, dead as a doornail. Since I was next to him, Murbles figured I did the killing."

"Couldn't he have died in his sleep?"

"Not bloody likely. His tongue was stuck out, and you could see the marks of fingers on both sides of his throat. Somebody throttled the bastard."

I couldn't resist a glance at Gardner's hands, which appeared quite strong. "Other than proximity, was there any reason to place the blame on you?"

"Aye, there was. Murbles searched the body, and when he saw he didn't have nothing on him, he had me turn my pockets out. I had Biggs's pipe and tobacco, and a gold-and-pearl ring he'd been wearing, plus some blunt I hadn't had before. But I swear I don't know how any of it got there."

It was a blow to the case, but not a fatal one. "The killer must have placed those things in your pockets to implicate you."

"That's what I told Murbles, but he didn't believe me. So they slapped me in irons and said they were going to maroon me. But the captain and I've been knowing each other since we came to sea, and he said the least they could do was give me a trial. Only nobody wanted to speak for me, and I was going to have to do it myself, until I remembered you were in the hold. Some of the crew were against using you, but Captain said it'd be a shame to miss a chance at seeing a real lawyer in action."

My first thought was that these men were fated to disappointment if they thought I was a real lawyer. My second was that the captain would not be pleased if I failed to adequately defend an old friend. My third, that Father would also not be pleased if I failed, though less likely to toss me overboard. And finally, I dreaded the blow to my sense of worth if I could not help this man.

With all those thoughts, it took a few moments before I could actually devote a few to the task at hand, but Gardner just sat patiently.

"Well," I said, as if I'd come to some momentous conclusion, "it seems that you had both the means and the opportunity, but did you have any reason to wish Biggs dead?"

He shook his head. "I don't know that I'd spoken two words to him before last night. He only joined the crew a fortnight past."

"Was he forced to join the crew?"

"No, he was a old member of the Brethren." When he saw my look of confusion, he explained, "The Brethren of the Coast, that's what we call ourselves. This weren't his first voyage, not by a long shot."

"But you had never sailed with him before?"

"That's right."

"What about last night? What transpired?"

"Well, after the captain got done dealing with the prisoners…" He had the good grace to look embarrassed at this, as if remembering how we prisoners had been dealt with. "Afterward, he gave permission for us to make merry, not that we needed him to tell us that."

"I believe I heard evidence of your merriment."

"It were a grand time, that's for truth. Plenty of grog, plenty of food. No women, but with the booty we've earned, there'll be time for that when the voyage is done."

"And in the course of your conviviality, you met up with Biggs?"

"That's right. I was playing dice with Crane and a couple of others—just for fun, mind, not for money, that being against the articles."

"Of course."

"While we was dicing, Biggs came to talk to Crane. The two of 'em had sailed together aboard the *Fair Wind*, off the coast of Venezuela. Biggs started talking about some of the prizes they'd taken, and I told him about some of mine."

"Comparing notes, as it were."

"That's right. I might have made it sound better than it were, mind you, but no more than Biggs, and his talk of sacks of doubloons and pearls from Margarita."

"Completely natural to exaggerate," I assured him.

"That led to talk of battles, and I told him about how we took a merchantman off Hispaniola just a month ago. Now that was a fight!" He smiled at the memory. "The tussle yesterday was nothing compared to that. No offense."

"None taken."

"Biggs knew he'd been outclassed—he got quiet as the grave after I told him how many men had died, and the injuries we took. That was the battle where Crane lost his hand, and that's a story worth telling."

"And after you finished relating war stories?"

"Then the singing started, and dancing, too."

"Perhaps more grog?"

"Plenty more. I don't remember much after that, truth be told, not until I woke up with a dead man next to me." He shuddered, and having recently shared sleeping quarters with a corpse myself, I could sympathize.

"Did you argue with Biggs?"

He shook his head. "He called me a filthy, lying son of a whore, but that's not the sort of thing you'd kill a man for."

"Any witnesses? Did anybody say they'd seen you kill him?"

"Nobody that I know of. Admittedly we were all the worse for drink."

"Then it seems to me that our case is secure," I said confidently. In fact, I was quite confident. There was no evidence against Gardner, other than the coincidence of being found next to the body, and there was no more reason to believe him guilty of killing Biggs than there was of me having killed the poor sailor in my cell. Less so, actually, since there were only three others with opportunity to kill the one, whereas any member of the pirate crew could have done in Biggs.

Just then, a pair of sailors came to escort Gardner and me onto the deck, where the trial was to take place. I had no doubt that my rhetorical skills would soon make mincemeat of whatever arguments that could be used against Gardner. After all, this was a pirate ship, not a proper court. How much of a challenge could the case present?

I continued to believe that right up until I saw the courtroom that had been erected on deck. The dock, the bench, the jury box filled with a twelve-man jury—all were in their proper places. Of course, they were only rough approximations, made from boards, crates, and barrels, but the fact that they existed at all was enough. I realized that these pirates quite likely knew more about courtroom procedures than I.

I turned to Gardner in amazement.

"Looks good, don't it?" he said. "You knew the Brethren like to act out trials, didn't you? And Captain Parker is a stickler for getting it right. He was in court himself, once or twice, and remembers how it was done. We don't always go to so much trouble for crew business, but being as we've got a real lawyer here…" He seemed uncommonly proud of the whole production, considering that it had all been put into place for his prosecution.

A burly pirate with a red beard approached us. "That there's your table," he said to me. "Gardner, you go to the dock."

I fervently wished it had been the other kind of dock before me, the kind that led to land and a well-appointed public house. As I took my place, I asked the bearded man, "Will you be acting as bailiff?"

"That's right."

"And the captain will be the judge?"

"No, he's sitting this one out, being that he and Gardner are old sailing mates."

I turned and saw Parker in the midst of the spectators, watching me with no little interest.

The bailiff went to the spot where I've seen so many bailiffs stand in Father's court, and said, "Be upstanding." Out came the judge, who turned out to be Crane, the one-handed pirate, dressed in a moth-eaten black robe and the most disreputable wig I'd ever seen, but strutting like any silk-clad magistrate. As he went behind the table that was to serve as his bench, I saw that the one missing prop was a gavel. A moment later, when he pounded on the table with his club, I realized that it was not needed.

"Be sitting," the bailiff intoned, and those of us with seats obeyed. I took the opportunity to see who would be serving as prosecutor, and was not pleased to see that dour quartermaster Mr. Talman was playing the role. A quartermaster is often the most educated member of a crew, which was the last thing I desired in an opponent.

Still feeling somewhat stunned by the preparations, I followed one of the first lessons I learned at university. I stalled. Standing once again, I said, "May it please the court, I would like to make a request before we begin the proceedings."

Judge Crane looked at the captain, and when he nodded, said, "You may make your request."

"Since your court is not ruled by the body of laws I have spent my career studying, might I have a few moments to examine the ship's articles on which your justice system is based?"

Again Crane looked over at the captain, and again he nodded. I heard an expression of impatience from the quartermaster, but he stomped away from his table and returned a moment later with the paper I'd seen men signing the night before.

"Thank you," I said, and took it up to read. It was a remarkable document, one I think even Father would admire. In its twelve tenets, it laid out the rules by which the crew lived and, depending on the severity of their infractions, died. Though I'd originally intended only to give myself time to think, I was fascinated. All food was to be divided equally, and booty divided into shares which were allocated according to rank. Those who lost a limb or joint were to be compensated from the company share—five hundred pieces of eight for hand or foot and eight hundred for a leg or arm. Gaming for money was forbidden, as my client had pointed out, as was bringing women or boys on board for dalliance, fighting on board the ship, and stealing from a crew member.

The harshest punishments were reserved for those who were careless with fire near the powder magazine, defrauded the company, or showed cowardice during battle. I finished reading, then waited as long as I dared for inspiration to strike. When it did not, and the crowd grew restless, I returned the paper to the quartermaster.

"A very clearly written contract," I said, "and in a handsome hand, as well."

Mr. Talman, evidently unimpressed by my courtesy, merely snorted.

Now the bailiff recited an approximation of the opening of court, and Judge Crane said, "The prosecution can now make its opening statement."

Talman stood, and in a bored voice, said, "Seaman Gardner strangled Seaman Biggs and stole his belongings, and should be marooned."

There was a murmur of discontent from the gallery, and Judge Crane said, "That's not the proper way to do it, Mr. Talman. You're supposed to say that you're going to prove all that."

Talman frowned, but said, "Very well. I intend to prove that Gardner strangled Biggs. Does that suit the court?"

"You're supposed to call him 'my Lord,'" the bailiff put in, but shriveled under Talman's glare.

"The defense may now make its statement," Judge Crane said.

"Thank you, my Lord," I said respectfully. "The defense intends to prove that Seaman Perry Gardner is completely innocent of the heinous crime of which he has been accused."

The crowd's reaction was much more approving, and I started to experience a bit of the same warm glow hitherto felt only while on stage.

Mr. Talman, still clearly uninterested in playing the game, called Murbles, the first mate, to the witness stand, and I was amazed to see that the bailiff actually produced a Bible for the swearing-in. The cover showed signs of wear, but the pages within looked pristine, as if the book were rarely, if ever, opened.

Murbles told his story straightforwardly enough, with minimal interruptions from the judge. I maintained a look of concerned interest until my time came to question him.

"You say you found the deceased lying next to Mr. Gardner?"

"That's right."

"But no witness saw the crime being committed?"

"Nobody that was sober enough to remember, anywise." There was laughter, quickly quelled by the judge.

I went on. "So other than the fact that the two were near one another, you have no reason to believe Mr. Gardner killed Mr. Biggs. Don't you find it unlikely that Gardner would strangle him, only to lie down next to the body? Wouldn't he instead have taken the first opportunity to absent himself?" I smiled winningly, giving the man a chance to admit his error in logic.

"I was thinking Gardner killed Biggs while he was drunk and then passed out."

"So your contention is that my client killed the man, robbed him, placed his ill-gotten gains into his pocket, and then fell asleep?"

"Only stands to reason," the man said. "If somebody else killed Biggs so as to steal his blunt, he wouldn't of put it in Gardner's pocket. What would be the point of killing him if he didn't make a profit out of it?"

"Men kill for many reasons, do they not? And having killed, do they not then try to cover up their crimes?"

"I wouldn't know about that," the mate said stolidly. "All I know is that Gardner was seen with Biggs, Gardner was next to Biggs's body, and Gardner had Biggs's blunt in his pocket. Seems plain enough to me."

I looked over at the jury, and sadly, it seemed plain enough to them, too. "I have no further questions for this witness."

Talman stood only long enough to say, "The prosecution rests its case, which I hope means that we can finish up this farce."

"Not until the defense gets a turn," Judge Crane said. He then asked me, "Do you wish to call any witnesses?"

I considered calling Gardner to the stand, but I didn't think there was anything he could say that would help his case. In fact, if he quoted Biggs calling him a filthy, lying son of a whore, it could well hinder his defense. But who else could I call? Any of the other pirates on board could have been the killer. As I looked at the men around me, inspiration finally struck. "My Lord, if pleases you, I would like to call a witness. More than one, in fact."

"Name 'em."

I made a sweeping gesture. "I wish to call the crew of the *Brazen Mermaid*."

The gallery erupted, and I heard Mr. Talman cursing me and, indirectly, Father. After much pounding with his club, the judge made himself heard. "You want to call every man jack on the ship?" he asked.

"Yes, my Lord. It is my belief that another crew member is the real murderer. Therefore if we can determine which man was out of the sight of his fellows for long enough, we shall know who killed Biggs. The only way to discover this is to verify the whereabouts of every man on board."

Crane looked over at the captain yet again, who in turn looked at the crew to see where their opinions lay. After informally polling those who were closest, he nodded at the judge, who said, "The court will allow it."

I requested a list of the crew members, and once it was ungraciously supplied by Mr. Talman, we began. I rather think the sailors enjoyed the process of coming to the witness stand, one by one. Most of them had been relegated to spectator up until then, so they relished the opportunity to swear on the Bible and become participants as well.

Considering the size of the crew, and the magnitude of the previous night's festivities, I would have wagered a handsome sum that I would be able to identify any number of men whose location during the hours in question would be in doubt, but as Father often points out, my luck in gambling is frequently bad. Somehow no man had escaped the attention of his fellows.

The captain had been drinking in his cabin, along with the first mate and the quartermaster. A small number of men, mostly those drafted from *Fortune's Daughter*, had been on duty to allow the others their pleasures. Other men had been gaming, eating, drinking, and dancing, but always in groups of five or more. And of course, we prisoners had been locked safely away.

At one point, I thought I had finally located another suspect, when a dour-faced specimen with an eye patch would say only that he'd been below-decks, and would not name a companion. But then one of the younger men announced, "He was with me." I asked that man what they had been doing, purely to verify his veracity, but the sniggers and catcalls from the rest of the crew drowned out any answer he might have cared to make. After a moment, I realized the truth, and let the matter drop.

I do not mean to be obscure, Mother, but… Actually, I do mean to be obscure. Let me say only that the men were thoroughly occupied during the time in question.

The patience of the crew was growing thin by the time I finished, and I was growing desperate. For though I questioned every man—including the members of the jury, the captain, the quartermaster, and the bailiff—I could find only three men who could not be alibied: my client, the deceased, and the one man on board who could not be guilty—Judge Crane with his missing hand. Two men who could have committed murder, but the marks on the dead man's throat spoke louder than words, telling me that my client was doomed.

Gardner was no doubt mentally preparing to meet his fate.

At this point, Mother, you may think I had doubts as to my client's innocence, but this was not the case. In truth, I'd never believed him innocent. Whether or not he'd killed Biggs, I had never lost sight of the fact that the man was a pirate. Killing was his livelihood. No, his despair did not concern me nearly as much as my own.

After years of education and my father's most ardent desires, I was no lawyer. Like the pirates around me, I was only playing a part, but unlike my bravura performances in *Hamlet* and *Titus Andronicus*, I had failed miserably, and was now likely to spend months in that cell below-decks. For a brief moment, I considered confessing my bachelor state, and signing the articles I'd so carefully perused.

Fortunately the moment passed, mainly because the thought of my theatrical triumphs woke something in my memory. Suddenly the truth revealed itself to me, as well as a way to share that revelation with the court.

Though my mental activity was great, to the outside observer it must have looked as if I was merely staring into space, because Judge Crane said, "Are you done?"

"Not quite, sir," I said. "There is one man left to question. You, our honorable judge."

Crane indignantly said, "You can't question the judge!"

"On the contrary. There are numerous precedents for taking such an action, notably in the case of Mortimer, the Sussex Bandit." Do not be surprised if you are not familiar with this case, Mother. I made it up. It has always been my belief that there are times when a lie is needed to serve the cause of a greater truth. And, might I remind you, I myself had not sworn to be truthful.

At any rate, my performance convinced the captain, who nodded as if the case I'd cited was one whose details he had only momentarily failed to recall, and said, "He's got the right of it, Crane." To me, he added, "Get on with it."

"Just as soon as our bailiff swears him in."

The obedient man approached the bench, then hesitated. "How's he going to put his left hand on the Bible? He's got none."

"In such cases, the law recognizes the former location of the append-age," I said.

The bailiff looked confused until Captain Parker barked, "He can put his stump on the Bible."

Crane dutifully raised his right hand, and gingerly put his wood-clad limb onto the Good Book in question.

"No, no, that won't do," I said. "Even the finest of ladies remove their gloves on such occasions." That reminds me, Mother. When the opportunity presents itself, ask my father what actually happens on such occasions, and inform me of his response.

Crane looked stubborn. "What difference does it make?"

I replied, "For the oath to be binding, there must be actual contact between your flesh and the Scriptures."

Still Crane made no move to remove the appliance. "It ain't fit to see."

"My dear sir, surely these combat-hardened men won't flinch at the sight."

He looked around as if to gauge the reaction, and must have realized that most of the crew were in agreement with me, and many were morbidly curious about his deformity. So he reluctantly loosed the straps that attached the club to the end of his arm, and pulled it off to reveal the stump of his hand.

It was a repulsive sight, a puckered scar streaked with angry red. He held it up defiantly for a moment, then gingerly laid it upon the leather binding of the Bible.

The bailiff, who had in fact flinched, recovered himself to administer the oath, and while he did so, I moved closer to the judge's bench.

Once Crane had repeated the words, "So help me, God," he looked at me and snapped, "Does that satisfy you?"

"Not quite." When I say my next motion was as quick as a whip, I assure you, I tell you only the truth. Before the man suspected what I was about, I grabbed that appalling stump and grasped it tightly.

Then I pulled it off, and revealed the perfectly whole hand that had been concealed.

After but a second of shock, Crane vaulted over the makeshift judge's bench, and threw himself onto me bodily, knocking me to the deck. His hands were on my throat—both of them—and had not other members of the crew recovered their senses quickly enough, he'd have squeezed the breath from me, just as he had Biggs. It provided an excellent demonstration of his guilt, but frankly, one I would rather have done without.

Moments later, while several sailors enthusiastically restrained Crane, Captain Parker examined the club and the stump, then turned to me in consternation. "How the devil did you know?"

Realizing that this was not an audience to appreciate modesty or understatement, I abandoned all thoughts of using either. "No one clue revealed the truth—it was all the facts taken together. One, I knew my client to be innocent of this crime. Two, only two men had the opportunity, and if it was not my client, it had to be Crane. Three, Crane was formerly an actor, an occupation that relies on deception, even more than piracy. The chopping off of a hand or arm is common enough on stage, and given sufficient preparation, I myself could produce a illusion convincing enough to sicken even your crew, as well as a much better prop than that." I flicked a hand at the "stump" the captain was holding, now revealed as nothing but wax and leather. "That would never have fooled anyone for long, had not the club concealed it."

"But why kill Biggs and leave the money on somebody else?" Mr. Talman asked.

"You know that Biggs and Crane sailed together before?"

"Aye. Are you thinking they had an old quarrel?"

"Possibly, but I suspect that this is not the first occasion Crane claimed payment for that hand. He could have repeated the trick any number of times. He joins a crew, pretends to lose his hand in battle, receives payment for same, and as soon as possible, leaves that crew, only to appear on another ship, his lost hand mysteriously healed. Biggs must have already seen Crane fake the injury, and was therefore in a position to reveal the scheme. Crane killed him to protect himself, and used my client as a scapegoat."

The captain turned to Crane. "Is that the way of it?"

Crane's only reply was to spit invective, and since some of his curses sounded suspiciously like the Bard's, I felt sure he had indeed been an actor.

Parker ordered him taken below, hopefully to a different cell from the one occupied by the prisoners from *Fortune's Daughter*, and set men to dismantling the courtroom. Almost as an afterthought, my client was released from his manacles and gave me a hearty slap on my shoulder that very nearly knocked me down.

"I suppose that wasn't a total waste of time after all," even Talman had to admit.

"Saved a good man," Parker said, giving Gardner a slap as firm as the one I'd received, "and got rid of a bad one. Cunningham, we are in your debt."

Perhaps it was foolish, but I could not let the opportunity pass. "As to that, there is my fee to discuss."

The captain eyed me. "Your fee?"

I nodded, endeavoring to assume the air of a man who'd said the most reasonable thing in the world. "It is customary. After all, Crane's share now returns to the ship's coffers, as does the money he was awarded for the loss of his hand."

"Are you claiming a full share?" Talman said in an alarming tone. In fact, it reminded me of Father when last I saw him, though perhaps you best not mention that to him.

"Absolutely not," I said firmly, and the tension eased measurably. "I ask for two things only. One, when my shipmate Squire Turow was relieved of his possessions, the proceeds included a necklace. I would like to reclaim it."

"The one he tried to hide?" Gardner said. "It went into the ship's coffers with the rest of the takings."

"Let's have a look at it," the captain said. A chest containing a tempting array of baubles was produced, and Gardner quickly located the correct one.

He handed it to the captain, who looked it over with a practiced eye. "This thing?" he said doubtfully. "It's naught but a cheap trinket."

"It has sentimental value."

He shrugged at my folly and tossed it to me. "Done."

"Thank you. One other thing. I would very much like to keep this." I held aloft the club Crane had used to conceal his hand.

"What the devil for?" he wanted to know.

"Just as a souvenir from my most unusual case." As my first, it was certainly the most unusual one.

Parker shrugged again. "We've no use for it. Nobody will be trying that trick again, not on this ship."

I thanked him again, and having no desire to return to the cell below, happily accepted when he asked me to join him for dinner. The cuisine was not refined, but it was plentiful, and the abundant wine surprisingly good. Though I don't remember details after a certain point, I am reasonably sure that the evening was spent pleasantly. I also have a dim memory of reciting the St. Crispin's Day speech from *Henry V*, but perhaps that was merely a dream.

The next day, the ship stopped at an island that was only barely deserving of the name, being nothing more than a spur of sand dotted with a few scraggly trees, where Crane's punishment was carried out.

Something that might surprise you, Mother, was that Crane was not sentenced to this fate merely for killing Biggs, which is not directly addressed in the articles. Fighting aboard ship is forbidden, but oddly enough, murder is not mentioned. No, to the pirates, Crane's more serious crime was his defrauding the company by collecting five hundred pieces of eight for the loss of a hand. In fact, more than one man suggested that the hand be severed in retribution, but the captain maintained that marooning him was enough.

I admit I had never before considered the horror of being marooned. Crane was left equipped only with a jug of water, a piece of hardtack, and a pistol with just one ball and enough powder for a single shot. He was allowed to keep his clothes, which I was told proves the basic humanity of Captain Parker, who could have ordered him stripped of every stitch. But dressed or wearing nothing but what God gave him, the man was doomed to a miserable death from starvation, thirst, and exposure to the elements.

Crane did not accept his fate with dignity. He struggled with the men tasked with ferrying him to the island, and cursed them with great imagination as they rowed back to the ship. I must admit to mixed emotions at seeing him abandoned, murderer though he was, and I watched him as we sailed away. As the island itself faded into the distance, I fancied I heard a gunshot, and I pray I was not mistaken.

That unpleasant task accomplished, Captain made good on his promise to release the other prisoners and myself. We sailed to Jamaica, and though we were not taken to any of the island's settlements, we were rowed ashore and left at a sunny beach only a few hours' march to Kingston. Gardner was among the pirates escorting us, and thanked me most sincerely for my efforts on his behalf.

"Especially," he said, "after what I threatened to do to your friend."

"But you would never have gone through with it."

"Of course I would have, if you hadn't told me where his gold was."

"But you said—"

"I said I take no pleasure in it. I take no particular pleasure from taking a piss, either, but I does it when I needs to."

Perhaps it was just as well I hadn't known that before the trial.

At any rate, I suspect it was due to his good wishes and those of Captain Parker that we were given a generous ration of water and hardtack to provision us. He also handed me a small sack of gold, an amount that more than made up for the funds I'd lost during the attack. I considered myself most fortunate.

As I write this, I am in my newly acquired offices, with a freshly painted sign proclaiming me to be WILLIAM CUNNINGHAM, LAWYER. Already I have met with several clients. Though it pains me greatly to admit it, perhaps Father was right in insisting that I take up law. If I can fool a crew of suspicious pirates into believing me to be an expert in legal matters, surely I can do the same with the trusting citizens of Port Royal.

I have also begun to make myself known to the members of society here, and upon two occasions, have spent time in the company of a most respectable lady: the lovely Miss Turow. This may surprise you, Mother, considering how Turow's opinion of me had plummeted, but I managed to win him over.

You see, once the pirates left us, and we began our overland trek toward civilization, I produced the necklace I'd claimed as part of my fee and presented it to Turow, along with the following words.

"Please, sir, give this to your daughter with my most heartfelt compliments. If she should bear me ill will for having revealed the location of these jewels to the pirates who attacked us, please convey my word as a gentleman that I did so only to preserve the safety and honor of her father, both of which are far more valuable to a dutiful daughter than even this treasure."

I was quite proud of this speech; it moved me nearly as deeply as it did Squire Turow, who could barely speak his thanks.

Then I added, "Retrieving this was the least I could do for you, after you aided me in my imposture."

"Imposture?" he said.

"Of being married. Of course, you knew differently, but held your tongue most admirably."

"I could do no less to protect a man of your quality," he said as if he had never doubted me.

From that moment on, he referred to me as "My boy," and spoke of his warmest wishes that I should soon be as dear to his daughter as I was to him. She has shown herself to be most appreciative of my efforts in retrieving her father and her jewelry.

Speaking of jewelry, you may be wondering about the gifts I enclose for you and my sister. I obtained them honestly, though the same cannot be said of their previous owner. You may recall that I asked Captain Parker for Crane's club, telling him that I wished it for a souvenir. That was true, but not complete.

It occurred to me when examining the thing after Crane's duplicity was revealed, that it was larger than it needed to be to conceal a hand. I also reasoned that if I were surrounded daily by dishonest men, I might well want to keep my valuables in a container that would never be separated from me. Close to hand, one might say.

Pirates, like university men, understand the value of a secure hiding place.

So please accept these pearls, liberated from the Spanish off the coast of Margarita, and fashioned into earrings to enhance your beauty. May they continually remind you—and Father—of the successful conclusion to my adventure.

I remain, your most loving and devoted son, William

Afterword

When I want a change from reading about circuses and carnivals, I have pirate books to keep me entertained. Three of the most unlikely aspects of the story are actually true. One, pirates did attempt to live by the articles they signed. Two, some pirate captains would only force single men to join their crews. And three, pirates did enjoy reenacting trials on board ship, vying for the roles of judge, bailiff, jailer, and hangman.

This story is an example of a story not going to the intended market. I intended to submit it to an anthology of courtroom dramas, but when I finished writing it, I realized I'd gone overboard on word-length requirements and sent it to *Ellery Queen Mystery Magazine* instead.

My original plan does explain why I had lawyers on my brain when I named the characters—most of them are named after fictional lawyers or authors of legal thrillers. Nathaniel Parker was Nero Wolfe's lawyer, and Murbles worked for Lord Peter Wimsey. William himself is named after my husband's grandfather, who was a lawyer, though he practiced in Connecticut and not aboard a pirate ship.

Kangaroo Court

The kids in the auditorium were goofing off, but they settled down when the bailiff stepped up to the microphone and said, "The Forty-Third Annual Session of the Jackson's Bridge High School Kangaroo Court is now in session, the Honorable Judges Dunbar, Reid, and Cuthbert presiding. Please rise."

We three judges were waiting in the wings, and as everybody else stood up, we hopped in, our kangaroo tails and ears flapping as we went.

I had never hated Jackson's Bridge High School more than I did at that moment.

***

In a way, it was my own fault that I got stuck with the tail.

I'd heard people talking about Rat Day before, but it wasn't until a couple of days before the big event that my home room teacher, Mr. Lilly, went through the rules, and I came to realize how lame it really was. Once a year, the seniors were allowed to spend the whole day telling every other student in the school what to do. Not just the way teachers get off on it, either. No, the seniors could tell us underclassmen to wear our clothes inside out or push a peanut down the hall with our noses or sing like the losers on *American Idol*. This was known as being "ratted," while the pranks were known as "rats." Those of us ratted were supposed to laugh merrily and go along with the gag.

"Are you serious?" I said when Mr. Lilly was finished. "People actually put up with that?" The rest of the kids in my homeroom, mindless sheep for the most part, looked at me as if I were the crazy one. "What genius came up with this bright idea?"

"My grandfather," a voice said from the door, where Principal Picket had materialized. I swear that woman moved like a cat. Not a sleek black cat or a street-smart alley cat, but a sneaky Persian with a smug expression on her flat face. She was always turning up in the middle of some class when I least wanted her around. And I never wanted her around.

"I see Mr. Lilly is explaining one of our most cherished traditions. You see, Garnet, my granddaddy first came up with the idea to help students blow off steam when spring fever hits, and I do believe the students would rise up if I ever even considered canceling it. Not that I would, of course. Doesn't it sound like fun?"

"Yeah, like a root canal with no Novocaine." I probably shouldn't

97

have said that, but there was something about that woman's tone and attitude that made me want to get myself in trouble. So I followed it up with, "I thought ritualized hazing was illegal. I'm surprised nobody's ever sued the school."

"Well, maybe people up North go to court over every little thing, but people around here don't resort to that kind of shenanigans." The way she said "up North" made it sound as if I'd been raised in New York or Boston, not Charlotte, North Carolina. "Some students do get a little carried away, which is why we have a court system in place to take care of any problems that might arise. So don't you worry. I'm sure you'll enjoy it, and in two more years, you'll be a senior yourself and then you'll be in charge."

"Only two years of torture—how nice," I said, already trying to decide if I was going to have a sore throat or menstrual cramps to keep me home on Rat Day.

But Picket was no fool and must have known what I was thinking. "Now you be sure and stay healthy. If you miss Rat Day without a verifiable illness or family emergency, you'll lose your Rat Day privileges as a senior."

As if I cared. But then came something I did care about.

"Not only that," she added, "but you'll be barred from all extracurricular activities for the rest of the semester. Which would include Mr. Lilly's drama club. Bye now!"

As she slimed away, I looked at Mr. Lilly and demanded, "Is that true?"

He nodded sympathetically. "That's the rule."

"Jesus freaking Christ!"

"Language," Mr. Lilly warned me, but he wasn't really mad. He was the only teacher I liked at all, and working on the drama club production of *Macbeth* was the most fun I'd had since my parents had forced me to move to Jackson's Bridge.

That meant that unless I wanted to kiss my shot at playing Lady Macbeth good-bye, I was going to have to endure a day of hell. I had no illusions that it would be fun. Not only was I the "new kid," meaning that I hadn't been in school with the same group of yahoos since kindergarten, but I was also known as "that weird goth girl" just because I happened to look fabulous in black. I was going to be a magnet for every sadistic senior in the school.

The bell rang, but as I was grabbing my bag, Mr. Lilly said, "Garnet, can you stay for a moment?"

There were a handful of snickers because people assumed I was in trouble, and a couple of busybodies tried to hang around to see what Lilly was going to do to me, but he sent them on their way.

"Sorry about the language," I said, semi-sincerely, "but this whole Rat Day thing—"

"I know. Look, there's one rule I didn't get a chance to explain." That's when he told me about the Kangaroo Court, which would be held the day after Rat Day to judge people who hadn't done their assigned rat or whose rats had gone too far. "I'm in charge of picking judges, and I thought you might want to be the sophomore class judge." He pulled out an honest-to-God badge from his desk drawer and held it out to me.

"And why would I want to do this?"

"Because in order to preserve their objectivity, judges are immune from being ratted."

"Seriously?"

He nodded.

Of course I took it. I'd have taken it even if he'd warned me about the ears and the tail, but it's probably just as well he didn't mention the pouch.

***

I didn't really know the other two judges, though it was a small enough school that I'd seen them around. The junior was fairly cool, in a geeky sort of way, and was working tech on *Macbeth*. I think he actually liked his kangaroo regalia; he was wearing a Qantas Airline T-shirt with it, and had stuck his iPod in his pouch. His name was Faulkner, of all things. His mother claimed distant kinship to the famed Southern writer, and Faulkner confessed that he was just relieved that she hadn't named him after a Confederate general like she had his brother.

The freshman was Mary Beth, who I'd tried to hate when I first got to Jackson's Bridge. She was perky, smart, and popular, and if that weren't enough to burn my buns, she was on the junior varsity cheerleading squad. Unfortunately, she was too damned nice to hate. Honestly and sincerely nice. I was hoping to find out she was a closet ax murderer or something equally disgusting, but in the meantime, I'd just have to be nice right back at her.

Then there was me, feeling like a complete asshole, and when a camera flashed, I realized that my judicial debut was being immortalized in the student newspaper or the yearbook. Maybe both. My pouch was overflowing with happiness.

At a signal from Stuart the bailiff, who was also the junior class president, we judges sat, and the students in the auditorium did, too. The court stenographer, also the junior class secretary, handed us copies of the docket and then returned to her table, ready to record our verdicts on a brand-new yellow legal pad she'd probably bought just to look official.

I looked at the table in front of me and rolled my eyes. I had an official legal pad, too, and two sharpened number-two pencils. I could die happy.

Stuart said, "The first case is Trask versus Mitchell. Annette Trask and Erin Mitchell, approach the bench."

As the two ersatz litigants made their way to the podiums set up in front of the stage, I tried to look as if I knew what I was doing. The way Mr. Lilly had explained the procedure, it shouldn't be too bad. There were only two kinds of cases. Either an underclassman had refused a rat, undermining some sainted senior's privileges, or a senior had issued a rat that was unsafe or inappropriate. Of course, very few rats were considered unsafe or inappropriate. As long as clothes stayed on, physical contact was minimal, and no bones were broken, most were considered good clean fun. I wondered how many psychologists had paid for their Porsches with the fees from the formerly ratted.

The bailiff swore Annette and Erin in, using a wildly non–politically correct Bible, and then they were ready to start arguing the case. I figured I better pretend I cared. There was no telling when Principal Picket might come sneaking around.

That first case was pretty straightforward. Annette, a senior and noted jock, had gone into the girls' locker room while a class was getting dressed after fourth period gym, and made them all sing "We Are Family" into her cell phone. Since the reception was bad in the locker room itself, they'd had to sing in the showers, but Erin stayed at her locker instead. I'd never noticed Erin before, maybe because she looked like a photocopy of half a dozen other juniors, only with less impressive curves. Erin claimed that she'd wanted to participate in the sing-along, but that she'd had to take care of a "female matter."

Once both girls had told their stories, we judges turned off our microphones and huddled together to deliberate.

"Erin's guilty," Faulkner said without hesitation.

"I don't know," Mary Beth said, sounding as nice as ever. "Maybe it really is her time of the month."

"No way," I said. "If she was on the rag, she'd have gone to the toilet stall to—" I saw that Faulkner was looking queasy, and decided to keep it clean. "If she needed to use a sanitary product, she'd have done so privately, not while standing at her locker."

Despite my effort to be delicate, Faulkner turned red, but he nodded and said, "Um, yeah. That's right."

Mary Beth looked unhappy, but agreed.

"What should we make her do?" Faulkner asked gleefully.

"You're not enjoying this a bit, are you?" I asked.

Faulkner shrugged. "I tried to get Rat Day banned last year, and Erin was one of the ones who made a stink about it. I figure it's only fair."

"You mean I wouldn't be wearing these ears if it weren't for her?"

"Well," Faulkner admitted, "she wasn't the only one. Caroline Hendry was the big one, but you know how Erin is always trying to suck up to her and the others in the so-called popular crowd."

I knew no such thing, actually, but I was all for going after *anybody* who'd worked to keep Rat Day on the calendar. "Let's throw the book at her!"

We went back and forth for a few minutes before deciding to make Erin sing "I Feel Pretty" over the loudspeaker during the morning announcements the following day.

The rest of the cases were pretty much the same. Somebody didn't do the rat they were supposed to do because it was embarrassing, and we made them do something even more embarrassing as payback. I might have felt guilty if I'd liked any of the people involved, but at least two of them had played the laugh-at-the-goth-chick game, and another one had written a racist screed for the school paper that had really frosted my shorts. In fact, it was almost alarming how much I got into the whole thing. My future therapist was going to have to spend months assuaging the guilt I was going to feel some day. In the meantime, I kept coming up with humiliating punishments, with the able assistance of Faulkner. That boy had a real mean streak—I was really starting to like him.

The only time we found in favor of the underclassman was when it turned out that the senior involved was the underclassman's ex-boyfriend. His story was that she wouldn't put on the old football uniform he'd told her to wear, but her witnesses pointed out that he'd had two other guys waiting nearby. One had a super-soaker water gun, and the other had a cell phone to get shots of the impromptu wet T-shirt contest, no doubt intending to post them online. That was the first time I saw Mary Beth get angry, and I was right there with her. We sentenced the jerk and his confederates to wearing cheerleader outfits and cleaning out the boy's bathroom for a week. The cheerleader outfits were my ideas, and I was rather proud of the enhancement.

Still, even dumping on people I dislike gets boring after a while, and the other kids in the auditorium were looking bored, too, until the bailiff called out the last case: Hendry versus Burns. All of a sudden, people sat up straight and got quiet.

Caroline Hendry was the head varsity cheerleader, and unlike Mary Beth, was exactly what a cheerleader was supposed to be: busty, blonde, vain, and mean. Roxanne Burns, on the other hand, had a figure that was as straight as her long brown hair. She wore glasses instead of contacts to prove her mighty intellect and edited the school literary magazine with an iron fist and a red pen that never seemed to run out of ink.

The two of them were like a snake and a mongoose—natural-born enemies. Having been unlucky enough to have encountered both of them my first week at Jackson's Bridge High, I hated each with equal enthusiasm.

Caroline had introduced herself promptly so she could start insulting my hair, clothes, and school supplies right away. At first she'd denounced me as goth, then decided I was emo, and finally settled for calling me a freak—she couldn't even keep her cultural stereotypes straight! As for Roxanne, when I attended a meeting for potential staff members and contributors to the literary magazine, she'd made it painfully clear that my help was not wanted. Apparently, genre fiction of any kind was not appropriately uplifting, which left me out in the cold.

I realized then that I was about to have a chance to cash in the karma points I'd earned for dressing like a marsupial in public, with interest.

Caroline, as the aggrieved party, went first, speaking with an accent that was eerily reminiscent of Principal Picket's. "I feel bad about having to bring all this up," she lied, "but it just wouldn't be fair to the other students who played by the rules if I didn't."

Roxanne snorted, and for once, I was in complete agreement with her, even though I had to keep my stern-but-fair judge face on.

Caroline tried to look shocked, but couldn't quite keep the flash of irritation out of her eyes. "Rat Day has always been real important to me, and I thought it might be fun to be more creative this year. To actually have rats. So I bought a dozen pairs of ears and tails." She reached into a Belk's shopping bag and pulled out a set. The gray ears were pretty convincing, but I personally thought the tail looked more like a opossum than a rat. "I had an eyebrow pencil to draw on whiskers, too."

The cheerleader looked so pleased by her own thoroughness that I wanted to slug her.

"Roxanne was one of the first people I gave one to. She put them on like she was supposed to, but when I saw her later in the day, she wasn't wearing them anymore."

"I had on the ears!" Roxanne said.

"But not the tail!" Caroline snapped, then went back into her sweeter-than-Tupelo-honey voice. "It just wasn't the same without the tail. Everybody else I told to wear them wore them all day long, and Roxanne should have, too." She sniffed in Roxanne's direction. "That's all I've got to say."

Faulkner said, "Roxanne, do you have a rebuttal?"

"I certainly do. Caroline was lying in wait for me when I arrived at school yesterday, and—"

"Objection!" Caroline said. "I was not lying anywhere. I just happened to see her."

"One, we don't have objections in Kangaroo Court," Faulkner said. "And two, Caroline, you had your chance. Now it's Roxanne's turn."

Caroline's eyes narrowed, but she didn't say anything else as Roxanne continued.

"As I said, Caroline was waiting for me when I arrived, and demanded that I put on the ears and tail. Which I did. And I let her draw whiskers on my face, even though I'm allergic to that brand of makeup." Now it was her turn to look pleased with herself, because she'd been such a martyr.

"Why didn't you keep the tail on all day?" Mary Beth asked. "Did you lose it?"

"Not exactly," Roxanne replied. "You see, I took it off at the beginning of gym class—"

"See!" Caroline crowed.

"School regulations clearly state that no accessories of any kind are to be worn with gym uniforms. Even if I'd been willing to break the rules, Coach Odo told me I *had* to leave the ears and tail in my gym locker. I was fully intending to put them back on after class, but when I got back to my locker, the tail was gone. Somebody had stolen it." She looked directly at Caroline, making it obvious who she thought the thief was. "I looked everywhere, but I couldn't find it. I did put the ears on, and was wearing them when I left the locker room, which is when Caroline saw me. I tried to explain, but she said she was bringing me up on charges. Quite a coincidence that she was lying in wait for me *again*."

"Are you saying I took the tail?" Caroline said indignantly. "You just threw it away because you didn't want to wear it."

"Don't be ridiculous. I'd worn it half the day already. Why throw it away then?"

"How do I know you didn't throw it away right after I gave it to you?"

Faulkner and Mary Beth banged their gavels on the table simultaneously. Personally, I'd been enjoying the carnage, even holding out a slight hope that it would get physical.

Mary Beth said, "Roxanne, can you prove you were wearing the tail before gym class?"

"Absolutely. I have witnesses," she said, and three juniors in the audience stood up and nodded.

"What about you, Caroline?" Faulkner said. "Can you prove you didn't swipe the tail?"

"I have Spanish fourth period," she said, "and I was there the entire time."

No witnesses were needed to confirm that. Señora Casali was infamous for not letting anybody leave class even *uno momento* before the bell rang.

"Then if neither of you has anything to add," Faulkner said, "we'll make our decision."

We huddled once more.

"This one's tricky," Mary Beth said.

"What's tricky about it?" Faulkner asked. "Roxanne didn't wear the tail, so she has to pay the penalty."

"But it's not her fault if the tail was missing."

"You don't really think Caroline managed to sneak out of Casali's class, do you?"

"Maybe it got lost."

"Come on. She just didn't want to wear it. Guilty."

But this time Mary Beth looked stubborn. "I don't think Roxanne would lie. If she says the tail was gone, then it was gone."

"Okay one vote for guilty, one vote for not guilty. That makes you the tiebreaker, Garnet."

"So it does." Caroline or Roxanne? Damned if I wasn't torn. I didn't know which of them to believe, any more than I knew which of them I disliked more. For a second I considered flipping a coin. What difference would it make really?

If I ruled for Caroline, Roxanne would have to do something embarrassing or forgo her Rat Day privileges the next year. Not exactly hard time at San Quentin. The only thing was, that would make Caroline happy, which I really didn't want to do.

So maybe I should rule in favor of Roxanne. Only that would be like putting out an ad that Caroline had stolen the rat tail and set Roxanne up, which wouldn't do much for her reputation. And in a school like Jackson's Bridge, reputation counted for a lot. Yeah, I hated her with a fiery passion and all that, but even if I had been willing to ruin her school career, I wasn't willing to do it unless I was absolutely sure she was at fault.

Faulkner and Mary Beth were still looking at me expectantly. In fact, everybody in the whole freaking auditorium was looking at me expectantly. I was stuck, and getting pissed about it. If only Caroline hadn't caught Roxanne without that damned tail!

That's when I figured something out. So I turned the microphone back on and said, "I have a few more questions." Caroline and Roxanne both looked irked at the delay, while Faulkner and Mary Beth looked confused, but I didn't let that stop me. "Roxanne, you said that Caroline was outside the locker room when you came out."

"That's right."

"And Caroline, you said you had Spanish while Roxanne was in gym."

"Yes, Your Honor."

"So what where you doing near the gym?"

For the first time, Caroline looked uncomfortable. "It was my lunch period."

"So? The gym isn't on the way from Señora Casali's classroom to the cafeteria."

She fidgeted a bit, then finally said, "I heard Roxanne wasn't wearing the tail, so I went to check."

"How did you hear this?"

"I got a text message."

No wonder she hadn't wanted to admit it. Cell phones were supposed to be turned off during school hours, and if she'd been caught receiving a message, hers would have been confiscated for the rest of the semester.

But enforcing that wasn't my problem. I said, "Who sent the message?"

"Erin Mitchell."

Better and better. Erin was the defendant from our first case. "Erin was in gym class with Roxanne?"

"I guess."

"Do you have your cell phone now?"

"Only on silent mode!"

"Let me see it."

She looked reluctant, but surrendered her top-of-the-line Razr, which I handed to Faulkner. "Can you check the call history to see when she received the message from Erin?"

It took a while, because apparently Caroline was a text messaging addict, but he finally located the record and announced, "She got the message at 11:58."

"Roxanne, what time does gym class end?"

"Officially at twelve, but Coach Odo sends us to the locker room at 11:45 to get dressed."

"So you left the locker room at the noon bell?"

"More like a quarter after. Between having to sing that abominable song Annette ratted us with and looking for the tail, I ran late."

"And Caroline was waiting for you?"

"Right."

"Was Erin with her?"

"I didn't notice, but she probably was." She rolled her eyes. "Erin's always following along behind Caroline."

I said, "Bailiff, call Erin to the stand."

After a moment, the scrawny junior came down to the stage, and arranged herself so that she was standing near Caroline.

"Just to remind you, you're still under oath," I said.

"Okay, fine," she said, not meeting my eyes.

"So Erin, when did you leave the locker room after gym class yesterday?"

"I'm not sure."

"Was it before or after you sent the text message to Caroline?"

"Um... I'm not sure."

"It must have been before 11:58," Mary Beth put in helpfully, "or you wouldn't have been able to send the text message. Everybody knows you don't get decent reception in the locker room."

I'd known that, thanks to the first case, but was happy to have Mary Beth point it out. "Is that right?" I asked Erin.

"I guess."

"So at 11:58 you sent the message that Roxanne wasn't wearing her tail, even though Roxanne was searching for it at that very moment."

The girl blanched. "She was already dressed before I left the locker room."

"Dressed, maybe, but still looking for the tail. How did you know she wasn't going to find it?"

Now all of those faces that had been watching me were watching Erin.

"I heard her tell somebody she wasn't going to wear it," she stammered.

"Who did she say that to?" I asked. "We can bring up the entire gym class to confirm."

"Um... Maybe I only thought I heard it."

"Or maybe you knew where the tail was. We already have sworn testimony that you didn't sing with the others in the shower room. Isn't it true that you disobeyed Annette so you could stay in the locker room, take the tail from Roxanne's locker, hide it, and then text Caroline to get Roxanne in trouble?"

She jerked her head around like a trapped rat, appropriately enough. "Well, Caroline said to—"

"You skank!" Caroline hissed. "Don't you dare try to pin this on me!"

"No, no! It's just that I knew that— I mean, everybody knows you hate Roxanne, and I was trying to help you."

"Help me? You call this helping! You douchebag!"

"Language," I said, but it was hard not to grin.

Faulkner gestured, and we three judges leaned away from the microphones to confer. It didn't take long.

Then I announced, "The case of Hendry versus Burns is hereby dismissed. Roxanne, would you like to press charges against Erin?"

"You bet I will!"

"No, I want to!" Caroline said. "She's the one who got me into this."

"You can be co-complainants. The case of Hendry and Burns versus Mitchell is now added to the docket." I turned to Erin. "Do you have anything to say in your defense?"

"I didn't mean— I just wanted—" Then she hung her head. "No."

"Then we will render our verdict. Erin, you have been found guilty of interfering in Rat Day proceedings. You are to retrieve the tail from wherever it was you hid it, and then to wear it to class every day for the next thirty days. If you are seen without it, or if you in any way try to avoid your sentence, you will lose all Rat Day privileges in the future." The three of us banged our gavels in unison, and Faulkner declared the session of Kangaroo Court complete. As the bailiff told the gallery to rise, the three of us hopped out the way we'd hopped in.

"I still think we should have gone ahead and taken away Erin's privileges for next year," Faulkner groused.

"No, this is enough," Mary Beth said with an uncharacteristic gleam in her eye. "Can you imagine how Caroline is going to treat her for the rest of the year? That's what she gets for trying to suck up!"

"You go, girl! Let that bad self out!" I said proudly.

Then she had to go and ruin it by saying, "Poor Erin's going to be really lonely from now on. Maybe I should go talk to her."

"Mary Beth, you don't have a bad self, do you?" I said.

She just smiled, and went along her decidedly non-bad way.

"She's too good to be real," I said wonderingly.

Faulkner nodded. "We'll have to keep an eye on her just to make sure she doesn't get taken advantage of."

I lifted an eyebrow at the "we" part, but didn't question it. I kind of liked the way it sounded.

"By the way, that was an impressive piece of deduction," he added.

"Thanks. Of course, it means that I've helped maintain Rat Day, which I despise, and missed my best opportunity to strike a blow at either of the school über-bitches."

"True. But you made sure that both über-bitches owe you, big-time."

I considered it. "So you think Caroline will let me be a cheerleader?"

"Please tell me you're kidding."

I grinned. "Then do you think Roxanne will let me submit to the literary magazine?"

"Forget that pretentious rag. I'm putting together an online zine that's way cooler."

"Yeah? Do you take genre fiction?"

"Is there any other kind?"

"I'll e-mail you a story tonight."

"Boffo." As we picked up our backpacks, he said, "You're going to drama, right? Want to grab a Coke first?"

"Sure."

We started out of the auditorium together, and I even forgot I was still wearing the kangaroo crap. Maybe Jackson's Bridge wasn't a complete hellhole after all.

Afterword

Rat Day was an actual thing when I was a student at Gulf Breeze Junior High School in Gulf Breeze, Florida, and I never realized how insane that event was until I described it to my daughters. We also had a Kangaroo Court to deal with people who didn't perform their assigned rats or who went too far. In fact, it was years before I heard the term *kangaroo court* in any other context. Sadly, I moved away from Gulf Breeze before I was old enough to impose rats upon underclassmen.

By the way, our Kangaroo Court judges did not dress in kangaroo suits, though I think it would have added considerably to the dignity of the proceedings if they had.

Kids Today

Jimbo French, a big man with more than his share of curly brown hair, was ringing up a check for a couple of truckers when I walked into French's Restaurant on Monday morning, so I just picked up my own menu from the wooden holder nailed onto the wall.

I could have skipped the menu. French's has been there for years, and the food never changes. They serve breakfast all day long, a decent selection of sandwiches at lunch, and at night, dinners like meatloaf and baked ham with two sides. Not that I care about their lunch and dinner. All I ever eat at French's is breakfast. The wife doesn't get moving until nearly noon, which means I get about an hour a day to call my own, five days a week, and I spend it at French's. It's about as cheap as any restaurant is these days, it's reasonably clean, and I don't need a dictionary to figure out what stuff on the menu is. I can't eat ambiance, so I don't see any reason to pay for it.

I headed for my usual table, which is close to the window for plenty of light and far enough from the TV mounted onto the wall that I don't have to listen to the talking heads. It wasn't until I was about to reach for my chair that I realized there was somebody there. A guy in pressed khakis and a dark blue shirt with an alligator on it was giving Sunny his order.

I muttered a few choice words under my breath, the way I do at home to keep the wife from hearing. There were other empty tables, of course—it was mid-morning, so the bulk of the breakfast crowd was long gone—but there was nothing open in Sunny's section. Digby, who considers himself the mogul of eBay, gave me a sympathetic look and Lilah May patted the empty chair beside her, but if I'd wanted somebody yammering at me while I ate, I'd have stayed home with the wife. At least the wife didn't expect me to pay attention the way Lilah May would. I just went to one of Marla's tables.

I looked at the menu to make sure that Jimbo hadn't changed anything, then slapped it shut and glared at the guy sitting at my table.

Sunny finished taking his order and came by to say, "Good morning, Mr. Anthony. How's the missus today?"

"Ill as a hornet," I said, "same as always."

"Is her arthritis bothering her again?"

"Nah, she's just mean."

"Let me get this order in and I'll bring you some coffee. Then Marla will be over in a minute to take care of you."

We both knew that a man could die of thirst while waiting for Marla, but Sunny was too nice to say so. Right about then, Marla came out of the kitchen, where she'd probably been talking to somebody on her cell phone when she was supposed to be working. Instead of coming to take my order, she sashayed over to Jimbo and started messing with him, pushing her titties at him as if they were something special.

Don't get me wrong. I'm not so old that I don't still appreciate a good pair, but that doesn't mean I want them shoved up in my face. Not that Jimbo seemed to mind, which the regulars all noticed. Lilah May was watching as if she couldn't wait to tell the story to some other blue-haired old lady, and even Digby glanced over. And naturally the two women who claimed to be sisters, but weren't, had to look.

What was Jimbo thinking, making a fool of himself over a cheap tramp when a nice girl like Sunny was crazy about him? Sure, Marla was a good-looking woman, if you liked blondes with plenty of makeup and short skirts, but the wife had been even better looking back in the day and look at what she'd turned into. Sunny was pretty enough, with brown hair kept neat and a good figure. Plus she kept her skirts down where they belonged. I shook my head and opened up my newspaper while I waited for Marla to notice I was there.

Eventually she wandered over and I gave her my usual order: two eggs scrambled, a biscuit with gravy, and crispy bacon. "*Crispy* bacon," I repeated.

"I heard you the first time," she snapped and grabbed the menu out of my hand. "You're the one wearing hearing aids, not me."

Naturally, when she finally brought my food over, the bacon was so limp I could have tied it into a knot. Not that my so-called waitress actually waited to see if I was happy—I think she'd have slung the plate to me like a Frisbee if she could have.

As slow as Marla had been with my breakfast, I wasn't surprised when my to-go order was slow, too. I'd long since finished reading my newspaper and was stuck watching some TV show about which TV star was sleeping with which movie star. Kids today. They think they invented sex. I was tempted to let Marla keep the damned order, but I knew if I showed up back home without the wife's two country ham biscuits and black coffee, I'd never hear the end of it.

Funny thing was, the new guy stayed around as long as I did, even though Sunny had brought him his food right away, the way she did for everybody. He'd pulled out a laptop computer and was typing away as if he was doing something important.

Eventually Jimbo brought over the to-go order because Marla had made herself scarce again. When I went to the register to pay, I said, "You know, Jimbo, I don't appreciate having to wait so long."

"Sorry about that, Mr. Anthony. The kitchen is a bit backed up today." He smiled as if he thought I believed him. He probably thought he'd got all the lipstick off his cheek, too. What a sap.

The next morning the new guy was at my table again, wearing a different-colored alligator shirt. I gave him the hairy eyeball, but he didn't even notice. That meant that once again I was stuck with Marla, my bacon was limp as a dishrag, and the wife's to-go order was slow in coming.

I gave Jimbo another piece of my mind, but he just apologized and gave me the wife's biscuits for free, which wasn't the point.

I made sure to get to French's earlier on Wednesday, and by the time the alligator-shirt guy showed up, I was already at my table crunching on bacon. Lilah May was running late so he took her table, and she had to put up with Marla. Thursday he got Digby's table. It looked like he was well on his way to becoming a regular, and he didn't seem to care that he was throwing off the rhythm of the place. Digby and Lilah May were as annoyed as I was, and the sisters were looking downright hostile, and I guessed they were thinking he might be coming after their spot next.

But on Friday, he beat me in and was back in my seat. The bastard gave me a smug look, too, sitting there in yet another alligator shirt. Dammit, there was a limit to how early I could get myself moving in the morning, let alone getting the wife situated. I was never going to get my table back!

I stomped over to Marla's section and stewed all through breakfast. Lilah May stopped by on her way out and said, "It looks like we may be losing a waitress soon."

"Hallelujah! When is Marla leaving?"

She tittered, which is one of the reasons I don't like eating breakfast with her. "No, silly, I mean Sunny. Don't you see how that new guy looks at her? He's smitten. I can read the signs."

How she knew anything about a man was a mystery to me, because as far as I knew, Lilah May hasn't been laid since Truman was in office. But after she left, I took another gander at the new guy. Even though he pretended he was working on that laptop of his or watching TV, every time Sunny came into the room, he was watching her. Unlike Lilah May, I really did know the signs. He was after Sunny, all right, and I had a hunch she'd be gone from French's sooner or later. There was no telling what kind of loser Jimbo would hire next, and I was in a black mood when Jimbo got around to bringing me the wife's biscuits.

I was walking to my car when I saw why Marla hadn't brought me the to-go order herself. She was outside with her cell phone glued to her ear, yakking a mile a minute.

"No, I've got time to talk. Jimbo doesn't mind," she said. "Wrapped right around my little finger … No, not yet, but any day now. … Work here afterwards? Not hardly. In fact, I'm thinking we'll sell this place. Jimbo told me one of the chains is dying for the location. I'm not sure which one, but it's one of the good ones, not like this dump. … I don't know how much they offered, but it's got to be enough to party on for a good long time."

She saw me listening and didn't even have the decency to look embarrassed. Just made a face and held her hand over the mouthpiece long enough to say, "Go on home, you old fart! And mind your own beeswax!"

I could feel my blood pressure rising as I went to my station wagon. Marla was going to talk Jimbo into selling French's to some damned chain? I wanted to think he'd have more sense, but I knew better. Not only was I about to lose the best waitress I'd ever had, but now Marla was going to take away the one place I could get a decent breakfast and country ham biscuits good enough for the wife. What was I supposed to do? Get biscuits from the Bojangles drive-through?

I sat and thought until the wife's coffee got cold, but the plan I came up with was good enough to be worth her fussing for the rest of the day. Maybe I am an old fart, but I still have a trick or two up my sleeve.

None of us regulars go to French's on Saturday or Sunday—there are too many people who go there for brunch—but on Monday I got the ball rolling. While the alligator-shirt guy sat in my chair, making cow eyes at Sunny, I sat with Digby and laid it all out for him. Come Tuesday, he sat with the sisters to explain everything to them, while I put up with Lilah May long enough to get her up to speed. It was none too soon. We all saw that Sunny was spending more and more time with the alligator-shirt guy, even making some of the rest of us wait for our coffee refills.

Wednesday morning, I didn't even try to beat the alligator-shirt guy to my table because for once, I wanted to be in Marla's section. As usual she was as slow as cold molasses, which meant alligator-shirt guy was long gone by the time she brought my to-go order. I said, "Huh, must be nice."

"What?"

"To have plenty of money."

"Like I'd know, working here."

"If that new guy keeps tipping like that, you can ask Sunny what it's like. He just slipped her a twenty."

"What?"

Since most of us only left a couple of dollars, a tip that big that sounded awfully good to Marla. I added, "Of course he didn't start out giving her that much, and it's not every day. Still, even twice a week is pretty good."

"I think you need to get your eyes checked, old man. Twenty-dollar tips in this place?"

I shrugged. "Just don't expect me to start throwing my money around like that."

"As if!"

The next day, when I sat at what was becoming my regular spot, Sunny came right over to get my order.

"Where's Marla?" I asked.

"Oh, she's here," Sunny said. "Jimbo rearranged the sections a little." She looked wistfully at the new guy, who was looking put out at having Marla waiting on him. But Marla was doing her best to show him how good a waitress she was—running back and forth every few minutes, bringing him fresh coffee whenever he took a sip out of his cup, and of course, shaking her booty for all she was worth. When he only left a so-so tip, she let her smile slip for a second, but since I'd warned her that he wasn't overly generous every day, she just sucked it up and kept on flirting.

The next couple of days were like musical chairs, with the alligator-shirt guy trying to make his way back to Sunny's section while Marla chased him around the dining room. I'd been hoping that he'd go ahead and fall for Marla, but he only had eyes for Sunny, no matter how many blouse buttons Marla left undone. Plus he hadn't left Marla any monster tips, so she was losing interest. That meant we were going to have to move on to the next phase first thing Monday morning.

This part involved all of the regulars. We were used to Digby talking about the stuff he bought and sold on eBay, and he was always telling us what our clothes and cars were worth. Now Digby told Marla how expensive alligator-shirt guy's watch and cell phone and computer were. He also made up some tale about the man owning his own business and being independently wealthy. I thought he was laying it on too thick, but Marla swallowed it hook, line, and sinker.

Since Sunny was still interested in alligator-shirt guy, too, she had to be redirected. Lilah May took on that job. Her being such a gossip anyway, it only seemed natural when she said, "You know, Sunny, maybe I should warn Marla about that man over there. Since he started eating here, I've heard him on his cell phone out in the parking lot making dates with three different women."

"Really?" Sunny said. "He seems so nice."

"Nice is as nice does," Lilah May said. "Now if I were a few years younger, it's Jimbo French I'd be looking at. He's a steady, trustworthy man. Cute, too."

"You're right about that," Sunny admitted.

Then, as if it had just occurred to her, Lilah May said, "You know, you two would make a real cute couple."

"I don't think he's interested in me."

"He could be. If you'd just wear a tiny bit of makeup and maybe spend just a little more time talking to him, I bet he'd be head over heels for you in no time."

"You think so?"

"I know so!"

Sunny had nearly given up on Jimbo because of him panting after Marla, but Lilah May's encouragement was all she needed to make her hopeful again.

As for Jimbo, he might not have been the brightest bulb on the circuit, but even he could tell that Marla was chasing alligator-shirt guy. So when Sunny started making an effort, it had an effect pretty quickly.

That left alligator-shirt guy, who still didn't like Marla, and that was the trickiest part. Since he never bothered to speak to any of us regulars, we couldn't very well suddenly strike up a conversation with him. Nor could we start yelling at one another across the tables, because the wrong people would hear what we were saying. That's where the sisters came in. They were both a touch deaf, so they usually spoke a little loud anyway and their table was the closest to alligator-shirt guy.

The brunette one said, "Have you seen what Sunny is up to this time?"

"Don't tell me she's catting around after another man," the redhead said.

"You know she is! This time it's Jimbo."

"I thought it was the cook."

"Oh, he was last week. You know she doesn't let moss grow under her."

"What about that linen delivery man?"

"He was just a one-time thing, I think. She kept the dairy man busy for nearly a month, but that's probably over now."

"I wouldn't put it past her to be seeing two at the same time."

"Two? Try three or four!"

They laughed.

I'd told them to not even look in alligator-shirt guy's direction, but I kept an eye on him as best I could over my newspaper. I don't think he wanted to believe them, but I caught him watching Sunny when she was talking with Jimbo, and I could tell he was becoming more and more convinced.

Of course, chasing him away from Sunny wasn't enough. If he just stopped coming to French's, Marla might start up on Jimbo again, and Jimbo might drop Sunny, and we could still end up losing our restaurant. So now we had to get alligator-shirt guy hooked on Marla. Making that happen was next.

First off, the sisters started talking about what a sweet girl Marla was. "She told me that she attends church every Sunday, and Wednesday night, too," said the redhead. Since we weren't sure what alligator-shirt guy's leanings were, we'd decided to take a chance and made her Protestant, which fit well enough. I figured Marla would be protesting as loud as she could if we ever tried to drag her into a church.

Next Lilah May shared a table with Digby, and of course she brought up the subject of Marla. "She's such a lovely, unspoiled girl," she said, emphasizing *unspoiled* enough that even a dummy would know that she meant Marla was a virgin. I had a hard time keeping a straight face at that—chances were that Marla hadn't been a virgin since her age hit double digits.

Then Lilah May said, "I just wish she'd dress a little differently. She's so innocent that she doesn't realize the effect her unfortunate outfits have on men."

I hadn't been sure that alligator-shirt guy would swallow that, but Lilah May can be pretty convincing when she wants to be.

The next day, Digby invited me to his table, saying he wanted to talk about something, man-to-man.

"You'll have to speak up a bit," I said. "My hearing aid battery is about to run out, and I didn't bring any spares."

"I've been thinking about asking Marla out," Digby said. "You know, like on a date."

"I can't say as I blame you," I said. "I'd ask her out myself if it weren't for the wife. Well, that and being forty-five years older than she is." Forty-five years older than Marla pretended to be, anyway. We went on to discuss where Digby might take her on this theoretical date of theirs, but I kept glancing over at alligator-shirt guy's expression. He wasn't liking our conversation one bit. There's nothing like a little competition to get a man riled up.

As for me, I sprinkled in random facts about Marla, saying what a shame it was that she didn't have any family in town and didn't even have a pet in the apartment where she lived all by herself. The other regulars weren't sure why that made Marla more attractive until I spelled out that it meant that he wouldn't have to get her parents' approval, didn't have to deal with a dog or cat in case he had allergies or phobias, and that they would have a place they could be alone. Even Digby got what they might want to do in private.

After a week and a half of our play-acting, I came into French's and saw that not only had Marla not come into work that day, but alligator-shirt guy never showed up either. None of us regulars said anything, but we were all grinning to beat the band.

Of course, that meant Sunny had to handle the whole dining room so she wasn't quite as good as she usually was, but that was only for a few days. A week later, when Marla still hadn't shown, Jimbo hired Annabelle. Annabelle wasn't as good as Sunny but she was a big improvement over Marla. After that, things quieted down, other than us regulars trying to guess when Jimbo was going to pop the question to Sunny.

Except a week after that, alligator-shirt guy showed up again. At my table. And while I was glaring at him, he was concentrating on Sunny. The other regulars were all kinds of agitated, wondering what was coming next, and Lilah May kept trying to get my attention to come talk to her. I acted as if I didn't see her, just read my newspaper and thought about the situation. By the time Annabelle brought me the wife's biscuits, I had my plan all worked out.

When I went to pay my bill, I said, "Jimbo, did that gal Marla ever pick up her stuff? I lent her a magazine right before she disappeared, and I was wondering if she left it here."

He looked doubtful, probably about the idea of Marla reading anything, but he said, "I don't know what she had. Sunny packed her stuff into a box in case she ever shows up. But she can forget ever getting her last paycheck, leaving me in the lurch that way." I had to listen to him complain about her for a few minutes, but in the end, he brought over a cardboard box that had once held bags of potato chips and said I could look through it myself.

I went slowly, knowing he'd eventually have to go check things out in the kitchen, but once he was gone, it didn't take me but a minute to find what I needed. I covered up what I took with my newspaper, and then headed for my station wagon to wait. When alligator-shirt guy came out and drove away, I followed his van, hoping he was going home. Luckily, that's where he went. Since my memory isn't as sharp as it used to be, I made a note of the address on an old envelope before continuing on to my house. Of course, the wife fussed and fumed about her coffee and biscuits being cold, but I just heated it all up in the microwave, put it in front of her, and turned off my hearing aids.

The next day, I didn't go to French's, even though it was a Thursday. That is, I went, but I didn't go inside. Instead I drove by to make sure alligator-shirt guy was there at my table. Then I drove back to his house, and left a little something under some leaves on his lawn. It took some doing to make sure it was visible, but not too obvious. I'd have been worried that somebody would see me, but naturally enough, alligator-shirt guy had an isolated house with no other houses near by.

Then I went looking for a public phone, which wasn't easy—the phone company doesn't have many anymore because everybody uses cell phones. I found one outside a busy grocery store, where nobody took any notice of me as I called the police and said I'd heard screaming coming from alligator-shirt guy's house. They wanted my name, but I hung up and went into the grocery store to get something the wife could eat instead of her country ham biscuits. She wouldn't like it, but she could lump it this once.

By the time I got back out to my station wagon, the police were at the phone trying to get fingerprints, and I wished them luck. What kind of moron leaves fingerprints in this day and age? I'd even wiped off the quarter I'd use to pay for the call.

And wasn't French's buzzing when I got there the next day? The regulars were all sitting at the same table, something I'd never seen before, and they waved me over to join them.

"Did you hear the news?" Lilah May asked, her eyes wide.

"I just got here—you know I haven't read the paper yet."

"They found Marla!" she said.

"Don't tell me she's coming back to work here."

"She's dead!" Digby put in, earning him a dirty look from Lilah May for spoiling her story.

"What was it? Drugs?"

"No," Lilah May said. "It was that *man*. The man with the alligator shirts. He kidnapped her and took her back to his house and he did *things* to her."

"You're shitting me."

"No, it's true," the sisters said in unison.

"And you know the worst part?" Lilah May said, lowering her voice to a stage whisper. "Marla wasn't the first."

Digby jumped in again. "The police found remains of three other women in his basement. Word is that they'd all been interfered with."

Why he couldn't say *raped* like anybody else, I'll never know. Jimbo and Sunny came out of the kitchen then, and I thought they were going to take my order, but no, they pulled up chairs so we could go over it all again.

With everybody talking over one another, I got most of the details without even opening the newspaper. The cops had received an anonymous tip the day before about screaming from alligator-shirt guy's house. The guy had just gotten home and said he didn't know what the police where talking about, but then a cop found a French's name tag with the name MARLA on it in the front yard. They called Jimbo, who told them what he knew, which was enough to make them suspicious. When they went inside, they found what was left of Marla and the other women, and now alligator-shirt guy was in jail where I hoped he would never get another bite of crispy bacon.

It took a week or two for things to really settle down. Sunny was upset, feeling guilty about Marla, so Lilah May pretended to be, too. And I saw Digby swiping some menus and things from French's, probably to sell on eBay—some people will buy anything. The sisters told anybody who'd listen that they'd known all along that there was something *terribly wrong* with *that man*, though they'd quickly change the subject when asked why they hadn't warned anybody. And of course nobody mentioned our efforts to point the guy toward Marla.

As for me, after that one day, I went back to my own table to eat my breakfast all by my lonesome while the other regulars kept on bleating about the horror of it all. Idiots! I'd known what the new guy was that first week. The signs are easy enough to spot, if you've got half a brain, and half a brain is all Lilah May had, thinking he was hunting for a wife. He'd been hunting all right, but not for a wife.

I couldn't believe what a fuss everybody was making anyway. Four women? Big fat hairy deal! Back in my prime, I went hunting every month, and I still managed one or two hunts a year—I'd have to check my scrapbook to find out what my latest tally was, but I was getting pretty close to triple digits.

Kids today. They think they invented serial killing.

Afterword

French's Restaurant is based on two real-life North Carolina restaurants: Finch's in Raleigh and Skyland in Charlotte. Finch's was where my grandfather ate breakfast every single day for as long as I can remember. The waitresses all knew his order by heart—two eggs over easy, streak o' lean, and dry toast—and to fix him two country ham biscuits and an order of grits to take home to my grandmother. The layout of French's, my fictional restaurant, is more like Skyland, where my parents ate dinner almost every day.

The real-life waitresses at both restaurants were wonderful, mind you, and as far as I know there was never a murder associated with either establishment. Blame that on the mystery writer's habit of seeing a nice place and thinking, "Hey, wouldn't it be fun to set a murder here?"

Bell, Book, and Candlepin

I should have noticed the curse as soon as I walked into the Candlepin Castle, but it's not like I've got a lot of experience with evil spells. Or with any spells. I'm Elspeth Allaway, and we witches of the Allaway Kith don't wave wands or spout magic words. We have Affinities. Sure, all of us can sense magic and smell lies, but the big action is in Affinities, and each one is different, as if we were a magical Legion of Superheroes. My mother can weave emotions into rugs and blankets, and my cousin Maura's thing is absorbing energy via phones. Another cousin is the Pied Piper of plants—I've seen vines reach for her when she walks by. My own Affinity was what was responsible for my being so eager to get to work that I didn't notice the curse.

Well, that and being pissed at my mother. She'd called just as I was heading out the door and had ripped me a new one. Oh, she hadn't yelled or screamed—I'd have preferred it if she had. Instead she used that calm, even tone of hers to tell me how disappointed she was that I'd used my Affinity in a non–life-affirming way the previous weekend. It hadn't been that big a deal, just a little prank, but she'd found out somehow—I was guessing my perfect cousin Ennis was behind it. Anyway, Mom decided I needed a refresher course in the Law of Return, as if she hadn't started brainwashing me the second after the midwife slapped me on the butt, and she ended up lecturing me for fifteen solid minutes. After that I was jonesing for some serious decibels.

See, my Affinity is for sound. I can block it in like a set of noise-canceling headphones or go the other way and amplify better than any woofer or tweeter ever made. I also collect sounds—from voices to squeaky doors to musical notes to special effects—and then replay those sounds at any volume from subliminal to ear-shattering. This lets me play great jokes or perform immature stunts, depending on whether you laugh at fart noises.

I like being around noise any time, but when I'm upset, nothing soothes me like a little cacophony. Hence my pleasure at arriving for my shift at the Candlepin Castle, West Sommers's premier candlepin bowling alley. In fact, it's West Sommers's only candlepin bowling alley, but that's no reason to abandon a semi-decent slogan. The pay is lousy and the hours are worse, and I don't even particularly like bowling, but you can't beat the noise. Balls crashing into the pins, bowlers cheering for their strikes or yelling at those last two pins to fall over even though it never works, the ball return smacking the balls together, and people talking over everything else. On weekends, you get loud music on top of that, and we host an awful lot of kids' birthday parties. That makes it heaven to those who prefer the noise-seeking lifestyle.

Somebody who'd never played might think the candlepin style of bowling New Englanders prefer would be quieter than ten-pin, but it's a trade-off. The balls are smaller, only about four and a half inches in diameter, but since they don't have finger holes, you get that satisfying thunk of solid balls. The pins are smaller, too, but the machines don't clear them away between the balls, so that gives an extra dollop of sound. Best of all, each bowler gets three balls in a box, which means more collisions for me to savor.

Since I'd had exams all week, I hadn't worked since the previous Saturday, so I paused just inside the door to soak in some of the glory. Though it was early in the evening and there wasn't much business, the Castle is a barn of a building, with creaking floors and echoes and clanking ball returns. I'd figured being a few more minutes late wouldn't matter, but my manager, Amar, really gave me the stink-eye as I clocked in.

I took a look at the schedule posted by the time clock and was glad to see that I'd be working the counter with Jake while Rayleigh and Belle had the snack bar. Rayleigh and Belle are fine, but they've been BFFs since kindergarten and when I work with either of them, they always seem vaguely disappointed that I don't know all their in-jokes. Jake and I, on the other hand, have our own in-jokes.

With Amar on duty, that was more people than we usually needed for a Thursday night, but we had a league championship scheduled.

Between one thing and another, it was probably fifteen minutes after five when I joined Jake at the front counter, where he was spraying disinfectant into rental shoes.

"Hey. What's up?"

"You're late," he said.

I looked around the Castle. There was one lone family foursome on lane one, and maybe half a dozen pairs of shoes still needed to be sprayed. "Dude, you could handle this in a coma."

"That's not the point, Elspeth!"

"Okay, I'm sorry." With anybody else, I'd have snapped back, but I'm usually willing to give Jake the benefit of the doubt. Werewolves get touchy at that time of the month. "Full moon coming?"

"Stupid much? It's just past the new moon. I'd think a witch would pay attention."

"Dude!" He and I were the only arcane types working at the Castle, and as far as we knew, the only ones at Cassidy College. We'd sniffed each other out during freshman orientation—literally, in Jake's case—and had been buds ever since. Normally that friendship included not mentioning each other's unusual abilities, but Jake seemed to have forgotten. Fortunately no other employees were close enough to hear, and the members of the foursome were squabbling too enthusiastically to hear anybody else. "If the moon isn't calling, why are you being such a butt?"

When he turned away from the shoes to glare at me, I felt his magic rising and could see his outlines start to blur, as if he were about to change into a wolf right in front of me. Then he took a deep breath and settled back into his usual lanky, gray-eyed, messy-haired self.

"Sorry," he said. "It's been a lousy couple of days. Hell, it's been a lousy week!"

"What's been going on?"

"All manner of crap. Amar got mad at Theresa Monday night and fired her in the middle of her shift. He said she was skimming from the cash register."

"Was she?"

"Maybe, but it wasn't cool to fire her in public like that. Then some douchebag accused us of rigging the scoring system. The man can't bowl for beans, and he blames us."

"Typical."

"On Tuesday, two guys in the Seniors League got into a fight over interference, and we had to call the cops."

"Seriously?"

"Neither guy would back down, even when the cops handcuffed them, but once they got outside and realized they were on their way to jail, they calmed down. Nobody pressed charges or anything."

"That's good. The last thing the Castle needs is players getting arrested."

"It gets worse. Last night there were two more fights—one started while the cops were on the way to deal with the first one. By the time it was all settled, the cops were making noises about shutting us down."

"Can they do that?"

"If they can't, the lawsuit might."

"What lawsuit?"

"A kid got his finger smashed in the ball return, and his mother is threatening to sue."

"That's insane."

"Then this afternoon, there were two birthday parties booked, and both birthday kids wanted the unicorn party room. Not only were the kids screaming, but I thought their fathers were going to throw down in front of them. So yeah, everybody is in a pissy mood. If it were up to me, I'd cancel tonight's championship, but you know Amar doesn't care about my opinion." His voice started to rise again. "Nobody listens to me!"

"Jeez, Jake!" I said. What was he sniping at me for? I hadn't even been there, so none of it was my fault. And why was everybody was acting like it was such a big deal for me to be a couple of minutes late? Maybe I should just walk out and let Jake work the counter by himself. Wouldn't it be funny if he lost it, went furry, and clawed up everybody in the place?

That's when I stopped myself. Not even in my most warped vengeful daydreams did I think it would be a hoot for a werewolf to attack innocent people, let alone what being found out would do to Jake and the rest of his Pack.

At last my magic-sensing kicked in, and I realized that something was seriously wrong. Not trusting myself to speak, I walked out from behind the counter and went out the front door and into the parking lot. Everything was normal, a little too quiet for my tastes, but good for most people.

I stepped back inside and felt myself growing agitated and angry. Out again. Calm. Inside. Bitchy.

That settled it.

I went back behind the counter, where Jake was spraying the last pair of shoes. Nobody was within range, but I used my Affinity to block anybody from hearing us—Jake calls it creating a cone of silence from some movie he saw. "We've got a problem. We've been cursed."

"Yeah, cursed by idiots," he snarled.

"No, I mean the Castle is under a curse."

"For real? Is that why we've had all these disasters?"

"And why you've been such a jerkface."

"I have not been—"

"Would you mind aiming the spray somewhere else?"

He looked at his hand as if he'd forgotten he was still holding the can of disinfectant, and carefully put it onto a shelf. "I guess I have been kind of an asshole. So is this curse like a spell? You told me you guys don't do spells?"

"We don't, but other witches can."

"Can you do a counterspell?"

"No spells, remember? And I don't think any of us Allaways have an anti-curse Affinity, even if there were any nearby." My family lived in Salem, Massachusetts—which is both funny and appropriate—but I go to college in West Sommers, which is a three-hour drive in good traffic. "Do you know anything about cursing?"

"According to my Pack, more than I should."

I resisted the urge to snipe at him for being a smart-ass, figuring my irritation was probably the curse affecting me. "I've never run into one before—"

"Then how do you know it's a curse?"

"Go outside for a minute."

He looked skeptical, but he did it. Then he did it again before coming back to the counter. "Man, curses suck. So what do we do?"

"No idea."

He continued to look at me expectantly.

I sighed. "I guess I can call my Aunt Hester after work. She knows a lot of things." She was the logical one to consult, but I was hoping I'd come up with a different plan before end of shift.

On lane one, the foursome's quarrel came to a head. The parents started screaming at each other as the smaller boy tackled the larger one and started pummeling him.

"On second thought," I said, "why don't I call Aunt Hester right now while you take care of that?"

Castle employees aren't supposed to make personal calls on the clock, and I didn't want to try to explain to Amar how talking to my aunt was actually work-related, so I took my cell phone into the staff bathroom. It's more private than the customer facilities and usually cleaner.

"Aunt Hester? This is Elspeth."

"Hello, dear. I've been waiting for you to call."

Aunt Hester is actually my great-great-aunt, and she creeps me out. Her Affinity is to see the future and she tends to rub it in. I've always wondered if she ever exaggerates how much she sees. I mean, how would I know if she was really expecting my call?

As if to stomp out my doubts, she said, "So you've got a curse. Nasty things, aren't they?"

I told her what was going on, and she told me as much as she was willing to. The thing about Aunt Hester is that she never tells everything she knows, which drives me nuts. It's a game of "I've Got a Secret" that never ends.

When I'd gotten all I was going to get, I said, "Thanks for the info. I'll call later to let you know how things turn out."

"I already know, dear. You better go now. Your friend is quite upset."

That was when Rayleigh from the snack bar burst into the bathroom, bawling like crazy.

I should have checked to see what her deal was, but crying is one noise I can do without. Besides, I figured that whatever she was crying about, it was likely another example of the curse at work, so it would be better to get back to Jake to make sure he was holding on to both his temper and his human form.

The fighting foursome had left, I was glad to see, so I didn't bother with the cone of silence. Jake was growling about some shoes that had been placed in the wrong slots, though not much more than usual. I exerted just a bit of my Affinity to conjure a creeper hiss from the game Minecraft right behind him, which usually gets a snicker. Today, he just looked impatient.

"Well?" he demanded.

"Aunt Hester said that it sounds like a Perturbatio curse, which messes with our emotions. It doesn't create meanness, but it does intensify any bit of nastiness you've already got. So instead of being a little irritated when somebody is late, you get über huffy."

"Come on, Elspeth! I'm under a curse. You can't hold what I do under a curse against me."

"You're right. The curse is just making me bitchy." He looked suspicious, so I kept going. "At least we don't have to worry about the roof falling in or the ball return throwing balls at our customers."

"What about the kid who got his finger caught?"

"Kids do that all the time. Maybe the curse intensified his tendency to stick his finger where it doesn't belong, or his mother's being sick of watching him every second. Besides, from what you said, it wasn't the finger that was the problem. It was the reaction that was way out of whack."

"You got that right. The woman was so mad I thought she was going to have a stroke. So how do we stop a curse?"

"If we're lucky, there's a cursed item hidden somewhere in the Castle."

"You've got a strange idea of lucky."

"If it's an amulet or something, all we have to do is find it and either destroy it or put it someplace where it won't bother anybody until the magic wears off." Aunt Hester had used that as an excuse for the day's second lecture on the Law of Return. As if I'd been seriously planning to put a cursed item under the bed of an ex-roommate who'd regularly eaten all my Cheerios and borrowed my clothes without asking.

"What if we're not lucky?" Jake asked.

"She said, and I quote, 'Oh, I can't break a curse, dear. If it were me, I'd just wait it out.'"

"That's it?"

"Pretty much." Okay, she had said some other stuff, but nothing that Jake needed to know. Still, I was glad it was witches who could smell lies and not werewolves, so he wouldn't notice that I'd left a detail or two out.

"Then let's hope we're lucky. How do we find the amulet or whatever it is?"

"That's where you come in, bloodhound boy." Even in human form, other than when lies were involved, Jake's sense of smell had mine beat by a mile.

"Man, I spend half my time trying not to inhale in this place. You have no idea how rank those rental shoes smell to me, and the nachos in the snack bar aren't much better."

"Sorry. I can't try to sense it because the whole building is affected. I could wander around and see where I'm most pissed off, but—"

"Never mind. What does it smell like?"

"Corruption and evil."

He gave me a look.

"That's what Aunt Hester said! Just see if you can smell anything more disgusting than the shoes."

Under the pretense of emptying trashcans, Jake spent the next half hour wandering around the Castle, but he was shaking his head when he came back.

"Nada."

"Did you check everywhere? The party rooms? The bathrooms? The trophy case?"

"I even sniffed our balls."

"Don't all werewolves do that?" I really shouldn't have said that to a guy under a curse, especially when I'd forgotten to put the cone of silence back up, but it just came out.

Fortunately, he laughed and unlike crying, laughter is a sound I like. I thought I felt the curse lift a little, just for a second, but it sprang back like a mystical rubber band.

That's probably why the other Castle employees looked at us as if we were crazy before going back to their curse-caused crankiness.

Jake said, "That means the building itself is cursed, right?"

"Which means we get to wait for it to wear off."

"How long will that take?"

"Aunt Hester says it depends on the experience of the practitioner, the strength of the motive for the curse, the phase of the moon…"

"She doesn't know?"

If she did, she wasn't telling, but I didn't tell Jake that. Nor did I tell him that he'd wasted half an hour sniffing when Aunt Hester must have known there was no cursed item. Getting him mad would only give the curse more ammunition to work with. "She did say that curses start out weak, grow stronger until they reach a peak, and then fade at that same rate." Extra casually, I said, "Didn't you say that things started to go bad on Monday?"

"I think so. I worked a half shift on Sunday, and it seemed normal."

"Are things better today, or worse?"

A pan or something clattered onto the floor in the snack bar, and this time it was Belle who ran for the bathroom crying.

"Worse," Jake said, which I'd already figured out. "Then we don't know if it's at its peak yet."

"So it could get worse?"

I nodded.

"Know what? I think I feel a bad bout of the flu coming on." He reached over and put his hand on my forehead. "If I'm not mistaken, you've got a fever, too."

I pushed his hand away. "Stop that. I'm not leaving."

"Elspeth, you said you can't get rid of the curse. What's the point of sticking around?"

"I don't know," I admitted, "but at least I can keep an eye on people and make sure they don't get hurt."

"Let Amar do it. That's why he gets the big bucks."

"He's as affected by the curse as anybody, Jake."

"And it's not getting to you?"

"It's making me a little crazy, but at least I know what's happening. The thing is, I feel kind of responsible. Being a witch and all." That wasn't the whole truth, and the smell of my lie wafted across the counter, at least for me. "Besides, I don't want the cops to shut the place down. It's the noisiest job in town." The only place close was the movie house, but the new manager liked showing deep, meaningful films without a single explosion or shootout. "But it's different for you, having to deal with all this as a werewolf. I don't blame you for wanting to get the hell out of Dodge."

"Are you saying you don't think I can control my wolf?" he said ominously, and stepped way inside my personal bubble. "Like I'm some kind of animal?" He stepped even closer, and I backed up against the counter as far as I could go. "Like I'm a monster?"

"No, no, you're good, you're cool, you're—"

"Psych!" He grinned as toothily as any wolf.

"You son of a bitch!" I said, shoving him back.

"Damn straight. And if you can take it, I can take it."

"Okay, then. We've got this covered."

We traded fist bumps, but he wasn't fooling me any more than I was fooling him. The league championship started in less than an hour, which meant that eight four-bowler teams would be arriving any minute, along with their families and friends. So we were about to have seventy to a hundred people in the Castle, all of whose emotions were going to be mangled and magnified by the curse.

It would have been nice if we could have relied on Amar, since he was the boss, but apparently the curse had intensified his laziness. Jake said he'd barely left his office all day. As for Rayleigh and Belle, they'd spent most of the week's shifts in tears, so we weren't expecting much support there, either.

"At least it's the Thursday night league," I said. Thursday's teams played for fun—they didn't take the game or themselves seriously. "They won't be too bad." If Aunt Hester had foreseen me saying that, she must have laughed her ass off.

Trouble started right after the teams and their supporters began showing up. First off, the Bowling Banshees and the Good Vibrations nearly came to blows over which team was going to bowl on lane one, even though it was no better than lane two or any other lane. We used a coin toss to decide that one, but only after each team inspected my quarter to make sure it wasn't double-headed.

Then the Sonic Boomers started screaming because their best bowler hadn't shown up, so our clock had to be wrong, even though every cell phone in the Castle showed the same time. When the guy finally arrived two minutes after the official start time, the other team captains wanted him disqualified. I got Amar out of his office long enough to wave around a copy of the league's rules that stated a player could be up to fifteen minutes late without penalty. That quieted everybody down for a few minutes.

The spectators were just as contentious. One woman tried to butt in line at the snack bar and ended up with soda "accidentally" spilled on her brand-new shoes. She couldn't decide who to hit up for a replacement pair—the woman who'd poured the soda or the Castle for not having tighter lids on our drinks. By that time the curse was getting to me enough that I had to resist the impulse to tell her that she should count herself lucky to have an excuse to throw the ugly things away.

Finally the serious bowling began, only fifteen minutes later than planned, which Jake and I considered a triumph under the circumstances. The format was simple. Each team would play three strings, and the team with the highest combined score won. All eight teams would start Game One at the same time, but as each team finished, it could move on to Game Two, and then Game Three. Each team had a judge to keep an eye out for foot faults, lob line penalties, deliberate fouls, and so on. Since the league wasn't usually that competitive—the prize was a six-pack of beer per player—they hadn't hired pro judges. Instead, they were using volunteers from another league, which was supposed to keep them objective. The system would have worked great any other night. As it was, fights with the judges began almost immediately.

Not only did the players argue with their own judges every time they were called out, but they tried to rat out the other teams for supposedly witnessed rule-breaking ranging from delivering the ball before the pinsetter had completed its cycle to violating right-of-way. Of course the judges were just as messed up by the curse as the players were— one of them insisted he had authority to ban a player from candlepin bowling for life.

It was a nightmare, and several times Jake and I were on the verge of pulling the fire alarm and clearing the place out. Only the knowledge that we'd lose our jobs kept us from it. Instead we kept fighting emotional fires as they ignited.

After a while we fell into a routine. I stayed at the counter and used my Affinity to listen for trouble. It was pretty slow there anyway, since most league players had their own shoes. The only problem was the one woman who kept asking for shoes that were smaller than her actual feet, and then complained that all our shoes were mismarked. Even without the smell of her lie, I could see that she wore at least an 8. But she swore her feet were tiny, and tried every pair of 6s we had before starting in on the 7s.

Once she'd squeezed into a 7 and a half, I could concentrate on listening in on everything happening in the building. Not everywhere at once, of course—that would have driven me insane. Instead I focused on one corner of the room at a time, or the snack bar, or the bathrooms, and so forth. It's hard to describe to anybody who doesn't have my Affinity—which is anybody else in the world—and the closest I could get when explaining it to Jake is that I was running a virtual cursor all over, and clicking on spots to listen in.

Jake stayed out on the floor, and whenever I heard something looming, I used my Affinity to tell him, making it sound as if I were right next to him but so that nobody else heard me. He said it was weird as hell to hear my voice coming out of nowhere, but it worked.

As soon as Jake knew where to go, he'd do his best to defuse the situation using his supernatural strength or that air of menace werewolves are so good at projecting. I think he growled one time.

I took care of any problems I could from a distance. When I saw a kid about to push another kid down, I pulled a sound snippet out of my memory to scare him—my old math teacher's voice saying, "Sit down immediately!" It worked on them just as well as it had on me back in the day.

I don't think we'd have survived if every crisis had needed intervention. Several of the upsets I overheard were pretty bad, but weren't likely to turn violent. One guy broke up with his girlfriend over the phone— if she'd been in the building, he'd have been in danger, but she was in Connecticut. An older man was convinced that somebody was out to steal his brand-new set of Epco bowling balls, but he didn't threaten anybody. He just kept his balls zipped up securely in his bag, watched the bag like a hawk, and used the Castle's balls, which probably didn't help his game any. One girl had a boyfriend with commitment issues, and apparently the curse was reinforcing her fear that she was doing something wrong. She spent the whole night asking her friends for advice, and from the things those women told her, either they were being extra-bitchy because of the curse or they were the worst friends ever.

By nine, all but the last two teams had finished bowling—the Wilhelm Screamers and Jan's Grapenuts had had so many arguments with the judges and each other that they were just finishing their second strings. Though I was starting to think we'd make it through the night relatively unscathed, I hadn't given up my arcane eavesdropping, and I let my focus float toward the back of the house while Jake played guard dog up front.

The party rooms were locked tight, Amar was holed up in his office with a six-pack he thought we didn't know about, and for the first time in a while, nobody was crying in the ladies' room. I switched my attention to the men's room in time to hear a conversation already in progress.

"That bastard Foley cheated! That was a clear foot foul in the third box of the first string and everybody knows it!"

"She doesn't love me anymore—I can tell something is wrong. I spent months saving for this ring, and another month waiting for the engraving, but there's no reason to give it to her now."

Okay, it wasn't really a conversation. More like dual monologues, one from a sore loser and one from a total loser.

Griper: "He knew just what he'd done, too. Did you see him laughing?"

Whiner: "If I propose and she turns me down, I don't know what I'll do. I've never loved anybody the way I love her."

Griper: "I wanted to wipe that smirk right off of his face, but I can wait. He'll be the last bowler tonight, and I've got it all planned."

Whiner: "How can I live without her?"

Griper: "I know damned well Foley rigged the game—there's no way some kid who just started bowling last year could be that good. You can bet that his last box will be a strike. That's all right. As soon as he makes that strike, it's payback time. With everybody looking at him, nobody's going to notice the gun. One shot and he's history."

There was a kind of gasp, and I guess Whiner finally realized what the other guy was talking about. "You're kidding, right? I mean, you wouldn't really shoot him, would you?"

Griper laughed. "Of course I'm kidding. I don't even have a gun."

A horrid stench crept across the counter. Griper had been lying both times. He hadn't been kidding, and he damned well did have a gun. And I didn't recognize the voice.

I rushed out from behind the counter, ignoring the woman who wanted to complain about having the wrong size shoes again, but before I could get to the bathroom, Amar grabbed me by the arm.

"How many times do I have to tell you kids that there are no personal phone calls allowed on the job?"

"What?" Was my mother calling with a fresh lecture, or had it taken him that long to find out about the call I'd made hours before?

"Your crazy aunt has called me six times, and said she wouldn't let up until I gave you this message. Do I look like a secretary?" He shoved a scribbled note at me. "One more call from her, and I'll fire your ass. You hear me? Now get back to the counter and do your job!" He stomped back to his office and the waiting beer.

Without stopping to read the message, I ran to the hall outside the men's room, hoping to get a look at the guy with the gun. But nobody came out, and when I listened in, I realized nobody was inside. The murderer-to-be was mixing with the other people in the Castle, and I had no way to track him.

Jake showed up at my elbow. "What's wrong?"

"Come back to the counter." Once we were there, I conjured a cone of silence to tell him what I'd heard.

"That's it," he said. "We've got to get these people out of here now. I'm pulling the fire alarm." He headed toward the nearest wall box.

At that moment, I finally looked at the piece of paper in my hand. All it said was, "Check your texts." I pulled my phone out of my pocket and a second later, screamed "STOP!" for Jake alone. He shook his head as if his ears were ringing, which they probably were, and trotted back.

"What is wrong with you?"

"Aunt Hester sent this." I showed him the message on my phone.

Don't pull the alarm. Fire alarm + Perturbatio = riot.
Cops = same effect.

"You've got to be kidding me! Now what do we do?"

"I don't know." I just knew we had to do something fast. The Screamers and the Grapenuts were starting their final strings. "Look, we know Foley is the target. All we have to do is keep an eye on him. If we see anybody aim a gun at him, we get between them."

"Screw that. I'm not letting you jump in front of a bullet. I am taking you out of here right now!"

He took my hand and started pulling me toward the front door. I yanked back as hard as I could, but I was no match for a determined werewolf.

"Stop it, Jake! I have to fix this."

"Let 'em fix it themselves."

"No, I can't let this happen! It's my fault!"

He stopped pulling me, though he didn't let go of my hand. "What are you talking about?"

"You said things started to go wrong on Monday, right?"

"Yeah."

"That's because Sunday night I did something I shouldn't have. A bunch of guys were having a party at my dorm, and they were so loud even I couldn't study with all the commotion, let alone sleep. And I had an exam first thing next morning. So I conjured up some sounds from a cop movie. Banging on the door, 'Open up, this is the police!' even a barking police dog."

"That's awesome. I bet you scared the crap out of them."

"Not awesome. One of them was on academic probation or something, and he was afraid he'd get expelled, so he climbed out of the window and fell."

"Was he hurt?"

"He sprained his ankle, but it could have been worse." In her lecture, my mother had told me in detail how much worse it could have been. "So the curse is my fault."

"How do you figure that? There's no way that guy could have known who did it. And why would he curse the Castle instead of going after you?"

"You don't understand. I know the guy didn't curse us—he's got no magic. It was the Law of Return."

He looked blank. Apparently werewolves live by different principles. I said, "The Law of Return says we should only send good energy into the world so that only good energy will return to us. It's like the Golden Rule on steroids. Instead of just 'Do unto others,' it's 'Whatever you do unto others will turn around and bite you on the ass.' When I played that prank, I let bad energy into the world, and the curse is bad energy coming back at me. In a karmic sense."

"I'm no witch, but according to my philosophy class last year, karma doesn't usually run on such a tight schedule."

"I know it sounds crazy—"

"Because it is."

"—but when I realized the curse started Monday, I asked Aunt Hester if the Law of Return had anything to do with what was going on, and she said, 'Of course it does.' That means it's my fault, and if I don't stop that guy, that murder will be on me, too. Now let go of me before I call for help. Really loudly."

"If I do, you're going to try to protect that guy Foley, aren't you?"

I nodded.

He made a face, but he released me. "Okay, let's do this."

"Jake, you're the best."

Though we'd never been anything but buds, I hugged him and gave him a kiss. It was just a quick one, but I could tell from his reaction that he'd have been happy to let it last a little longer. Come to think of it, so would I, had it been a better time.

Jan's Grapenuts and the Wilhelm Screamers were playing on lanes nine and ten, so everybody in the Castle was clustered around them. Half of them could have had weapons drawn and I wouldn't have known it. Will Foley, a tall man who was normally completely laid back, was pacing back and forth while waiting for his turn to deliver.

"Any ideas other than throwing myself on top of Will Foley?" I said.

"Maybe I could smell the gun oil or bullets or something," Jake said.

"Do you know what a gun smells like?"

"Not really. For some reason the Pack doesn't like guns. Keeping them within reach of a bunch of people who lose it every month seems like a bad idea."

"We're not big on having them around either." A couple of generations back there'd been a member of the Kith with an Affinity for guns. It hadn't ended well.

Unless any of the bowlers started more arguments with the judges or themselves, we had maybe half an hour to figure out who Griper was and stop him from shooting Foley.

Jake and I separated to make our way through the crowd, sniffing and listening respectively. Every few minutes I'd send him a message asking if he had anything, and each time he growled a negative. With people crammed so close together, and the game reaching its end, emotions were running high and the curse was at its most powerful. We had to stop twice to head off minor violence, which meant we had that much less time to spot the killer.

The Grapenuts had finished their last string, and they were in the lead, but the Screamers could still take it if they bowled well. And assuming Foley didn't get shot and default on the game.

Jake and I were getting desperate, and for the first time since my Affinity had made itself known, I wished I had a different one, something that would help me find the shooter. There were so many people, and any one of them could have had a hidden gun, except maybe the one gal in a mini-dress—she didn't have room to hide a Kleenex.

Then time ran out. As Griper had predicted, Foley was the last bowler of the night, and the Castle was nearly silent as he lined up his shot. He was known as a great bowler and I didn't need Aunt Hester to tell me he was expecting to make a strike—it was in his every movement. He bent over to make his delivery and…

And I conjured the loudest, juiciest fart I'd ever produced, making it seemingly come from Foley's butt.

At first there was only shocked silence as the sound echoed through the building, so I added a giggle from the middle of a clump of people and a chuckle from some people in the back. While I was trying to decide which snicker to use, somebody laughed for real. An instant later, so did somebody else, and an avalanche of hilarity began. It was as if all the tension of the night had been released at once.

For a second I hoped the curse had been dissipated or dissolved or whatever verb applied to reversing a curse, but I felt the magic spiraling up and then down, no longer spread all over but instead targeting one person: Will Foley. His face was deep red, he was holding a two-pound-plus purple pearl Starline ball in both hands, and unless I missed my guess, he was about to lob it at somebody.

Everybody likes laughing—nobody likes being laughed at.

I walked toward him, hoping he wouldn't decide I'd make a good target. "High five, dude!" I said, raising my hand, and amplifying my voice just enough to cut through the continued chortles. "That was awesome! I don't know how you managed to set it up, but people are going to be talking about that for years."

"I didn't—" he started to say.

"And fixing it so you'd be the last bowler? Pure genius!"

I could see Foley's shoulders loosen, and he transferred the ball to his left hand so he could slap the hand I still had up in front of him.

"It was pretty funny, wasn't it?" he said tentatively.

"I just wish I'd videoed it for YouTube. It would have gone viral. Warn me next time, okay?"

"This was probably a one-time thing."

I nodded as if understanding his self-restraint, then stepped back. "Let me get out of the way so you can finish the string. Good luck!"

"Thanks." He got into the spirit enough to turn and bow to the crowd, getting a round of applause in return.

As soon as I could, I looked for Jake, and sent my voice to him. "Did you spot him?"

"No. You?"

"No, damn it." I sat down in an empty chair, closed my eyes, and really let my Affinity loose. There were so many conversations that it actually hurt to listen to them all, but I eliminated as fast I could, blocking people talking about funny farts, the games, ice cream after the game, an extramarital quickie in the parking lot—eww.

Finally I heard a voice I recognized from the bathroom. Not Griper, but the love-struck Whiner. He was bleating to somebody about how much he loved his girlfriend and that his life would be over if she didn't love him back. I opened my eyes to look at the guy, and realized I knew him. Klip, Klips, Klipt… That was it, Rob Klipsch. He bowled regularly at the Castle but was one of the worst bowlers I'd ever seen. I squeezed my way to him, tapped him on the shoulder, and conjured a cone of silence around us.

"Mr. Klipsch?"

"Yes?"

"When you were in the men's room earlier, did you drop a hundred-dollar bill?"

"What? I mean, yeah, that was me."

I didn't need to smell that—he lied as well as he bowled. "Seriously, it must have been somebody in there with you. Who was it?"

"Paul Harmon? I don't think he dropped any money either."

"I'll go check with him." I left him mourning the lost C-note along with his girlfriend.

"Jake," I asked, "do you know a guy named Paul Harmon?"

"Yeah, he was last year's high scorer for the league. He's on Foley's team."

I'd assumed the killer had to be from one of the other teams. Killing one of your own teammates was just wrong. "He's the one with the gun!"

"Shit, he's right behind Foley. I'm on it! Stall!"

But it was too late. Though I tried to throw a bee buzzing right behind Foley's ear, it didn't distract him from delivering the ball, and as I watched, he made the most perfect strike I'd ever seen. The Castle erupted in cheers and Harmon started to pull his hand out of his pocket, but Jake had managed to get in front of him.

"You're blocking me," Harmon was saying, but Jake said, "Give it up, man."

"Get out of my way!"

Almost instinctively, I threw a cone of silence up around the two of them.

Meanwhile, having made a strike, Foley got an extra shot. Another strike. The cheers were even louder that time, and I was petrified Harmon was going to use the opportunity to take his shot, but Jake was still keeping him occupied.

Foley had one last ball, and everybody was watching him. He delivered, the ball rolled, and… Another strike!

The cheers were loud enough for me to get drunk on, but my attention was on Jake and Harmon. It looked as if they were arguing, but I couldn't penetrate my own cone of silence without everybody else hearing what was going on. Then an impressively tall, wide guy got in my way, and I lost sight of them for a minute.

When the wall-that-walks-like-a-man finally moved, Harmon was gone and Jake was sitting down, looking winded. I dropped the cone of silence and used my Affinity to say, "What happened?"

"He's gone," Jake said.

I glanced toward the door and saw Harmon's back—he must have been running to get there so quickly.

"Then we're good?" I asked, but for some reason, I felt the power of the curse spike. Voices were suddenly higher pitched, people were breathing in panicked gasps, and I could tell we were on the edge of pandemonium.

"Shit!" I said. "The curse is peaking!"

"Harmon must have spooked people. You've got to distract them!"

"How?"

"I don't know. Make some noise!"

I couldn't seem to think. Laughter had held the curse back before, but as I'd seen with Foley, it could go either way. What else would calm people or make them happy? If YouTube was any judge, I needed cute cat videos, or a soldier surprising his kids on his return home, or…or a proposal.

I grabbed an empty water bottle and strode out into the middle of lane six, way past where I should have been without proper shoes.

"Ladies and gentlemen," I said with Affinity-fueled amplification, my hand wrapped around that water bottle in hopes everybody would think it was a microphone. "Give it up for Will Foley. He's made Candlepin Castle history by making three end-of-game strikes during league championship play." I had no idea if it was history-making or not, but it was enough to get people clapping.

"For another piece of Castle history, I would like Rob Klipsch to please come up here."

Klipsch looked startled when I called his name, but when his buddies started pushing him, he gave up and came over.

I put my hand over the water bottle and shut off amplification to say, "Have you got the ring with you?"

"Yeah, but how—?"

"What's her name?"

"Whose name?"

"The one you're proposing to. What's her name?"

"Deb. Deborah Benoit."

I went back to my water bottle. "Deborah Benoit, this gentleman has something he would like to say to you."

A cute brunette wearing a Quiet Willow Nursery polo shirt came up, looking nervous and confused. I was eighty percent sure it was the same woman I'd heard bemoaning the fact that her boyfriend was commitment phobic, but if I was wrong, things were about to get worse.

"Take it away, Rob." I held the phony microphone under his mouth.

"Um, Deb. Deborah. There's something I've been meaning— Something I've been wanting to—" He fumbled at his pants pocket and pulled out a ring box covered in soft gray velvet. "Will you marry me?" He even dropped to one knee, though it might have been because his legs buckled.

Deb pressed her hands to her mouth in time-honored fashion, then nodded furiously.

"You will?" he said incredulously.

Before he could queer the deal, I announced, "She said yes!"

The crowd cheered, and as a tide of well-wishers surged forward to pat Klipsch on the back and hug the bride-to-be, I played salmon-swimming-upstream to get to Jake. Except he was gone, and I saw something I hadn't seen from a distance. There was blood on the chair where Jake had been sitting. Harmon had shot him!

Now everybody else was happy, but I was panicking as I listened for Jake. From the staff bathroom I heard a horrendous assortment of noises—popping, cracking, panting. I ran, pushing people out of my way like a fast ball through pins. If I'd needed any more confirmation that the curse's power was broken, I got it when nobody pushed back.

There was more blood on the bathroom door, and I was almost afraid of what I'd hear when I went inside. "Jake? Are you…?"

There was a wolf on the tile floor, surrounded by a pile of Jake's clothes. He was looking at me, and if it's possible for a wolf to smile, he was smiling.

"Can you talk?"

He gave me a look that was pure Jake.

So no talking. "He shot you?"

He nodded his muzzle, and nosed the bloody shirt on the floor. There was a hole in one sleeve. Then he lifted his right hand…paw.

"You changed. Did you lose control?"

A shake of the head.

"Then why… Did changing help you heal?"

A nod.

"And you're all better now?"

A particularly emphatic nod.

"Jeez, Jake, you scared the hell out of me!" I'd known that werewolves were tough, but I hadn't realized that they could heal from a freaking bullet wound within minutes.

He shrugged.

I stopped to listen to the goings-on in the Castle. Friends were congratulating the happy couple, and if Foley was peeved that his historical game was no longer in the spotlight, he wasn't saying so. Most people were packing up and leaving.

As for the curse, I could still feel it, but it was about as dangerous as a kitten. It might make somebody annoyed, but only if they were halfway annoyed already. "I think the worst of it is over."

He held up one paw.

"Fist bump?"

He nodded.

I went with it, and said, "Shouldn't you change back?"

He looked pointedly at the clothes.

"You think you've got anything I haven't seen before?"

He stood and stalked toward me, growling deep in his throat.

"Okay, okay," I said. "I'll go see if I can find you a clean shirt." After the door was safely shut, I threw my voice into the room to add, "And some kibble."

Amar finally emerged from his office, looking embarrassed, and told me to take a break while he herded the rest of the people out the door and locked up. Belle and Rayleigh were as thick as thieves again, and happy to oblige with Cokes and a fresh batch of onion rings for Jake and me.

While I was waiting for Jake to do whatever it was he had to do, I called Aunt Hester.

"Hello, dear. You have had an exciting evening, haven't you?"

"Aunt Hester, you lied to me."

"Elspeth Allaway, I did no such thing."

"You told me I couldn't break the curse!"

"I did not. I said *I* couldn't break a curse. And I can't. Seeing the future doesn't do a thing against curses."

"But you knew what I thought you meant."

"I can't tell you everything, dear. You have to learn some things for yourself."

"Aunt Hester, Jake got shot! That's a lesson I could have done without."

"I am sorry about that, but I knew he'd be all right. And that man who shot him threw his gun into the lake and then went straight to his therapist—he'll be fine, too. So no hard feelings?"

I was trying to think of what I could say that wouldn't get me in hot water with my mother when she added, "Let me make it up to you by explaining something else you might have misunderstood."

"Okay," I said, not sure if I wanted to hear what she wanted to tell me.

"Remember how you asked me if the curse had anything to do with the Law of Return, and I said it did?"

"Right, because of the prank I pulled."

"How is it you'd put it? Self-centered much? The sprained ankle was the boy's own fault—he shouldn't have been out that night and he certainly shouldn't have jumped out a window. No, the curse was brought on by your boss's actions."

"Amar?" I thought back to something Jake had told me. "Because of firing Theresa?"

"He handled that very badly, and something was bound to happen. It turns out that girl's aunt is a practitioner, and frankly, not a nice woman. She cursed the Castle."

"So it was nothing to do with me?"

"That's right."

"And I don't have to worry about anything happening because of the prank?"

"Oh, no, you're going to have misfortune because of that. And very soon, too."

"Great."

"Don't fret. It'll be far overshadowed by the good fortune because of the people you helped tonight. You know the Law of Return doesn't run on a schedule, or you would know if you'd pay more attention to your mother, but this time you'll get both punishment and reward right away."

"Aunt Hester, you seriously creep me out."

"I know, dear."

She hung up just as Jake joined me, which she had no doubt foreseen.

The two of us chowed down, and then helped clean up the unusually messy Castle before clocking out and heading for the parking lot.

"Crap!" I said, looking at my car's front end. "I've got a flat tire."

"You want me to help change it?"

"Thanks, but I can do it." Except that when I went toward the trunk, I saw another flat. "Jeez! Another? I've only got one spare."

"Have you got Triple A?"

"Yeah. Let me find my card." Only it wasn't in my wallet. "The Law of Return strikes!" I muttered. Having two flat tires was worlds better than a curse, but it was a pain just the same.

"Why don't I give you a ride home?" Jake said in an all-too-casual way. "I don't have classes tomorrow, so I can help you get squared away in the morning."

"You wouldn't mind?"

"No, it's no big." As we were getting into his car, he said, "You know, I was thinking about hitting the Sonic for something else to eat. Changing and healing take it out of me. You want to come?"

I was pretty sure the Law of Return had struck again. It was the best thing I'd heard all night.

Afterword

The candlepin bowling alley in this story is based on a real candle-pin place here in Massachusetts. I bowled there many times, and had a great time even though I'm a terrible bowler. The bowling alley closed several years ago, but I remember it fondly.

Making a bowling alley home to a witch with an Affinity for noise seemed appropriate because it truly was a noisy place to be. It's also why I named the various bowling teams after sounds and/or noises: Bowling Banshees, Good Vibrations, Sonic Boomers, Wilhelm Screamers and Jan's Grapenuts. (Grape-Nuts is the loudest cereal known to man, and the team name is an homage to mystery writer Jan Grape.)

Though I really don't try to link all my work, I admit that this story is a double-spinoff. Jake the werewolf was the protagonist in "Keeping Watch Over His Flock" (published in *Wolfsbane and Mistletoe*, edited by Charlaine Harris and myself) and I wrote about members of the Allaway Kith in "For a Good Time, Call…" (published in *The Wild Side: Urban Fantasy with an Erotic Edge* edited by Mark L. Van Name).

Now Hiring Nasty Girlz

I'd told Amber Blaine to come in for an interview at ten in the morning, when the bar was quiet. Most of the people in Rocky Shoals at least pretend to go to church, and Nasty Girlz Bar-n-Grill isn't the kind of place men take the wife and kiddies to for Sunday dinner, so we wouldn't be opening until mid-afternoon, when the ballgames started. That meant the opening crew wouldn't show for another couple of hours. J.Z. Wilson likes nothing better than being alone in a building with a pretty girl.

Amber knocked on the bar's back door at ten on the dot, and I watched her on the security cam as she got more and more nervous. Only after she'd fidgeted for a solid five minutes did I finally let her in.

"Amber?" I said, offering a hand. "I'm J.Z. Wilson, owner and manager of Nasty Girlz Bar-n-Grill. It sure is a pleasure to meet you."

She smiled at first, but her expression faltered when I let my hand linger on hers just a shade longer than she wanted. And I gripped tightly enough that she couldn't break loose without making a fuss. J.Z. Wilson likes to show people who's boss right away.

"Come on in," I said, and stepped back so Amber could enter. She was a pretty thing, with freckles everywhere I could see and a head full of red curls. Her jeans and top showed off her figure well enough to demonstrate that she wasn't as busty as the ideal Nasty Girl, but exceptions have always been made for the right attitude.

Though I'd told her to dress casual, I had on a shiny blue suit with the jacket cut loose enough to make my shoulders look wider and the pants cut tight to show off assets down below. Wearing duds like that is another way J.Z. Wilson shows the girls who's the boss.

She stopped just inside the door, probably waiting for her eyes to adjust from the bright sunlight to the dimly lit storeroom, and jerked as I slammed the door behind her and locked it. Then I moved right up behind her, putting my hand on the small of her back so I wasn't quite copping a feel.

"This way," I said, grinning when she tried to move fast enough to evade my hand as I guided her to my office. Oh yeah, she was nervous. She was clutching her black pocketbook so tight the tips of her fingers were white.

"Have a seat."

Some bar owners don't spend a lot of time and money on their work space, but that's not the way J.Z. Wilson does business. The desk and file cabinet were solid mahogany, the computer was top of the line, and the boss chair was upholstered in dark red leather. There were pictures of Nasty Girlz girls lining the walls, and right in the center, so you couldn't miss it when you came in, was a framed magazine cover from *Rocky Shoals Living*. The photo of the bar along with the headline, "J.Z. Wilson Makes a Splash," had been worth every one of the comped meals it had taken to get it.

The only piece of furniture in the room that wasn't impressive was the guest chair, which was a ramshackle reject from the restaurant, and Amber sat down gingerly, as if she was afraid the stains were fresh.

Instead of taking my place in the desk chair, I picked up a file folder and leaned against the front of the desk, standing just a few inches in front of Amber. That put her at the perfect eye level. She could either stare at my crotch or look up at my face. Either approach suited me fine.

"I appreciate you coming in so soon," I said. "I'll be honest with you, Amber, I wasn't really planning on hiring anybody this week, but your application changed my mind." I opened the folder, making a show of reading what was on the printout. "I see you haven't held a job in a good while."

Amber had opted for looking up at me, so I could see her mouth tighten a bit. "I haven't been in the work force for several years," she said. "I was a homemaker."

"Is that right? So why do you want a job now?"

"My husband and I broke up."

"Man, I can't imagine anybody letting a cute little thing like you get away." I gave her a sly wink. "Don't tell me you've been a nasty girl."

"I beg your pardon!"

"Just kidding," I said, grinning wide. "This is Nasty Girlz, you know."

"Oh right, of course."

I looked back at her application. "I'm not seeing any food service experience."

"No, sir, I mostly worked retail before, but you know retail doesn't pay much. I heard that the pay is better here, with tips and all."

"It can be, if you know how to treat customers."

"I'm a hard worker, Mr. Wilson."

"Call me J.Z."

"All right."

"All right, J.Z."

"All right, J.Z." There was just a hint of resentment in her voice.

"Here's the thing, Amber. Men don't just come here for wings and beer. They want a girl who makes 'em think."

"Who makes them think?"

"That's right. Our girls make the customers think all kinds of nasty thoughts, and you'd be surprised how much they're willing to pay for that."

"You're not saying—"

"I'm just saying that our customers like to be treated right. Do you think you can handle that?"

"I'm a hard worker," she said again, "and I'll do my best."

"All right then." I closed the folder and slapped it onto the desk.

"All right? Then I've got the job?"

"Don't be getting ahead of yourself. We've still got to check out how you look in the official Nasty Girlz outfit. It's all part of the package, you see. Just let me find you a uniform. What are you, size six?"

"Eight."

I frowned. "Is that right? I don't know that I have one that big."

"I've been dieting," she offered quickly. "I'm really between 6 and 8 right now."

"Let's try the 6. I bet you can squirm into it if you work at it."

I got a pair of black faux-leather booty shorts and a low-cut, blood-red tank top from the cabinet and handed them to her. "We supply the uniforms, but you have to buy your own thong and push-up bra." I gave her my best leer.

She stiffened as she took the clothes from me, but managed to fake a smile. "Where can I change?"

"The ladies' locker room is right next door."

I showed her the way, turned on the light in the locker room, and made sure nothing was blocking the hidden camera before going back to the office. I had the feed up on the desktop computer in time to see her lock the door. As if I didn't have a key, if I decided to use it. But J.Z. Wilson likes to get a good look at the merchandise before he makes his move.

I watched as she looked around the locker room for peepholes, managing to completely miss the trio of hidden cameras that gave a good view of every inch of that room. Only when she thought she had a shred of privacy did she start to undress. The system recorded everything she revealed, including the wire taped inside her bra. Which was not, as it happened, the push-up kind.

My hunch had been right on the money. Amber—though I was ninety-eight-percent sure that "Amber" wasn't her real name—was a ringer.

I'd been going through email the previous day, including a handful of job applications sent in via nastygirlz.com, when the software I'd installed on the bar's system flagged Amber's email as suspicious. It hadn't taken long to figure out that that email address had only been set up a day earlier, that her street address was phony, and that her phone number was for a burner. My first thought had been to delete the application and forget about it, but then I decided I could use it to my advantage. If there's anything J.Z. Wilson likes, it's taking advantage of unsuspecting young women.

While Not-Amber tried to get herself into the uniform, which was closer to a size four than a six, I took a screen shot of her face and plugged it into a facial recognition program to find out who she really was. I knew she wasn't a local cop and J.Z. Wilson knows how to stay under the radar for anything federal, so that left four likely possibilities: a PI, somebody settling a personal score, a woman in trouble trying to create a new identity, or some kind of reporter.

After a couple of minutes, I had my answer. Amber Blaine was actually Annabelle Ballantine, and she worked for an online investigative news magazine with strong feminist leanings. No doubt she'd heard the story of Gloria Steinem going undercover at the Playboy Club before planning her exposé on the way things were done at Nasty Girlz. The site was fairly new, and since she was listed as a contributor rather than as a staff member, that probably meant she didn't have any backup. Just to be sure, I checked the security feed for the parking lot. There was nobody around, and the only cars were hers and the Nasty-Mobile: a black SUV with the Nasty Girlz logo plastered all over it. J.Z. Wilson believes in advertising himself as much as possible.

On camera, I could see Annabelle had finally gotten herself dressed, but had given up on continuing to wear the wire because there was no way to conceal it in that too-small uniform. She settled for putting in an outer pocket of her pocketbook. When she opened it to stuff in her jeans and top, I saw J.Z. Wilson wasn't the only one who liked hidden cameras. Since there was no way of knowing if she was streaming off-site or just recording to a memory card, I had to assume I wouldn't be able to get the footage away from her, but I could work around that.

After a bit of primping to convince herself that she wasn't really stalling, Amber finally came out of the locker room. I put an innocent-looking spreadsheet up on my computer screen, and came back around to the front of the desk to meet her as she came through the open door.

"Is this what you're looking for?" she said.

"Well, now, it just might be. Put that bag down so I can get a *good* look."

She carefully propped her purse up in the guest chair, making it plain where the lens was. I made sure I was in the frame as I looked her up and down, leaving no question as to what J.Z. Wilson was contemplating, and motioned for her to spin around.

She did as she was told.

"Not so fast, little girl. Nasty girls know how to take their time."

She turned more slowly, biting her lip.

"Well, the shoes aren't right, and you're going to have to do something about your…" I paused. "Your lingerie, should I say? But I think we might just have something."

"Great," she said with a combination of enthusiasm and relief. "When can I start?"

I lowered my voice. "You can start by coming a little closer." When she didn't move, I did.

What happened next pretty much matched what was shown on the majority of the video files stored on a very special external hard drive tucked away in the desk. Of course, the way the girls reacted varied: some went along willingly with what J.Z. Wilson wanted, some went along unwillingly, some fought, and some froze. Amber—or Annabelle—froze at first, but just about when it was time to start pulling down pants, she broke free and pushed me away.

"Hey now, do you want the job or not?" I said.

"I applied to be a waitress, not a—" She didn't have a good way to finish her sentence.

"You applied to be a nasty girl, and I need to see how nasty you can be." I made a grab for her.

She jumped back. "Don't you touch me. I'm leaving, and you better not try to stop me." Her voice was hoarse and I thought she was about to break down into tears. She stumbled away, and managed to find her way through the back rooms to the exit, with me following.

Just as she pushed the door open, I said, "That uniform belongs to me. You better take it off before you go!"

She turned just long enough to glare at me, and flipped me a bird before fleeing into the parking lot. I watched through the security cam as she nearly ran to her car and threw herself in.

Butch, the fry cook, pulled into the lot just then, and Annabelle nearly hit his pickup as she squealed away.

Butch had been working at Nasty Girlz for over a year, so he didn't even look surprised. He just came on inside, and raised an eyebrow at my disheveled appearance and the fresh scratches on my face.

"New hire not working out?" he asked.

"Mind your own damned business," I snapped. "And get to work. You're late."

He was actually half an hour early, but nobody argues with J.Z. Wilson when he's in a mood. I stomped off to the office, where I stayed for the rest of the day and into the night. I knew Butch would spread the word to the rest of the staff not to bother me any more than absolutely necessary. That meant that nobody came to the office other than to bring me register drawers to cash out, and to deliver the food and numerous bottles of Coors I demanded as the night wore on. I didn't waste words on any of them.

I needed the time on my own to finish some work on the computer. I was on a deadline. I figured Annabelle would be writing about our encounter in a cold white fury, and it might well be posted online before dinnertime. Along with the video she'd taken, of course. Luckily for me, she was either a slow writer or had a lousy internet connection because the post didn't show up on the web until nearly ten. Within an hour, all of the staff and some of the customers had heard about it, and by midnight, it had gone viral.

It was time for me to go.

There was still a handful of customers in the dining room, even that late on a Sunday night, so I had an audience as I lurched out to the front of the bar, slurring my words as I muttered about nosy, lying bitches.

"Give me a beer!" I said.

"You sure you want another, J.Z.?" Marley, the bartender, said. "You've got a long drive home."

I narrowed my eyes. "I'm J.Z. Wilson, and this is my place. If you ever want to see another paycheck, give me the damned beer."

She gave me the bottle, and I chugged it down. Marley needn't have worried—it was my first beer of the night. The others had just been for stage dressing. I'd spilled part of one on my desk and suit, and poured the rest down the sink before throwing the bottles around the office to make a convincing mess.

"I'm going home," I announced when I'd finished and wiped my mouth on the suit's shiny blue sleeve. "I want this place cleaned and stocked before you lock up, and if everything isn't in apple pie order tomorrow, you all better start looking for another job. You hear me?"

"Yes, J.Z.," replied a chorus of Nasty Girlz, who knew they wouldn't make it home until four at the earliest. I felt a little guilty about that, since they'd soon need to find new places to work no matter how spotless they got the place.

I wove my way to the back door and kept pretending to be drunk in case anybody was watching me get into the Nasty-Mobile. Only after I'd careened out of the parking lot did I allow myself a smile. My job was nearly done.

Marley had warned me about the long drive home, but I only had to go half a mile away from the bar before I turned off onto a side road and flipped the lights off so nobody would see me as I approached a small drugstore that had shut down when the new Walgreens opened in town. I waited and watched for a couple of minutes to make sure nobody was nearby, but that was overly cautious. I had proximity alarms set up and would have known if anybody had come around. Still, I kept a sharp eye out as I walked to the back door and unlocked the padlock that only looked rusty.

All the windows were completely blacked out, but I still only allowed myself a dimmed flashlight as I went inside and checked on my guest.

The real J.Z. Wilson was lying on an air mattress, sleeping like a baby, and the IV line keeping him that way was still in place. All he was wearing was a pair of Depends, so I removed those and cleaned him up before I stripped off his stinky suit and dressed him in it.

I wouldn't have minded a good wipe myself, but that could wait until I got to my hotel room, where I would take a nice long shower and wash off the makeup and hair dye that helped convince people that I was J.Z. Wilson for the past two days.

I did remove the padding I'd used to give the illusion of J.Z.'s manhood and took off the wrapping that had held my breasts down, which felt wonderful. I wasn't big-chested enough to be a Nasty Girl, but I wasn't flat, either. I was lucky J.Z. Wilson favored loose suits in a vain attempt to convince people that he had a manly chest. Otherwise the impersonation would never have worked.

When I took the job, my initial thought had been to go undercover as a Nasty Girl to get to J.Z., kind of like what Annabelle had tried, but when I got a good look at the man, I realized it would be just as easy to pretend to be him. Faking the voice had been the hardest part, but I've had training and practice, and his voice was about as manly as his chest. It didn't hurt that J.Z. wasn't the kind of boss to chat with his employees. Other than the interaction with Amber/Annabelle, all I'd had to do was bark orders as needed.

Grabbing J.Z. had been easy, and once I had him in storage, I could take my time going through his secret hard drive. The trick had been to edit the video files enough so that women J.Z. had secretly filmed over the past few years couldn't be identified, while leaving plenty of evidence for the police to realize what he'd been up to.

Of course, I'd removed every trace of my client's niece and what had happened to her.

I kept the IV in place while I packed up my equipment and took it all out to my rental car, which was parked in the store's former loading dock, covered with a tarp. Only then did I remove the needle from J.Z.'s arm. Before he could start to come to, I started pouring Coors down his throat, and he must have been thirsty because he drank it down so fast he passed out again. Then I took one last look around to make sure I hadn't left anything and lugged him out to the Nasty-Mobile. As late as it was, I still had a drunken car crash to stage. I reminded myself to make sure his arm got a good whack in the process. That would hide the needle mark from the IV in case the medical examiner was especially thorough.

Though J.Z. was a drinker, most of the time he didn't overdo it, so if Annabelle hadn't shown up, I'd have gone with a scenario like a robbery gone wrong or a jealous boyfriend. But nobody would question him going on a bender after first being attacked by a woman he was trying to nail—I stopped to scratch his cheek to match the marks I'd made on my own face—and then finding out she was a reporter who'd publicly exposed his nasty secrets.

Annabelle's sting operation had come at just the right time for my purposes. Of course, it'd have been a lot better for my client's niece if the reporter had gone after J.Z. a year earlier. That was when the niece had been hired at Nasty Girlz, and ended up harassed and abused to the point that she ODed on crack. My client hadn't been sure if her niece's death had been suicide or an accident, and she had no proof about what had been going on, but she knew it was J.Z. Wilson's doing. So she hired me to take care of him.

Assignments like this are what I do for a living.

I started driving toward the spot I'd picked out the day before. About a mile from J.Z.'s house, there was a sharp curve, a steep incline, and a deep lake that would be perfect for him to crash into.

There's nothing J.Z. Wilson likes better than making a big splash.

Afterword

I don't often write twist-at-the-end stories, but every once in a while, I just can't resist trying to fool the reader, at least for a little while.

The setting, Rocky Shoals, is the neighboring town to Byerly, North Carolina, where I set my Laura Fleming books. I keep using it because I just like the way it sounds.

Rage Warehouse—
Ire Proof

"How much further is it?" I asked my sister, Becky.

"We're nearly there," she said.

"How did Aunt Peg even find this place?" our cousin Janice asked from the backseat of the car.

"There probably weren't as many self-storage places around back in the day," Becky said.

"Or it was cheap," I added.

"Mama always was careful with her money." Becky made it sound like a virtue, which I guess it was, but there'd been a whole lot of occasions when I was growing up when I'd wished our mother had been a little less virtuous.

When the road made a jog to the left and I finally got a glimpse of the place, I knew it couldn't have cost much. There was no other reason to pick such an out–of–the–way monstrosity. I've used self–storage places, but they were long, low concrete buildings with roll–up doors, like a row of garages. This was a tall brick structure I suspected had started out life as a hosiery mill, and instead of having a light-up sign, the words *Storage Warehouse—Fire Proof* were painted above the front door. At least they had been until the *Sto* and the *F* wore off.

"Rage warehouse. Ire proof," I read. "Must be where you put stuff you're angry about."

Janice laughed more loudly than it deserved as we turned into the parking lot.

"I just hope it's air-conditioned," I said. It was North Carolina in August, the kind of hot, humid weather I'd avoided as much as possible since moving away from Rocky Shoals. Just the idea of digging through boxes while dripping with sweat made me tired.

"We should wait until tomorrow," Janice said. "There's a storm coming tonight, and that'll cool things off."

"Gail's leaving in the morning," Becky reminded her, then gave me a look. "Unless she could change her flight and stay a little longer?"

"Sorry, but I've got work," I said, which was half-true. Yes, I had a job to get back to, but my boss had told me I could take as much time as I needed after my mother's death. I just didn't feel like I needed more. I'd come for the visitation on Monday, the funeral on Tuesday morning, and the reception at Becky's house Tuesday afternoon. I'd helped clean out Mama's room at the nursing home, and I'd written thank-you notes for the funeral flowers and food left at the house because Becky thought my handwriting was prettier than hers. That fulfilled all my obligations. I'd loved my mother, but we hadn't had what anybody would call a warm relationship. Honestly, I didn't think any of Mama's relationships had been all that warm.

Janice said, "Becky, you and I could come tomorrow or even later this week. Mama would be happy to lend a hand, too."

Becky looked at me and rolled her eyes. The last person she'd want around was Aunt Jenny, Mama's sister-in-law. Helping didn't interest that woman nearly as much as nosing around. Janice wasn't quite as bad, but we'd only brought her with us because Aunt Jenny had heard about our expedition via the family grapevine, and she'd volunteered Janice's help. Which is to say that Aunt Jenny was expecting her daughter to provide a detailed report of what we found. I was just as glad Aunt Jenny had had other plans, so she hadn't been able to tag along, too.

Janice went on. "If we find the ring, we can mail it to Gail."

"I wouldn't trust Mama's ruby to the mail," Becky said. "What if it got lost?"

"You could insure it. How much do you suppose it's worth, anyway?"

Sometimes Janice sounded just like her mother.

Becky scoffed. "You can't insure sentimental value. That ring has been in the family for generations, and now it's Gail's."

"I never did understand how that worked," Janice said. "My daddy was younger than Aunt Peg, so why didn't he get it?" Or in other words, why hadn't it gone to Aunt Jenny, who would then have passed it on to Janice?

Becky said, "Because it passes from youngest daughter to youngest daughter, not youngest child to youngest child." My big sister always was more patient than I was, and she went through the whole story again, even though we both knew darned well that Janice had heard it before.

Family legend was that our multi-great grandmother, the youngest in her generation, was outraged when all the family property went to her big brother, the oldest child, and she'd sworn that anything she left would be divided up among all her children, with something special for the youngest daughter. That something was a vibrant ruby set in a gold band that had been bequeathed to youngest daughter to young-est daughter until it reached Mama. That meant it was coming to me, whether I wanted it or not.

Which I didn't.

Mama's ring just didn't mean as much to me as it did to Becky. Where she saw a family legacy, I just saw an old-fashioned piece of jewelry that didn't go with anything else I owned. Of course I'd intended to dutifully take the ruby home to my place in Connecticut, but when it turned out that nobody knew where Mama had put it, I wasn't overly concerned.

Becky, on the other hand, was upset enough for both of us.

She was bound and determined that I was going to have that ring, and had been driving me crazy with her attempts to locate it. While my big sister didn't insist on getting her own way often, when she did, nothing would change her mind.

"Well, it's not going to get any cooler today, so we may as well go on inside," Becky said.

There weren't any other cars in the parking lot, if you could call a dusty square of red clay a parking lot, and until I tested the door to make sure it was unlocked, I wasn't even sure the place was open. To my relief, there was at least the hint of cooler air inside, though I couldn't tell if it was air conditioning or just a benefit of the thick walls and few windows. There was a counter right inside the door, but nobody seemed to be on duty. Instead there was a rusty call bell and a sign that said, "Ring if needed."

"I think Mama's unit is on the second floor." Becky led us up a steep flight of dimly lit stairs.

"Haven't you been here before?" I asked her.

She shook her head.

"Really?" Between being nine years older than I was and having stayed in Rocky Shoals her whole life, Becky had been a lot closer to Mama than I had.

"I didn't even know Mama had anything in storage until after she got sick. I only found out when I checked her mail so I could pay her bills and opened a notice from this place. Then when I recorded the payment in her ledger book, I realized that she'd been renting out here since I was in high school."

"Then you don't even know what she had stored?" Janice said. "Don't you think it's peculiar that she had so much stuff that her own daughters didn't know about?"

"Mama liked her privacy," Becky said, again making it sound like a good thing.

"Why do you think the ring is out here? Did Aunt Peg say this is where she'd put it?"

"Not exactly," Becky admitted, "but one day toward the end, when she couldn't talk very well anymore, Mama started fussing about her keys until we brought them to her." She pulled out the key ring Mama had always kept in her purse, including several keys that nobody knew the source of. "Then she pointed to the one for this place and said, 'Hidden' and 'storage room.' What else could she have been talking about but her ring? Besides, it's not anywhere else." Becky shook her head sadly. "Mama would be so got away with if she knew we'd lost it."

"It's not your fault," I said. The doctors had told us Mama had likely had multiple strokes before anybody realized it. Since she'd lived alone, nobody had noticed her increasing confusion until she burnt a roast down to the charred bones. A neighbor saw the smoke and called the fire department, and the firefighters got there in time to make sure the house didn't burn down. By then the neighbor had called Aunt Jenny as well, and when she came rushing over, she knew right away something was bad wrong. Mama was a meticulous housekeeper her whole life, but not only was the kitchen a filthy mess, the rest of the house looked as if a tornado had hit it. As for Mama herself, she was so addled that she hadn't even noticed the sirens—the firefighters found her in her spare bedroom, rummaging through boxes of old shoes.

Aunt Jenny had called an ambulance to get Mama to the hospital in Hickory, and after a few weeks there, we'd moved her to a nursing home, where she died a month later. In all the confusion, the ring had gone missing, though nobody was sure exactly when or where. Becky had gone through the house with a fine-tooth comb and spoken to the firefighters and the folks at the hospital before I got back to town, and we'd questioned the nursing-home staff, too. But we hadn't found hide nor hair of it. I said, "She could have thrown it in the garbage for all we know."

"No, it must be out here," Becky said stubbornly.

I sighed and followed her down the hall to the door marked #24. Becky unlocked it, pushed it open, and said, "Lord have mercy."

The windowless room was stuffed with furniture, boxes, bags, and old suitcases and, as I'd expected, it was hot and stuffy. "The ring must be in one of the front stacks, right?" I said, hoping.

Becky patted me on the shoulder. "Don't you worry. We'll go through every bag and box in here if we have to."

"Great," I said, thinking that that was exactly what I'd been afraid of.

There was so little free space in the room that we decided to each grab a box and take it out into the hall, where the light was better and the air fresher. We still hadn't seen a soul other than ourselves, so it wasn't like we'd be in anybody's way.

"Pay dirt!" Janice squealed as she opened up her box.

"You found the ring?" Becky said.

"What? Oh, no, I found toys. I wonder if there are any Cabbage Patch dolls. I read that those sell for big money."

I knew darned well that neither Becky nor I had ever owned a Cabbage Patch doll—Mama had thought they were ugly, and I couldn't say I disagreed—but I said, "You never know." If it would keep our cousin quiet for a while, I was all for it. Then, when Janice pulled out a battered teddy bear, I had a thought. "Let me know if you find a stuffed Mickey Mouse."

"Is it a collector's item?"

"No, just a toy. I called him Mr. Mouse."

Becky gave me a look. "You don't think Mama would have left Mr. Mouse out here, do you? After how upset you were when you lost him?"

"You said Mama put stuff in here over thirty years ago, right? That would be about when Mr. Mouse disappeared. Maybe she packed him away by mistake." I would hate to think Mama had done it on purpose, but I didn't remember her being overly sympathetic when I cried about Mr. Mouse's absence. She'd just told me to find a different toy to take to bed. "Anyway, let me know if you find him."

"Will do!" Janice chirped and continued pulling out toys.

The box I'd picked was filled with paperback books, without the first sign of anyplace to hide a ring. "Were these yours?" I asked Becky.

She looked at the Nora Roberts book I was holding up. "Oh, no, those were Mama's. She used to read a lot of romances."

"Really? I never knew Mama to read anything like that." Sometimes those nine years between Becky and me seemed like a lifetime. The mother she remembered was nothing like the one I'd known.

I closed up the box, pulled a pen out of my purse to mark it with an X so we'd know it had been searched, and went back to the storage room to pick out another one. I was working my way through an assortment of plastic bowls and plates when Becky said, "Well looky here." She pulled out a lavender tutu and ballet slippers that had been spray-painted to match.

"My gosh, I can't believe Mama kept those," I said. If I remembered correctly, I'd worn the costume in a dance recital when I was in first grade.

"You were so cute!" Becky said. "Mama was just beaming when she saw you prancing on the stage."

I'd loved dance class, but I'd only taken one year's worth because Mama had said the lessons were too expensive.

"Now I think I know where this stuff came from," Becky said. "Remember that big white house we lived in for a while?"

"The house in the country?" I didn't remember my first home because I'd been so young when my father died in a car crash and we had to sell it, but I had fond memories of the house we lived in after that. It was out in the middle of nowhere, and I'd spent hours playing outside, having imaginary adventures.

"That's right. Well, the apartment we lived in next wasn't all that big. Mama must have needed somewhere to put things."

"I remember moving into town, but I don't remember why." I knew I hadn't been consulted, and that I'd hated that cramped, smelly apartment. "Was it to save money?"

Janice gasped theatrically. "You don't know? Aunt Peg was afraid to stay out there after *it* happened!"

"After what happened?"

"After Old Man Cunningham disappeared!"

"Old Man Cunningham? Wait, you mean Uncle Lonny?" His house had been the only house within sight of ours.

"You know he wasn't really our uncle, don't you?" Becky said. "He was the landlord."

"I guess I knew that, but he said I could call him Uncle Lonny. Come to think of it, he's the one who gave me Mr. Mouse. We used to play a game where we were looking for Mr. Mouse's mousehole and—" I saw that Janice was grinning at me, not altogether kindly. "What happened to him?"

"Nobody knows," Janice said in a sepulchral voice. "One day somebody came to his house, and he'd disappeared. His bed had been slept in, there were traces of his breakfast in the sink, and his car was still there. But he was never seen again."

Not that I didn't believe Janice, precisely. It's just her story sounded like a ghost story, not something that happened in Rocky Shoals. But Becky was nodding.

"Mama said she'd seen him a couple of days before, just to wave at, but he seemed all right then. And none of us heard anything the night he went missing. The cops didn't have a clue. Everybody was talking about it for ages, but Mama wouldn't let anybody mention it in front of you. You asked about him once or twice, but she made up some excuse about him having gone away or being sick. Mama was mighty protective of you."

In some ways, that sounded less believable than the story of the disappearing landlord, but after seeing the tutu Mama saved, I was starting to think that there were a lot of things about her I'd never known.

"I don't know if Mama was scared to stay out there," Becky said, "but

I sure was. I didn't sleep for weeks afterward. So Mama found the best place she could afford, which wasn't very nice, but I could sleep there."

Janice was all set to share bizarre theories about Uncle Lonny's disappearance, but Becky said finding the ring was more urgent than old gossip, and we got back to work. Over the next couple of hours, we made it through the first row of boxes and most of the way through the next, unearthing baby clothes, most of a set of fine china, a battered wooden high chair, several spectacularly ugly lamps, three kitchen chairs, and a box of tools that must have been my father's. We found jewelry, too, rhinestone pins and all kinds of necklaces and bracelets, but though Janice examined every piece for identifying marks, it was all costume stuff, nothing valuable. And to Becky's growing disappointment, Mama's ring was nowhere to be found.

After I sneezed my way through a suitcase filled with musty clothes, I said, "Becky, it doesn't matter. We can look some other time."

"When? When are you coming back home?"

"I don't know. Next summer, maybe?"

"Or maybe the one after that." She held up a hand to forestall my protest. "That's fine, you've got your life up in Connecticut, but I don't want you leaving without Mama's ring."

"It's just an old tradition. Do you really think she'd care?"

Becky put her hands on her hips, looking so much like our mother that I blinked. "The day you were born, Mama told me that her engagement ring and her wedding band would be mine some day, but that her ruby was to go to you. And I promised her I'd make sure you got it."

What could I say to that but, "I'm going to get another box." I was halfway through a collection of novelty salt-and-pepper shakers when Becky went into the room and yelled, "Will one of you give me a hand?"

"Can you go?" Janice said, scrolling on her phone. "I'm trying to see if these Happy Meal toys are worth anything."

"Sure." I squeezed my way into a small space Becky had cleared out in the middle of the room. "What's up?"

"I can't lift this on my own," Becky said.

It was an old-fashioned cedar chest, with a shiny, rounded top. "Where'd that come from?"

"Don't you remember Mama's hope chest? She used to keep it at the foot of her bed."

I tried to lift one end, grunting at the weight. "Why don't we open it up in here?"

"Good idea."

When we lifted the top, the first thing I saw was a plush Mickey

Mouse wearing a vest and a top hat. "Mr. Mouse!" I picked him up, but resisted hugging him. There was a dark brown stain on his chest that I didn't remember.

Underneath where he'd been was a manila envelope and a large bundle covered in black plastic trash bags. An unpleasant smell mingled with the scent of cedar.

"I don't think that's a ring," I said.

"I don't know what it is," Becky said, puzzled. She started pulling at the plastic, and finally tore off a chunk about six inches around, enough that we could see a piece of plaid fabric, like part of a man's shirt. "It's just clothes." Then she pulled more plastic off, and I think we realized at the same instant what we were looking at.

"Is that—? Is that—?" she stuttered.

It was.

I should have screamed, or thrown up, or cried, or something. Instead I froze, looking at the exposed bit of skin below the sleeve, and the Mickey Mouse watch around the shriveled wrist.

I knew that watch. I knew who'd loved Mickey Mouse.

"Jesus Christ, Becky. It's Uncle Lonny."

I don't know how long the two of us would have stood there staring if Janice hadn't called out. "You two having any luck in there?"

Though I had no idea what I should do, I did know that I didn't want Janice to see what was inside the chest. I lowered the lid seconds before she stuck her head in the door.

"What's that?" she said. "Is that the toy you were looking for?"

"Um, yes, that's it."

"Good for you," Janice said. "Becky, are you okay?"

For once, she wasn't just being nosy. My sister's face was mighty pale.

"I think the heat is getting to her," I said.

"Maybe we should come back another day," Janice said.

"I just need a break." Becky swallowed hard.

I said, "Janice, would you mind taking the car and going to town to bring us back some cold drinks? My treat." Janice loved being treated.

"Sure! Should I get us a snack, too?"

I repressed a shudder, but said, "How about some cookies? Whatever you want." I went to where I'd left my pocketbook to get some money.

"Y'all let me know if you find anything good while I'm gone. I'll be back in two shakes."

"No rush."

I waited until I heard her go down the stairs, then went partway down myself so I could see the cloud of dust from the parking lot that confirmed that she'd driven away. Then I went back to Mama's storage room, this time closing the door behind me. Maybe the building was empty, but I wasn't taking any chances.

I started to lift the lid.

"What are you doing?" Becky asked.

"I want to see what's in that envelope."

I could tell she was relieved when I closed the chest, hiding the body from sight. I was, too. It was bad enough that I could still smell it, or imagined that I could.

The envelope wasn't sealed, just had the flap folded down, and I pulled out a piece of notebook paper with Mama's handwriting on it.

To Whom It May Concern:

If you're reading this, then you've found the body of Lonny Cunningham. I killed him.

Lonny was my lover, though we never told anybody because we didn't think people would approve. After a while, I decided to break up with him, but when I told him, he lost his temper and grabbed a knife from my kitchen to attack me. So I hit him with a blue onyx ashtray from the coffee table. My younger daughter was asleep upstairs, and my older girl was spending the night with friends, so neither of them ever knew what I'd done.

I didn't mean to kill him, and I'd have told the police what happened if it weren't for my girls. I'm a widow, my parents are dead, and my little brother has a house full of kids, so my girls would have had no place to go. So I cleaned up all the blood and hid the body in this chest. The ashtray is in the bottom. Then I made it look like he was still living in his house. The police never searched my house because they didn't know about our relationship.

After a few weeks I brought the chest out to this storage place, and it's been here ever since.

I'm sorry it happened this way.

Margaret F. Greer

It's funny. I never doubted that Mama could kill a man if she had a mind to. It was just the circumstances that confounded me. "Mama slept with Uncle Lonny? I know any adult looks old when you're a little kid, but wasn't he a lot older than Mama?" In 1988, she'd been in her thirties, while Uncle Lonny had been a white-haired old man. "Unless the age difference was why she wanted to break up with up with him."

"I don't believe it," Becky said. "You may have been little, but I would have known. Mr. Cunningham never showed the least bit of interest in Mama, and she was still in mourning for Daddy."

"Maybe she was lonely." When my father died, Mama had had to go to work fulltime, and with me and Becky to care for, she didn't have time or energy for a social life. "Maybe he took advantage of her being a widow."

"Gail, are we talking about the same woman? You really think any man could take advantage of Mama, and not have her do something about it?"

"What if he tried, and that's why she killed him?"

"Then why didn't she say so in her letter?"

"I don't know. Look, your memory of that time has got to be better than mine. What kind of man was Uncle Lonny?"

Becky shrugged. "He seemed nice. Mama knew him from church, and somehow he heard that we couldn't afford to keep our house, so Mr. Cunningham said we could rent the one next to his. She invited him for dinner every now and then, and he'd baby-sit you when Mama was working nights so I could go out with my friends. He said you reminded him of his own little girl, so you probably spent more time with him than I did. What do you remember?"

I pulled out one of the kitchen chairs we'd found, and sat in it, still holding Mr. Mouse. "I remember him giving me Mr. Mouse, and us playing the mousehole game when he came over to watch me. He'd let me stay up late to watch cartoons and gave me Coke to drink. Mama said it kept me up at night, but most of the time I fell asleep on the couch. Then Uncle Lonny would carry me to bed, get my nightgown on, and put me to bed with Mr. Mouse." I looked at the stain on Mr. Mouse's chest. "Christ, I think that's blood." I dropped him onto the floor.

"How could blood have gotten on him? Mama wouldn't have been fighting with Mr. Cunningham in your bedroom."

"Maybe Uncle Lonny left Mr. Mouse downstairs when he took me to bed that one time." I rubbed my forehead, as if I could coax the relevant memories to the surface.

"Gail, tell me about that game," Becky said hesitantly. "The mousehole game."

I wasn't sure why she was asking, but I said, "It wasn't much of a game, really. Uncle Lonny would hold Mr. Mouse and imitate Mickey Mouse's voice. 'I need to go to my mousehole and I can't find it. Where could it be?' And then Mr. Mouse would look in my ear, and under my arm, in my mouth, and in my belly button."

"Your belly button?"

"Yeah, he'd lift up my shirt."

"Then what?"

"He'd look down my pants, and between my legs, and—" I stopped, looked at Becky, and saw the expression on her face.

That time I did throw up, but at least I was able to grab an old bucket half full of sponges in time.

Becky patted my back until I was done, then went to find a bathroom where she could wet down a paper towel to wipe my face, and she washed and filled an old cup with water so I could rinse my mouth. I tried not to think while she took care of me, but eventually I had to say, "Mama caught him with me, didn't she?"

"I read an article about pedophiles. They do something called grooming, where they find a vulnerable victim—"

"Like a little girl whose father had died and whose mother had to work a lot."

"And whose big sister was off with friends instead of watching her!"

"Stop that right now! Nothing like that would have occurred to any of us thirty years ago, and you know it."

"Anyway, pedophiles groom children with games and special treats and toys."

"Like Mr. Mouse." I didn't think I'd ever want to touch the thing again.

"Then at some point they decide it's safe to… to do more."

"Do you think he did more to me?"

"Did you ever notice any signs of damage down there?"

I suddenly laughed, making Becky look at me as if I was crazy. "Jesus, we're grown-ass women and we're afraid to say the words. No, I never noticed any injuries to my vagina and my gynecologist never noticed scarring or tearing. Mama must have caught him in time. But why didn't she call the police?" Then I answered my own question. "Because it was thirty years ago. Nobody would have believed her. They might not believe her if it happened today."

"You're probably right, but knowing Mama, that's not the only reason."

"What do you mean?"

"She must have come in and saw him about to hurt her baby, so she defended you. Plain and simple. She even lied in her letter to protect you, in case the body was ever found."

"Now it has been. What would she want us to do? You knew her so much better than I did."

"You keep saying that, but she was your mother, too. What do you think?"

The Mama I'd known had been self-contained, private, and very strong. She hadn't trusted easily, and given her experience with "Uncle Lonny," maybe I finally understood why. Most of all, she'd defended and protected me, even knowing what it could have cost her. Could I do any less for her?

"We're going to keep her secret," I said firmly. "For now, we'll leave the body here and keep paying for storage. That will give us time to figure out a safe way to get rid of what's left of the body."

By the time Janice got back with Cokes and a package of Oreos, Becky and I had returned everything to the storage room and locked the door behind us.

"What are you doing?" Janice asked. "Aren't y'all going to keep looking for the ring?"

"We decided that—" Then I stopped. Why had she assumed we were giving up? "How do you know we didn't find it while you were gone?"

She flushed dark red. "I don't. I just thought you would have told me if you had. And you don't look, you know, happy or anything."

"We just decided that it probably isn't out here," I said.

"Why do you think that? I mean, you don't know where it is, do you?"

"No, we don't. Do you?" Her face got even redder, and I didn't think it was because of the heat. "You do, don't you?"

"That's ridiculous," she sputtered. "How could I know?"

Maybe I had an answer for that. "Becky, didn't you tell me that Aunt Jenny was the first family member to get to the house the day Mama nearly set it on fire?"

Becky nodded. "I went to the hospital with Mama, but Aunt Jenny stayed at the house. She said she wanted to help straighten things out."

We turned to look at our cousin. "Janice," I said, "did your mama take that ring?"

"Why would you even think…?" Janice started to say. "I mean, Daddy is the youngest, and Mama said… Aunt Peg might have told her she'd changed her mind about who should get it… Besides, Gail, you don't care about it anyway and…" We just waited her out while she tried to decide which excuse to use. Finally, she must have realized that there was no story on earth good enough. "Now that you mention it, Mama did say Aunt Peg had given her some things for safekeeping. Strangers were trooping through her house, and things disappear at hospitals and nursing homes all the time."

"You never know when something is going to get stolen," I said dryly.

"If Mama does have the ring, it must have slipped her mind, what with the death in the family and all. Tell you what. I'll call her and—"

"Better yet," Becky said, "let's go ask her about it in person."

For once, Janice had nothing to say as we drove to Aunt Jenny's house.

I couldn't bring myself to be overly angry at either of them. Janice had been protecting her mother, and she really had thought I didn't care about the ring. I hadn't realized I cared either. And it was thanks to Aunt Jenny's "safekeeping" that we'd gone into that warehouse and found a legacy that was worth a whole lot more to me than any piece of jewelry.

Of course, as I told Becky later, that didn't mean that I wasn't going to go claim Mama's ring as my own.

Afterword

The title for this story came from a real building in Cambridge, Massachusetts. The Metropolitan Storage Warehouse was so proud of being fireproof that it painted that onto the building under the title. But if you were driving down Massachusetts Avenue and looked up at just the right angle, two of the letters were hidden and the building seemed to say "Rage Warehouse Ire Proof." I couldn't resist using that for a story.

The building is now owned by MIT, and I don't think it's ire proof anymore.

Nasty

Nobody made me take on the role of official black sheep in the family, but sometimes I wonder if things might have been different if I'd had a different name. You see, my name is Natasha—Tasha to my friends—but my sister, Hailey, was only six when I was born, and according to family legend, she started calling me "Nasty" because she couldn't pronounce my name correctly. Funny thing is, she didn't seem to have any trouble pronouncing anybody else's name. And she never did stop calling me Nasty.

I spent a lot of years trying to live up to that name, or maybe down to it. Lousy grades, toking behind the bleachers at football games, drinking at parties with black sheep from other families. My parents would probably have been happier if they hadn't known what I was up to, but my snitch of a sister made sure they heard about every class I skipped, every visit to the principal's office, every boy I made out with, and every lipstick I shoplifted from the drugstore.

Hailey's biggest score was when she somehow found out that I was flunking out at Catawba Valley Community College. I'd been on my way back to Rocky Shoals to break the news myself, but Hailey got to the house first, so by the time I got home, they'd had an hour to get riled up. Mama cried, Daddy thundered at me, and though Hailey didn't say anything, when she was sure nobody else but me was looking, she smirked.

I know from therapy sessions I took much later that I shouldn't blame anybody else for my behavior getting even worse after that, but I've got to tell you, my sister's smirk got under my skin nearly as much as her continuing to call me Nasty.

After half an hour of the crying and yelling—and of course the smirking—I'd had it. I flipped them all off, packed up as much of my stuff as I could fit into a duffel bag, and called my best friend Addalyn to give me a ride. I didn't even care where I was going, but it turned out to be Asheville, a couple of hours away from Rocky Shoals. For the next few years, I alternated between couch-surfing and renting cheap apartments while working junk jobs. I also started taking drugs.

Hailey told people in Rocky Shoals that I'd become estranged from the family. I guess she thought that sounded better than advertising the fact that nobody in the family wanted anything to do with me. For a long time, I didn't want anything to do with them, either. Even after I finally got my head out of my butt and quit the drugs, I stayed away.

My wake-up call was when I found out Mama had died. I hadn't even known she was sick—no one bothered to tell me. Daddy said I didn't have to come to the funeral if I didn't want to, and when I showed up, he barely spoke to me other than to make it plain that I wasn't welcome at the house. He wouldn't believe that I'd been off the drugs for years. Mostly, anyway. I was still smoking pot. It wasn't legal in North Carolina yet, but everybody knew it was just a matter of time, and I had a tiny patch behind my house in Asheville to grow my own.

I'd never gotten into twelve-step programs, but I knew about making amends. After Mama died, I started doing just that. Maybe Daddy and Hailey weren't interested, but I did reconnect with some of my old friends. If I hadn't, I'd probably never have known when Daddy got cancer a few years later.

It hit him bad, and I suspect him knowing that he didn't have much time left convinced him to give me a chance. When I showed up at his door unexpectedly one day, he actually let me in and we really talked. It wasn't easy—there had been a lot of hard words between us over the years—but it was a good visit. He even asked me to come back. After that, I came every chance I got.

I cooked for him a few times, but the doctors were giving him chemo and it made him so sick he couldn't eat. I'd heard that weed would help with nausea, so I brought him some and got him to try a joint, and he said it did settle his stomach. He even got the munchies afterward.

Knowing that the arthritis in his hands would make it hard for him to roll his own joints, I made up a bunch for him and filled the cigarette dispenser on the coffee table.

The dispenser had been his mother's, and I'd always loved that thing. It was made of wood, and the front looked like a tiny bookcase. When you wound it up and pushed the button on top, a song played and a dog's head popped out of the top with a cigarette in its mouth. Daddy never smoked, but he'd kept it filled with candy cigarettes for years, and every kid who came into the house had played with it.

Daddy wasn't entirely happy with the idea. He said he didn't know that he wanted to keep illegal drugs in his house, but when I came the next week, he asked if I had any more.

He and I would smoke and talk for hours during those visits. He confessed that he'd thought I'd done a lot worse things than I actually had. That was Hailey's doing. She'd made up all kinds of tales. Sure, I'd taken drugs, but I'd never dealt coke or cooked meth the way she said I had.

The only times I'd been in trouble with the cops was minor stuff from when I was running around with my fellow black sheep. Most of those kids had grown up to be solid citizens, no matter what Hailey claimed: Gail was a lawyer, Randi had her own hair salon, and Addalyn was a cop in Rocky Shoals. I was only a woodworker, but I had my own business designing and installing custom cabinets, with a waiting list of potential clients. One day Daddy told me he was proud of me. We both cried.

I started coming more often to give him rides to the doctor. Hailey lived less than a mile away, but when Daddy called her, she was always busy with work or church or something. He swore that she did come sometimes, but she never showed up when I was there. Though he never said so directly, I was pretty sure she was trying to get him to shut me out of his life again.

Not long before he died, Daddy told me he wanted to change his will. He'd left everything to Hailey because she'd convinced him that I'd take my share of the estate to buy drugs and I'd either end up in jail or dead from an overdose. Now he'd decided that he wanted to give me half of everything.

I thanked him, but told him not to. I had a house and money in the bank, so I didn't need anything. Besides, I didn't want Hailey claiming that I'd bullied him or forged his signature after he was gone. The only thing I wanted was that cigarette dispenser.

Daddy got worked up over that. He said that wasn't fair because the dispenser wasn't even worth anything. Back when he'd been able to hit the local flea markets, he'd seen the same thing selling for fifty bucks at most, and ours was likely worth less because we'd played with it so much. But I insisted that the dispenser was what I wanted, so he finally relented and promised that it would be mine.

We had a year and a half to make up for lost time before the cancer took him. I was there at the hospital with him at the end and saw Hailey for the first time in years. We hugged for his sake, but I don't think either of us really meant it.

My sister hadn't changed a bit. Maybe she was older and had a husband and grown kids, but she still hated me as much as ever. When Daddy told her he hadn't changed the will, so she could have everything except the cigarette dispenser, she demonstrated that she could still smirk like a boss.

I spent the night before the funeral in Daddy's house so I wouldn't have to drive from Asheville so early in the morning. Besides, I knew it would be my last chance. Hailey would have kicked me out before we finished picking out the coffin if she hadn't known how it would look to everybody in town, but I knew that as soon as Daddy was buried, she'd make sure I never set one foot inside that doorway again.

The funeral was small, but some of those old friends Hailey still sneered at came to pay their respects. Addalyn even arranged a police escort. She and I spent a few minutes talking over old times after the burial, which meant Hailey got back to Daddy's house before I did.

She was smirking big-time when I came in the front door. I would have thought she was just rubbing it in that she was going to inherit the house if the cigarette dispenser hadn't been missing from its usual spot on the coffee table.

I asked Hailey where it was, and at least her husband, Joe, looked embarrassed when she pretended she didn't know what I was talking about and then asked if I was sure it had been on the table. When I reminded her that Daddy always kept it there, she just shrugged and said she'd look for it and let me know if she found it. When I offered to help her look, she turned me down flat. After all, even if she did find the dispenser, the will said that the house and all its contents were hers and hers alone. As for Daddy's last words, she said that there was nothing in writing, so she didn't have to pay any mind to anything a dying man might have said. That's when she brought out the smirk again.

In years past, I'd have been tempted to wipe that expression right off her face, but I didn't want my last memory of my childhood home to be of me beating the crap out of my big sister. So I just left, and didn't even respond when she called me Nasty one last time.

I didn't go straight back to Asheville, though. Instead I found a place where I could park and watch the house while I used my cell phone to call my cop friend, Addalyn, and have a little conversation with her. When Hailey and Joe left the house, I called Addalyn again to let her know, then followed them back to their own home and parked in a shady spot where they wouldn't notice me.

Addalyn drove up just as Hailey and Joe pulled into their driveway, and climbed out of her patrol car to tell them that she'd received a reliable tip about something illegal in their car. Hailey sputtered and fumed, but Joe saw the neighbors were watching and told her to be quiet and let Addalyn look.

It only took Addalyn a couple of minutes to find the cigarette dispenser—Hailey hadn't bothered to hide it. She also hadn't taken time to open it, so it wasn't until Addalyn pushed the button and the doggie's head popped out with a joint in its mouth that Hailey realized she'd laid claim to a hefty stash of weed.

I hadn't asked Addalyn to arrest Hailey, just to scare her good, but my sister got angry. When she tried to grab the dispenser out of Addalyn's hand, and then pushed her away, Addalyn got mad, too. That's when she pulled out her handcuffs. I left then because I was laughing so hard I thought sure Hailey would hear me. I kept grinning for most of the drive back to Asheville.

Addalyn called me a day or two later and asked if I wanted her to "lose" the dispenser out of the evidence locker so she could send it to me, but I told her she didn't have to. What I didn't tell her was that the one at the police station wasn't Daddy's dispenser anyway.

I'd had a hunch Hailey would pull something, so before Daddy passed away, I'd gone on eBay and bought one just like his. The night before the funeral, I hid the real one in my car, and left the replacement on the table for Hailey to find. And of course I'd filled it up with a fresh batch of weed, just for her.

It was kind of a nasty thing to do, but sometimes you've just got to live up to your name.

Afterword

The cigarette dispenser described in this story really exists. My grandfather gave it to my grandmother, and since the statute of limitations has long since passed, I can admit that there are rumors that the cigarettes he filled it with were not tobacco.

The Skeleton
Rides a Horse

I didn't even want to go riding. I'd rather have spent the day relaxing at the hotel until the convention began, but Sid had a hankering to go on a horse, and obviously he couldn't go alone.

Sid is a skeleton.

Unlike most skeletons—at least those without skin and flesh—Sid is alive. Ish. He's alive enough to walk, talk, and be my best friend, but not enough to be seen in public.

That's why I couldn't take all of him with me. Instead his skull, one hand, and his phone were in my bag, which enabled him to see, hear, talk, and text. The purple satchel had decorative sugar skulls on both sides and while it was often admired, nobody had realized that the eyeholes were black netting for Sid to peer out of.

I'd gone riding once or twice as a kid, but didn't even remember how to mount properly. Eve, the resort's wrangler, almost stifled her sigh while helping me climb onto the black horse, but didn't try as hard when I insisted on tying my bag to the saddle horn.

My boyfriend, Brownie , was already in the saddle, looking annoyingly comfortable. Though he hadn't ridden since his parents' carnival ran a pony concession, apparently riding a horse was like riding a bicycle.

I wished I were on a bicycle.

After a few minutes of instruction, I managed to stay on as we ambled around the corral, which reassured Eve more than it did me. "Don't worry, Georgia. Minnie here is used to new riders."

Minnie turned her head and sneered. Clearly being used to new riders and liking them were two different things.

Eve opened the gate and mounted her own horse. "Just yell if you have any trouble." She and Brownie rode off.

I squeezed my legs as I'd been instructed, but Minnie only went five steps before stopping. I squeezed again. Nothing. I jiggled the reins. Nothing. "Giddyup?" Worse than nothing. She took a lazy 180-degree turn and headed back toward the stable.

"Whoa! Whoa!"

Minnie ignored my existence as she went through the open door, walked straight to a stack of hay bales at the far end of the building, and began noshing.

Dismounting went no better than mounting had. My foot got caught somewhere it shouldn't have been, maybe because I was trying to hold onto the sugar-skull bag, and both the bag and I tumbled onto the straw-covered floor.

From ground level, Minnie looked alarmingly tall, and I scuttled into an empty stall before she could step on me, stopping only when I collided with something I thought was a sack of oats or other horse-related supply.

It was Sid who realized what it really was.

"Coccyx, Georgia!" he said from inside the bag.

I looked behind me and saw a man, lying on one side. He wasn't moving.

***

I'd just wanted Brownie and Sid to get along. How was I to know that my efforts would lead to a dude ranch, horses, and murder? It was a testament to my unusual hobby that the horses bothered me the most—I've gotten used to murders.

The problem was that while my two best guys had met months before, the only things they'd found in common were me and the afore-mentioned interest in crime. With my parents and daughter out of the house for the evening, I'd thought it the perfect opportunity to rectify that, but it didn't work out as planned.

Given Sid's limitations, we stayed home to watch TV, which could have been great if we'd been able to agree on a movie or program, but after thirty minutes of negotiation, all we could come up with was *Chopped*. A cooking show. Sid doesn't even eat!

Nobody was thrilled, so as the chefs combined natto, popsicles, feta cheese, and scrapple, we played on our phones until Sid said, "Huh. There's going to be a *Cowtown* convention at a dude ranch near here."

"There's a dude ranch in Massachusetts?" Brownie said.

"It's news to me, too."

"What's *Cowtown*?" I asked.

"A classic TV Western," Brownie said. "Eight seasons of Wild West adventure!"

Sid said, "You know *Cowtown*?"

"Sure. I coauthored a paper comparing it to Icelandic sagas."

Like me, Brownie is an adjunct professor, but while my field is English, his is American Studies, which apparently includes TV Westerns.

"It's great, isn't it?" Sid enthused.

"Since when do you like Westerns?" I'd never known Sid to watch one.

"I watched *Cowtown* reruns after you moved out."

Though Sid had lived with my family since I was six, I'd spent several years chasing jobs across New England, so he'd spent a lot of time alone.

Sid fiddled on his phone. "Hey, Netflix is streaming the whole series."

"Then let's saddle up!" Brownie said, and switched the station.

Cowtown was a fifties-era TV Western series with guest stars coming through town to tell their stories to Arabella, the saloon owner with a heart of gold. Though I wouldn't have picked it myself, I was glad to ride along if it made them happy, and silently yelled *Yee-haw!* when Brownie and Sid wanted to get back together to watch more episodes.

The next weekend, Sid grabbed the TV remote as soon as Brownie arrived, but my boyfriend said, "Hold your horses! Remember that *Cowtown* convention? You guys are looking at the latest addition to their speakers list."

Sid's jaw dropped. Literally. "Seriously?" he said after snapping it back into place.

"I spoke with the organizer today. He loves the idea of an academic presentation, and after I dazzled him with my professorial credentials, offered me free registration and a hotel room. With a plus-one."

"Outstanding!" Sid said. "Ruben Timmons, the last surviving cast member, is Guest of Honor and he's selling the new edition of *Cowtown Companion*. Can you get me a copy?"

Brownie said, "Dude, do you think we'd go without you?"

Sid was speechless for so long that Brownie asked, "You do want to come, don't you?"

"Do I want to come?" Sid hummed the theme to *Cowtown* while performing moves that might have resembled a cowboy boogie if he'd had chaps to tuck his phalanges into.

"He wants to come," I confirmed.

***

Brownie's perks included an invitation to preconvention drinks and dinner with the other speakers and a preview of the exhibits. So three weeks later, Brownie and I walked into the saloon at the Round-Up Resort, with Sid's usual travel team of skull, hand, and phone in my bag. He was vibrating with excitement, which I hoped anybody noticing would attribute to a buzzing phone.

A dark-haired man wearing an extravagantly embroidered Western shirt tucked into brand-new Levis greeted us. "Howdy! I'm Terry Turner, head honcho at the Round-Up. You must be Dr. Brownlow Mannix."

"Please, call me Brownie. This is Dr. Georgia Thackery."

"Another Cowpoke?"

Thanks to Sid's detailed briefing during the drive to the resort, I knew that *Cowtown* fans were known as Cowpokes.

"Just a tenderfoot," I said. "I only recently discovered the show."

"Well, we're plum tickled to have you both. I can't tell you how delighted I was when Brownie called. There just hasn't been enough scholarly work on *Cowtown*."

Brownie said, "It's a shame. Westerns offer a fascinating reflection of the country's values."

"Absolutely! That's why I opened the Round-Up."

"That and getting the place cheap after the previous owner went bankrupt," said a petite brunette whose jeans and checked shirt looked lived-in.

Terry managed to keep smiling. "This here is Eve Wilson, our chief wrangler."

"The only wrangler."

"Well, we just opened a few months back—we're still rounding up our herd. Eve, would you get these folks something to wet their whistles?"

"Sure," she said unenthusiastically, and stepped behind the gloriously carved mahogany bar to pour our beers.

"The place looks great," I said.

Eve grimaced. "Just like on TV."

She wasn't wrong. From the wagon-wheel chandeliers to the carefully aged tables and chairs to the wall display of branding irons, the place was as determinedly rustic as Terry's figures of speech, and just as authentic. Since I prefer frontier living with running water and Wi-Fi, I didn't mind.

"I assume chief wranglers don't normally wrangle drinks," Brownie said.

"No, but we're running a skeleton crew until we get more business."

I felt Sid wriggling in appreciation. "What do wranglers do?"

"Tend to the horses and take people out on the trail. If you want a ride, I've got time tomorrow before the convention gets going. No charge for speakers and their guests."

Brownie said, "Sounds like fun. Georgia?"

"You go. I'm not much of a rider."

Eve said, "It's an easy trail, and I'll put you on Minnie. She won't give you any trouble."

I felt my bag vibrating again, which meant Sid wanted to go. "Okay, I'll give it a shot."

As we chatted with Eve, we found out that she wasn't a fan of *Cowtown*, dude ranches, or Terry. She'd only taken the job because she'd moved back east to help her ailing grandfather, and there weren't many horse-related jobs available. When Terry herded three newcomers in our direction, she used that as an excuse to escape.

Terry said, "Dr. Brownie Mannix, Dr. Georgia Thackery. This here's Mark Quale, Marco Panello, and Marcus Baxter."

Thanks to Sid's rundown, I knew *not* to make a Marx Brothers joke. The three Marks were well known as the *Cowtown* community's premier dealers and collectors, but were as brotherly as Cain and Abel, and rarely appeared at the same event.

Quale had suspiciously dark hair for a man his age with an equally unconvincing mustache. Despite being the biggest seller of *Cowtown* memorabilia, rumor had it that his wares weren't always as genuine as advertised.

Panello wore Western regalia from his white Stetson to his tooled leather boots, but when he said, "Pleased to meet you, ma'am," I heard an Italian accent. Sid said he'd come to the U.S. to explore the American West and stayed to peddle historical-style clothing.

Baxter gave me a quick handshake and smile, seeming too shy for somebody sporting that head full of red curls. As *Cowtown* fandom's favorite artist, he produced drawings of the show's characters and replicas of the more famous props.

We'd just gotten past introductions when a man called out, "Howdy, folks! Am I old enough to come in?"

Given how long ago Ruben Timmons had acted in *Cowtown*, I hadn't expected to recognize him, but he had the same mischievous gleam in his bright blue eyes, even if his hair was now pure white.

According to Sid, Cowpokes took their name from Ruben. In the second episode, his character tried to sneak into the saloon but Arabella told him, "Sorry, cowpoke, not until you're older." It became a running gag, and the Cowpoke Kid only entered the saloon at the end of the last episode. The role was the pinnacle of Timmons's acting career, but he took advantage of it by appearing at collectible shows and conventions.

Ruben came to the bar, accompanied by two women, and started shaking hands. "Mark, you old rascal, did you bring my books? Marco, mighty fine duds. Marcus, always a pleasure."

After Terry introduced Brownie and me, he said, "Perfessors?" Yes, he said it that way.

One of the women cleared her throat, and Ruben said, "Tarnation, where are my manners? This is my wife, Lulu." He smiled proudly at the short, plump redhead in an emerald green pantsuit. "Most of you already know my daughter, Melody." She looked like Ruben, though her hair was still brown, and was dressed in jeans and a *Cowtown* polo shirt. "Now what does a man have to do to get a drink around here?"

"Name your poison, Mr. Timmons," Terry said.

"Just Ruben, and I wouldn't say no to a beer." Melody wanted the same; Lulu asked for a glass of wine.

After serving them, Terry excused himself, and Quale pulled Ruben aside to talk about signing books while Panello discussed history with Brownie and Baxter listened silently. That left me with the womenfolk.

"Isn't this nice?" Lulu said.

"I'm having a great time," I said, "but you must go to a lot of these events."

"Ruben does, but this is the first time I've been away from home since our honeymoon."

"That long?"

"Oh, it's only been two years." Though I didn't ask, she said, "I'm not Melody's mother. Ruben's first wife passed away long ago." She took a sip of wine as if it were a treat. "Melody's the one who travels with Ruben."

"And makes the arrangements," Melody added, "deals with convention staff, handles the website and social media, works with the publisher, reminds Dad to take his heart medicine, and does whatever else comes up." As if to prove her point, Ruben called her name. "Coming!"

Lulu said, "Before Ruben and I got married, I had no idea how much work it takes to be a celebrity. I only saw the glamour."

I didn't consider being a perennial convention guest the height of glamour or celebrity, but Lulu explained that she'd rarely left the small Alabama town she'd grown up in until winning passage on a TV nostalgia cruise. She met Ruben the first night on board, and by the time they docked, he'd already proposed. "Such a whirlwind!" she said. "Now did I hear that you teach English?"

Before I could answer, there was a horrendous clanging. Terry was whacking on a metal triangle while hollering, "Chow time!"

Brownie and I found seats at the long table with Marks to either side and the third across from us. After a nudge from my bag, I checked my phone and found a text:

SID: Ruben's wearing Arabella's IOU!
Get him to show it to you!

In *Cowtown*, Arabella's tragic backstory involved a beau who gave her a heart-shaped locket engraved with *IOU* to say he owed her a happy life, then went to fight in the Civil War, never to return. She wore it forever after.

GEORGIA: I'll try after dinner.

SID: You waste so much time eating.

Fair, but I wasn't giving it up. Given the announcement style, I'd halfway expected baked beans with brown bread, so was happy to be served salad, steak, and a baked potato. Brownie and I also got a show of sorts as the Marks squabbled their way through dinner.

First Quale tried to convince Baxter to let him sell his art on commission, but Baxter insisted on cash up front because he'd been underpaid before. Then Panello said one of Baxter's drawings included a gun that postdated the milieu of *Cowtown*, and as Baxter sputtered indignantly, added that the DVDs Quale was selling weren't authorized. That led to a truce between the merchant and the artist, but only until Quale again pushed for commission sales.

Had Lulu been listening, she might have reconsidered her opinion about the glamour. Then again, maybe glamour is in the eye socket of the beholder. Midway through dinner, Sid texted.

SID: This is great!

After finishing our sweet potato pie, we went to view Ruben's exhibit of costumes, props, and other *Cowtown* memorabilia. The display was set up in a large function room, with the other half of the space filled with the Marks' merchandise tables.

Brownie said, "Maybe we can get a peek at Ruben's locket."

"Did Sid text you, too?"

"Just a little."

We oh-so-casually sauntered toward Ruben.

"The perfessors!" he said, making me wonder if he'd been cast in *Cowtown* because of how he spoke or if he'd adopted the style afterward. "I'm sure looking forward to your presentation, Brownie. Are you giving a talk, Georgia?"

"Actually Brownie only recently got me hooked on the show," I said.

"A true Cowpoke shares the things he loves." It could have sounded corny and/or contrived, but Ruben was sincere.

My bag bounced. "Speaking of sharing, could I get a peek at Arabella's IOU?"

"Happy to oblige." He fished it out of his shirt and held it out for me to see. The gold locket showed signs of wear, but was polished so that the engraved IOU was easy to see.

After I took photos with my phone, including several close-ups, Ruben said, "How about one of us two? Brownie, would you mind?" He put one arm around me, still holding out the locket, and I put my bag front and center so that Sid would be next to his idol.

"Dad, what did I say about pictures?" Melody walked up, looking annoyed.

"Oh, honey," Ruben said, "it's just a couple of snapshots."

"Remember our contract with the photographer? If you pose for selfies with every attendee, nobody will pay for a formal photo shoot."

"I'm sorry," I said, "I didn't realize—"

Ruben patted my arm. "No, this was my doing. Of course, since the convention hasn't started yet, these pictures don't really count, do they?"

His daughter sighed. "I guess not, but at least hold the IOU right side up."

He adjusted it, saying, "My eyesight isn't what it used to be."

Melody said, "Brownie, Terry wants to talk to you about equipment for your presentation. Can I show you to the meeting room?"

"Sure thing." He followed her out.

Ruben said, "Since you're new to *Cowtown*, Georgia, can I show you the displays?"

"I'd like that," I said, even before my bag vibrated.

It was charming. Ruben had stories about every cowboy hat, tomahawk, and phony stick of dynamite. Then we visited the Marks' sales tables, ending up at a stack of books under a *MEET THE AUTHOR* banner.

"Take a gander at the hot-off-the-press edition of *Cowtown Companion*," Ruben said, handing me a copy.

I held the book where Sid could see as I turned pages, paying special attention to the section of color photos.

Ruben said, "It's like a brand-new book. I've added pictures, guest-star interviews, and all kinds of stuff."

Lulu, who stood nearby with Melody, cleared her throat pointedly.

Ruben said, "Of course I couldn't have done it without Melody! No true Cowpoke takes credit for another Cowpoke's work."

"That's all right, Dad," Melody said. "It's your name on the cover."

I started to put the book back, but Ruben said, "It's a gift for a new Cowpoke!"

"No true Cowpoke gets another Cowpoke in trouble with his daughter," I said, "but I would love to buy a couple of copies."

"Can I at least sign them?" Ruben asked Melody plaintively.

"Sure, Dad. I'll get a pen after I ring them up."

When I looked inside my bag to find my wallet, I saw Sid grinning. Of course he always grins, but this one was particularly happy.

After Ruben autographed the books and Brownie returned, Lulu said, "I don't know about you jet-setters, but we homebodies go to bed early."

That started a mass exodus, but on the way to our room, Brownie and I detoured to the parking lot. We'd driven to the resort in Brownie's camper so Sid would have a place to amuse himself overnight without disturbing those of us who require sleep.

Brownie opened the door wide enough to slip in the sugar skull bag so Sid could reassemble himself. A moment later, Sid's bony hands returned the bag and reached for his signed copy of *Cowtown Companion*. "Sleep tight!" he said.

As soon as we got to our room, Brownie went to the desk and booted up his laptop. "I'm going to go through my slides again."

"I thought you prepped last week."

"I did, but I want to do a good job for Sid."

"He'll love whatever you do."

"A true Cowpoke always gives his best." He carried it off nearly as well as Ruben had.

The next morning, we went to the stable for the ride that ended so sadly.

***

"It's Ruben!" Sid said.

I scrambled toward the old man and put a hand on his chest. He felt cold and stiff.

"Can you do CPR?"

"It's too late, Sid," I picked up the bag and backed out of the stall as Brownie and Eve came into the stable.

"Are you okay?" Brownie asked.

"It's Ruben Timmons—he's dead."

"What the—?" Eve pushed me aside to see for herself as I explained how I'd found him. "I must have walked right past him." She cursed under her breath as she went to a phone on the wall.

"Terry, Ruben's in the stable. He's dead." She talked over his reply to add, "I'm calling nine-one-one. Get his family."

She was still on the phone with the operator when I heard voices coming our way. Brownie said, "There's nothing we can do—let's give them some privacy."

We slipped past quickly enough to avoid witnessing Lulu's and Melody's reactions, and went to our room. As soon as the door was shut behind us, Sid unzipped the bag from the inside. "Georgia, are you okay?"

"Coccyx, that was horrible," I said.

When I reached into the bag, his hand briefly squeezed mine before I plopped his skull on a bed pillow.

"Do you think he had a stroke?" Brownie said.

Sid shook his skull. "Probably a heart attack. Remember the chapter in *Cowtown Companion* about his heart surgery?"

"Right. I forgot."

"I know this has been a shock," Sid said, "but get ready for another one. When Georgia fell off the horse and dropped me—"

"I'm sorry about that."

"No worries—if I break, you can glue me back together. The point is that I was nearly on top of Ruben's body, with Arabella's IOU in clear view. Only it wasn't the same locket as last night."

"What do you mean?" I asked.

"Georgia, how closely did you look at the IOU when Ruben showed it to us?"

"Not very. I was busy making sure you could see."

"Which is why I was close enough to notice a scratch under the *U* in *IOU*. The locket I just saw didn't have that scratch."

"So someone stole the real IOU and substituted a cheap copy?" I said.

"Not cheap. It looked as good as the original—better, without the scratches."

Brownie said, "Sid, how sure are you?"

He sniffed for effect. "I have excellent eyesight, eyes or no eyes. Besides, we can confirm by comparing the one Ruben's wearing to Georgia's pictures. There's an illustration in the *Companion*, too."

"Granted that you're right," I said, "would an old TV prop be worth stealing?"

They gaped at me.

"Arabella's IOU is the Holy Grail of *Cowtown* collectibles!" Brownie said. "The costumer engraved an authentic Victorian piece, so it's the only one in existence. Any Cowpoke would want it!"

"Then why not just steal it?"

Sid said, "It was Ruben's prized possession. He never went anywhere without it! There's no way it wouldn't have been missed."

I put up my hands. "I surrender to your superior Cowpoke wisdom."

They looked sheepish, and might have apologized had Brownie's phone not buzzed.

He read the text. "Terry wants to talk about the convention."

Sid said, "See what you can find out about Ruben's death, and if anybody noticed it's the wrong locket."

As soon as Brownie left, Sid's fingers started drumming nervously in the sugar skull bag. "Georgia, I have a confession to make. I'm not a real Cowpoke."

"Sid, you don't need a membership card as long as you love *Cowtown*."

"That's the thing. I don't. Until we started talking about it that night, I'd only watched a few episodes."

"Excuse me?"

"Brownie and I hadn't been connecting, so when he said he'd studied *Cowtown*, I thought we could have the show in common."

"What about the trivia you've been force-feeding me?"

"I binged the show and researched online. Plus I read the *Companion* last night. You might say I was boning up." He tried for a grin. "I'm sorry. Are you mad?"

"More like exasperated. I appreciate you working so hard to bond with Brownie, but you should never pretend to be something you're not."

He widened an eye socket, which is as close as he can get to raising one eyebrow.

"Okay, sometimes you do, but not with Brownie."

"Are you going to tell him?"

"I think you should."

He was considering it when my phone buzzed.

BROWNIE: Convention still on. Lunch in saloon.

I showed the message to Sid and said, "Investigating now—confessions later," before loading him back in my bag and heading for the saloon.

Sandwich fixings were waiting so I helped myself before joining Brownie. Though nobody was near our table, I kept my voice low as I asked, "What's the word?"

"The EMTs think that given Ruben's history, it was almost certainly a heart attack. There will be an autopsy, but nobody's investigating."

"What about Arabella's IOU?"

"Lulu has it, but nothing else has been said."

"Maybe she hasn't noticed the switch." At normal volume, I said, "So Terry decided to go ahead with the convention?"

Brownie nodded. "People are already arriving, and the resort would take a big hit if it was canceled. Plus Melody and Lulu said Ruben would want it this way. Terry is putting together a memorial video to show in place of Ruben's introductory speech, and for the other schedule gaps, Baxter will do a drawing demonstration, Panello will talk about costuming, and I'll give a second presentation."

"On the fly?"

"Hey, I've run seminars with less warning. Though I could use a topic."

Our phones buzzed.

> SID: How about the story of Arabella's IOU?
> Might get a reaction from the thief.

"Perfect!" Brownie said. "I'll go back to the room to get cracking."

Meanwhile my skull-in-a-bag and I went sleuthing.

Quale was still eating, but when he saw me, said, "Georgia, how are you? Finding Ruben must have been a shock." I was touched until he added, "You realize those books he signed for you were his last autographs, so if you want to rid yourself of that sad memory, I'll happily take them off your hands."

"No, thanks." I moved on as Sid vibrated angrily.

Terry was talking to Eve at the bar, and as I approached, he left her with several boxes and a disgruntled expression.

"How are you doing?" I asked.

"Just dandy," she said in a tone that meant the opposite, and started yanking manila envelopes out of a box.

"Want some help?"

"Yes, but no. You're a guest."

"Technically I'm a plus-one, and I've got some free time." I pulled up a barstool. "What's the job?"

"The attendee packets need new schedules inserted."

"Couldn't we add errata sheets?"

She glowered in Terry's direction, which was enough of an answer. I'd had bosses like that myself.

Though I'd planned to ask leading questions as we worked, Eve was irritated enough to jump in without prompting. "You know, I'm sorry about Ruben—he seemed like a nice guy—but it wasn't my fault."

"Who thinks it was?"

"Oh, Terry didn't say so outright, but he kept asking why I didn't see him. As if I've got time to mess around in empty stalls!" She stapled a packet aggressively.

"How did Ruben get into the stable anyway? Wasn't the door locked?"

"Nope. If there's a fire, the horses have to be able to get out. I don't lock a stable unless there's somebody on watch, which requires more staff."

"That makes sense."

"So Lulu said Ruben always got up early, and loved horses. Apparently he left while she was asleep, went to the stable, and collapsed. Nobody knows exactly when."

"Since rigor had set in, it had been at least an hour, though the average is two to six hours."

She stopped stapling to blink at me.

"I looked it up." I wasn't lying. I'd done the research after Sid and I started encountering murders.

Terry rushed by, and I said, "I guess a lot's riding on this convention."

"Only everything. Terry bought the Round-Up just before the pandemic hit, so we couldn't open for months, and now that we have, we're not getting the bookings we need to stay in business. This convention is the first time we've had a full house—if Terry cancels, he'll have to sell the horses, and without horses, this place is just a hotel in the middle of nowhere."

I imagined that fencing Arabella's IOU would help keep the resort open, and since Eve couldn't be a wrangler without horses, her motive was as strong as Terry's. If, that is, they knew that the locket was valuable. "So why a *Cowtown* convention? Is Terry a Cowpoke?"

"I doubt he ever watched the show," she said, "but he was looking to market to Western fans when he found a *Cowtown* fan site. He figured that anybody that devoted to an old TV show would pay to play cowboy."

We finished and I helped Eve carry the packets to the table in the exhibit/sales room where Terry would be greeting attendees.

"Unless he pawns that off on me," she groused. The hotel was getting busy, and dodging clusters of chattering Cowpokes only made her grumpier. So after I grabbed Brownie's and my packets, I scouted for a fresh information source.

Baxter sat at a display table, alternating between staring intently at a pair of spurs and sketching, so I decided against disturbing him.

Panello was in the room, too, but also unavailable. A man I hadn't seen before was taking photos of him against a Western street backdrop.

I was moving on as my phone buzzed.

SID: Panello's dressed as Rusty O'Donnell!

I whispered back, "Explain the significance later." Since there was nobody else around to talk to, I added, "I'm going to check on Brownie. Want to come with?"

SID: Drop me at the camper. Research time!

The parking lot was bustling, which meant I had to move quickly to ensure nobody saw me delivering Sid's pieces, so I had no time to ask about Panello's costume. When I found Brownie hard at work in our room, I decided to look Rusty up myself, but couldn't find my new book.

"Brownie, have you seen my *Cowtown Companion*?"

"Sorry. I borrowed it." He retrieved it from the morass of papers on the desk. It was bristling with sticky notes.

"Did you mark every page?"

"Um, just refreshing my memory."

"Then who's Rusty O'Donnell?"

"Rusty who?" He scrambled through notes.

"Never mind, here it is. O'Donnell was the lover who gave Arabella the IOU." I realized Brownie hadn't gone back to work. "Don't worry, I won't move your bookmarks."

"It's not that. It's— Georgia, I'm sorry."

"About what?"

"I lied about being a Cowpoke. I'd never watched *Cowtown* before."

"But you coauthored a paper!"

"I wasn't coauthor—I was second author."

"Oh." Academics routinely return favors by giving secondary credit to people who had little or nothing to do with actually writing the paper. "Did you do any of the research?"

Brownie shook his head. "A colleague's hard disk crashed, and I helped him recover his files."

"That's it?"

"I caught some typos."

"Then why did you pretend to be an expert?"

"So Sid and I would have something to talk about. I want him to like me."

"He does!"

"Yeah, because you like me."

"Ahem. I love you."

"Which I appreciate and reciprocate, but I want Sid to like me for myself."

I didn't know what to say. Would revealing that Sid was also faking make the situation better or worse?

Brownie said, "Are you going to tell him?"

"I'd rather you do it, but are you going to be able to handle your presentations?"

"Absolutely. I'm doing my homework."

"Good enough. But take the book back—you need it more than I do."

***

Brownie and I collected Sid and got to the lobby just before six, when the convention opened. Since we already had our badges, we could bypass the registration line, but were stuck in the crowd waiting for the programming room to open.

A wide array of Western attire was on display, with those in regular clothes mostly wearing *Cowtown* T-shirts. From snatches of overheard conversation, I figured word about Ruben had gotten out, which was confirmed when the crowd fell silent as Lulu and Melody arrived. Everyone wearing a cowboy hat placed it over their heart, and Lulu thanked them as a path opened up for them to enter first when the door opened.

Once inside, Brownie and I made our way up front to the VIP section, where the women were already seated. Lulu was wearing the IOU, but I couldn't tell if there was a scratch.

To cover my staring, I said, "I'm so sorry for your loss."

"Thank you. And thank you for finding Ruben."

I considered responding *It wasn't my first dead body* or *I didn't do it on purpose,* before going with, "I just wish it had been sooner."

"It wouldn't have made any difference," Melody said, sounding almost matter-of-fact. "They told us he died almost instantly."

"At least he didn't suffer," Lulu said. "That's a comfort."

Melody shrugged. Maybe she didn't want comfort.

Quale arrived, taking the seat next to Melody. "Lulu, Melody, I'm devastated. If there's anything I can do, just ask."

"That's very kind," Lulu said.

"Have you decided what to do about the *Cowtown* exhibits?"

"Christ," Melody said, "can we bury Dad first?"

"Of course, but if you need any help disposing of anything…"

She turned her back on him.

Brownie looked as uncomfortable as I felt, so we were relieved when Terry came to the platform and the audience quieted. After announcing Ruben's death, he explained the resulting schedule changes and then played a video combining clips of Ruben in *Cowtown* and photos of him at events over the years. He'd done a great job for such a tight deadline, and I don't think there was a dry eye in the house, except Sid's.

Since that was the evening's only event, once Terry escorted Melody and Lulu out of the room, most of the Cowpokes went to tour exhibits, shop at the Marks' tables, or watch *Cowtown* videos. Brownie and I picked up burgers at the saloon and adjourned to the camper, where Sid could use all of his bones for body language.

"Let's talk suspects!" he said as he straightened his skull.

"Should I leave you sleuths to it?" I think Brownie was trying for nonchalant, but he sounded wistful to me.

"Don't you want to help?" Sid didn't hide the wistful—he may even have played it up.

"If you don't mind—"

"Suspects!" I said briskly before they got mushy. "Who had the opportunity to switch lockets?"

"Lulu could have done it overnight, or anybody from last night's dinner could have found Ruben in the stable before Georgia did," Sid said.

"Stealing from a dead man?" Brownie said. "That's unsettling."

I had to agree. "The theft must have been planned because the thief needed to get the replica ahead of time—the lockets being sold here aren't nearly convincing enough. How long ago was the convention announced?"

Sid grabbed his laptop and typed with his usual speed and noise. "Nine months. Any of our suspects would have had time."

"Motive?" Brownie asked.

Sid replied, "Lulu or Melody? Unknown. Terry and Eve? Money."

"Terry and Eve don't know enough about *Cowtown*," I said.

"So Eve says," Sid argued. "She could be lying or Terry could be faking."

Brownie said, "Except there wouldn't be that much profit after buying a replica. It's got to be a collector."

In unison, we said, "The Marks," but unity was short-lived.

Sid said, "It's Panello. He's dressed as the man who gave Arabella the IOU."

I countered, "I think it's Baxter. He's the only one who could have made the replica."

"Anybody could have commissioned one," Brownie said. "What about Quale? I've seen his type—he'd gaffe a kids' hanky pank ." Whatever that meant, it sounded bad.

To stave off squabbling, I said, "It could be any of them. Let's snoop around tomorrow and see what we find out."

***

Sid analyzed the schedule overnight, and by Saturday morning, had a timetable that provided maximum observation of our suspects. While Brownie performed scholarly duties, Sid's skull and I went to demonstrations and talks, shamelessly eavesdropping when any of the Marks came within range. Unfortunately, we didn't learn much beyond art techniques, costuming tips, and low-ball bargaining.

During Brownie's presentation about Arabella's IOU, I sat up front to help with his slides but more importantly to observe the Marks' reactions. It wasn't helpful. Quale dozed, Panello was entranced, and Baxter sketched. Nobody jumped up to admit guilt.

We kept at it until the non-themed pizza-buffet dinner, when Brownie and I grabbed slices and sodas, and retreated to our room to debate.

"I'm still thinking Panello," Sid said. "He's dressed as Rusty again, and left his table to watch the two-part episode about Arabella's and Rusty's romance when he has to have seen it before. That says obsession."

I said, "Baxter is just as obsessed. He sketches from life, and wanted the IOU as a model. Plus his replicas are amazing."

"Then he would have included the scratch," Brownie objected. "I say it's Quale. I listened to his talk about collecting, and his attitude is that the more expensive something is, the more desirable it is."

"Guys, the convention ends at noon tomorrow!" I said. "We have to figure this out."

"I've got a plan!" Sid said cheerfully. "We'll skip tonight's square dance and search the Marks' rooms. Whoever has the IOU has to be the thief." I'd grown so used to Sid's investigative zeal that I didn't even try to talk him out of it.

Sid's scheme wouldn't have worked had the Round-Up used keycards like most hotels, but in order to simulate Western charm, they had actual door keys, and thanks to my locksmith sister, Sid and I knew how to pick locks. So we could split up to search Panello's and Baxter's rooms.

"What about Quale?" Brownie asked.

"I'll give you a hand." Sid meant it literally. He intended to pick the lock at a distance.

Brownie and I put in an appearance at the square dance, but only stayed until we saw the Marks enjoying the festivities. Then I slunk off to Baxter's room and Brownie went to Quale's. Meanwhile, Sid went through Panello's window—we'd decided him wandering around inside might cause more heart attacks.

Baxter's lock was easy to pick, and I swiftly got inside and bolted the door behind me. I'd been nervous about leaving traces, but after one look around the room, stopped worrying. Since checking in, Baxter had created a makeshift studio by filling every surface with scattered sketches and pens, stacks of prints, a scanner, and both regular and 3-D printers.

Despite the clutter, it wasn't hard to find Arabella's IOU. It was in plain sight, nestled on a piece of red velvet, and the nearby pile of crumpled drawings showed Baxter wasn't satisfied that he'd captured its likeness.

Once I was sure the IOU had the identifying scratch, I took a slew of photos and exited in triumph while humming the theme to *Cowtown*. Not that it was a competition, but if it had been, I'd just won it.

Sid was waiting for me in the camper, and though I'd expected him to be disappointed by not having found the IOU, he looked smug.

"Why are you so pleased?" I asked.

"Why do you think? Panello had the IOU. It's part of his freaky altar to Arabella: photos, candles, yellow roses, and the locket."

"So how does Baxter have it?"

Then Brownie arrived and after returning Sid's hand, said, "Prepare to be impressed!"

"Don't tell me," I said. "Quale has Arabella's IOU, too."

"That's right— Wait, what do you mean *too*?"

We had to hear one another's stories and look at the pictures—all of which showed the telltale scratch—before accepting the fact that there were three IOUs.

"Maybe they're in it together," Brownie said.

"And share the real IOU?" Sid snorted. "The Marks?"

The Marks… Something clicked into place. "Hang on," I said, and explained my newborn theory. Getting them on board was easy—the hard part was deciding what to do next.

***

Once the convention ended and the Cowpokes took off, the weekend was scheduled to end as it began, with drinks for the special guests, but only Melody, Lulu, Brownie, and I joined Terry in the saloon.

"No Marks?" Melody said.

"They wanted to hit the road right away," Terry said. "What can I get everybody?"

Once we were served, Brownie said, "I propose a toast: To Ruben."

We clinked glasses and sipped.

A few minutes later, Eve showed up. "Sorry I'm late. I had something to take care of." I didn't need the nudge from Sid-in-the-bag to recognize my cue.

I said, "What will you do now, Melody?"

She shrugged. "I've got books to sell, and I'll keep the website going, plus some shows are still interested in the exhibits. Dad always said *Cowtown* was his life—I guess it's mine, too."

"What about Arabella's IOU?"

"Dad wanted Lulu to have it."

The older woman patted the locket she still wore. "I'll treasure it always."

"Lulu," I said, "you told me you didn't usually travel with Ruben. Why this time?"

"It sounded like such fun. And maybe I had a premonition that this might be the last time…" She sniffled and put a napkin to her eyes.

"So it had nothing to do with the Marks?"

"Excuse me?"

"It's just that while Ruben crossed paths with all the Marks on the convention circuit, this was the first time in a while that the three were together. Quite a coincidence that it happened at the event where Arabella's IOU went missing."

"What are you talking about?" Melody said. "Lulu's wearing the IOU."

"She's wearing *a* locket, not *the* locket. That one is a phony." I had my copy of *Cowtown Companion*, and opened it to one of the photo pages. "See that scratch under the *U*? And here's a picture from Thursday night. Same scratch. Does that locket have one?"

I'm sure Lulu didn't want to hand the locket to Melody but couldn't think of an innocent excuse not to.

Melody examined it long enough to make me nervous before finally saying, "You're right—there's no scratch."

"I noticed it when I found Ruben," I said, taking credit for Sid's observations, "but wanted to be sure before saying anything. So Brownie and I started asking around, and we found out who has the real IOU."

"It's Quale, isn't it?" Melody said. "Him and his fake sympathy!"

"Quale has it, but he didn't steal it. He bought it. Isn't that right, Lulu?"

She'd had time to prepare for the question. "I'm sorry, Melody. Georgia's right. I did sell it to Mark."

"How could you?"

"I need the money. You must realize your father didn't leave much."

"It didn't take you long to figure that out!"

"Ruben would understand. He's still taking care of me, even now."

"What about the phony IOU?" I asked.

"Ruben gave it to me that last night to commemorate my first *Cow-town* event. Then we celebrated by—" She looked demurely away. "Of course, Ruben took the locket off for *that*. He must have picked up the wrong one afterward." Lulu glanced around, gauging our reactions. "I hope our… I hope our celebration didn't bring on the heart attack, but we'll never know." She sniffled again. "I know it seems heartless, but since Ruben left Arabella's IOU to me, I had every right to sell it."

I raised my voice to ask, "To three different people?"

Lulu froze as all three Marks emerged from where they'd been hiding, awaiting my signal. Quale was red with anger, Panello's jaw was clenched, and Baxter had gone pale. When I first met them, I'd resisted Marx Brothers references, but totally missed the other joke. The three men had been marks for Lulu's con game.

"You had four replicas made," I said, "three with scratches to sell to the Marks, one without to 'prove' that you were keeping a fake. Then you asked them to keep their acquisitions secret so as not to tarnish Ruben's memory. You knew they'd slip up eventually, but by then you'd be long gone with the genuine IOU."

Since Lulu didn't respond, I continued. "Melody, did you know that Lulu had three husbands before your father? Each was wealthier than the last, and they all gave her generous divorce settlements." Sid was a whiz at online research. "I'm guessing she went on that cruise looking for Number Four. Ruben didn't usually get gigs that plush, did he?"

Melody said, "Most of the time it was crappy convention centers."

"So Lulu must have thought Ruben had more money than he did. Of course, she could have divorced him once she realized the truth, and probably intended to, but not without getting something out of it. She figured that Ruben owed her. Arabella's IOU was her IOU."

Melody said, "I want the real locket back, Lulu!"

"This locket?" Eve pulled the IOU out of her pocket and handed it to her. As soon as Lulu had left her room, Eve had gone inside to search. For once, she hadn't complained about doing something outside her job description. "You better hang onto it until the law decides who really owns it."

I thought that would be the end of it, but Melody said, "One thing I've got to know. Lulu, did you remind Dad to take his heart medicine?"

Lulu's hand tightened on her wineglass stem until it snapped, but she didn't speak.

***

Dealing with the police's questions filled the rest of the afternoon. It would take time for the medical examiner to determine the level of heart medicine in Ruben's body, but after the police saw that the pills in his bottle weren't the ones he'd been prescribed, they took Lulu into custody.

I expected to head home after that, but Brownie said, "Why don't you and Sid take a last look around while I haul the bags out to the camper?"

Sid was delighted, of course. With the Cowpokes long gone, the place was so empty I wouldn't have been surprised to see tumbleweeds blowing past—maybe Terry would order some. A little while later, Brownie texted.

BROWNIE: Meet me at the stable.

Considering my last visit, I was glad he was waiting outside. I was less pleased that he was accompanied by Eve and two horses, one of whom was Minnie.

"I thought we'd finally go for that ride," Brownie said.

I didn't love the idea, but my bag was vibrating. Brownie got me up on Minnie, making sure I had Sid positioned for optimum viewing, before mounting himself. Then Eve helped him tie a canvas laundry sack and a shopping bag to his saddle.

"Hey Georgia, don't fall off this time," Eve said before going inside.

"What's in the bags?" I asked.

"Hey! That's the rest of me!" Sid said. The sack started wriggling.

"Stop, you'll spook the horses," Brownie said.

The wriggling subsided. "What's the big idea of bone-napping me?"

"I thought you might enjoy a full-body horseback ride," Brownie said.

"Oh. Thanks, pardner."

Brownie set off, and fortunately Minnie followed. Once we were out of sight of anything but flora and fauna, he slowed to a stop.

"Now what?" I asked.

"Wait and see." He dismounted, helped me do the same, got the sack from his saddle, and put it on the ground. "The coast is clear, Sid."

The rest of Sid clambered out, and I gave him his skull and hand. His bony face looked mighty confused.

"Ready to ride?" Brownie said.

"You mean I can actually sit on the horse?"

"If you want to."

"Coccyx, I've wanted to ride a horse my whole non-life! Georgia, get a picture!"

While I played paparazza, Brownie explained the basics of mounting and controlling Minnie, who seemed to like Sid more than she did me. Once Sid could handle the reins, Brownie handed him the shopping bag. "A true Cowpoke needs a hat."

Smiling as widely as I'd ever seen him, Sid pulled out a white cowboy hat and settled it on his skull.

"Georgia, you can ride with me," Brownie said.

"No, thanks," I said, heading for a handy boulder.

"Are you sure?"

"Positive. Riding is a Cowpoke thing."

Brownie remounted. "Which way, Sid?"

"West, of course. I've always wanted to ride off into the sunset."

And away they rode!

Eventually they'd find out that neither one of them was a true Cowpoke, but not from me. Nor would I mention that they were actually going southeast.

Afterword

"The Skeleton Rides a Horse" is part of the Family Skeleton series, which I write as Leigh Perry, and takes place after the events of *The Skeleton Stuffs a Stocking*. Since it was originally written for an anthology of stories inspired by the Marx Brothers, the names came from Marx Brothers movies and trivia. (Minnie was the Marx Brothers' mother.) But once again, I blew the word length, so I sold it to *Ellery Queen Mystery Magazine*. I really ought to pay more attention to anthology requirements.

In the afterword for "Sleeping with the Plush" I mentioned that Treasure Hunt from that story appears in the Family Skeleton series, but there's also a connection with my Where Are They Now? books. In *Who Killed the Pinup Queen?*, the actress who played Arabella in the fictional TV show *Cowtown* is murdered and two characters in that story are building a dude ranch in Massachusetts. That dude ranch became the setting for this story.

The Skeleton Rides a Horse and Other Stories

THE SKELETON RIDES *a Horse and Other Stories* by Toni L.P. Kelner also writing as Leigh Perry is printed on 60-pound paper, and is designed by Jeffrey Marks using InDesign. The type is Garamond, a group of fonts named for French engraver Claude Garamond. The cover is by Gail Cross. The first edition was published in a perfect-bound softcover edition and one hundred copies of the clothbound edition accompanied by a separate pamphlet of Toni L.P. Kelner's "An Unmentionable Crime." *The Skeleton Rides a Horse and Other Stories* was printed by Southern Ohio Printing Company and bound by Cincinnati Bindery. The book was published in July 2024 by Crippen & Landru Publishers.

Sources

"Murchison Solves a Mystery" Originally published in *Murderous Intent Mystery Magazine*, Spring 1995.

"Where Does a Herd of Elephants Go?" Originally published in *Midnight Louie's Pet Detectives* edited by Carole Nelson Douglas, Jan. 1998.

"Security Blanket" Originally published in *Riptide: Crime Stories by New England Writers* edited by Skye Alexander, Kate Flora, and Susan Oleksiw, Fall 2004. Reprinted in *The Mystery Megapack: 25 Modern and Classic Mystery Stories*, April 2011.

"Sleeping With the Plush" Originally published in *Alfred Hitchcock Mystery Magazine*, May 2006.

"Skull and Cross-Examinations" Originally published in *Ellery Queen Mystery Magazine*, Feb. 2008.

"Kangaroo Court" Originally published in *Alfred Hitchcock Mystery Magazine*, May 2008.

"Kids Today" Originally published in *Damn Near Dead 2: Live Noir or Die Trying* edited by Bill Crider, Nov. 2010.

"Bell, Book, and Candlepin" Originally published in *Games Creatures Play* edited by Charlaine Harris and Toni L.P. Kelner, April 2014.

"Now Hiring Nasty Girlz" Originally published in *Ellery Queen Mystery Magazine*, Jan./Feb. 2020.

"Rage Warehouse—Ire Proof" Originally published in *Ellery Queen Mystery Magazine*, May/June 2020.

"Nasty" Originally published in *Shattering Glass* edited by Heather Graham, June 2020.

"The Skeleton Rides a Horse" Originally published in *Ellery Queen Mystery Magazine*, Sept./Oct. 2022.

CHAPBOOK

"An Unmentionable Crime" Originally published in *Magnolias and Mayhem* edited by Jeffrey Marks, Jan. 2000. Reprinted in *Crooked as a Dog's Hind Leg*, Sept. 2015.

Crippen & Landru, Publishers
P. O. Box 532057
Cincinnati, OH 45253
Web: www.Crippenlandru.com
E-mail: orders@crippenlandru.com

Previous
Crippen & Landru
Publications

Challenge the Impossible: The Impossible Files of Dr. Sam Hawthorne by Edward D. Hoch. Full cloth in dust jacket, signed and numbered by Josh Pachter, $45.00. Trade softcover, $19.00.

Nothing Is Impossible: Further Problems of Dr. Sam Hawthorne by Edward D. Hoch. Full cloth in dust jacket, signed and numbered by the publisher, $45.00. Trade softcover, $19.00.

Swords, Sandals And Sirens by Marilyn Todd. Full cloth in dust jacket, signed and numbered by the author, $45.00. Trade softcover, $19.00.

All But Impossible: The Impossible Files of Dr. Sam Hawthorne by Edward D. Hoch. Full cloth in dust jacket, signed and numbered by the publisher, $45.00. Trade softcover, $19.00.

Sequel to Murder by Anthony Gilbert, edited by John Cooper. Full cloth in dust jacket, $29.00. Trade softcover, $19.00.

Hildegarde Withers: Final Riddles? by Stuart Palmer with an introduction by Steven Saylor. Full cloth in dust jacket, $29.00. Trade softcover, $19.00

Shooting Script by William Link and Richard Levinson, edited by Joseph Goodrich. Full cloth in dust jacket, signed and numbered by the families, $47.00. Trade softcover, $22.00.

The Man Who Solved Mysteries by William Brittain with an introduction by Josh Pachter. Full cloth in dust jacket, $29.00. Trade softcover, $19.00.

Constant Hearses and Other Revolutionary Mysteries by Edward D. Hoch. Full cloth in dust jacket, signed and numbered by Brian Skupin, $45.00. Trade softcover, $19.00.

SUBSCRIBERS AGREE TO purchase each forthcoming publication, either the Regular Series or the Lost Classics or (preferably) both. Collectors can thereby guarantee receiving limited editions, and readers won't miss any favorite stories.

Subscribers receive a discount of 20% off the list price (and the same discount on our backlist) and a specially commissioned short story by a major writer in a deluxe edition as a gift at the end of the year.

The point for us is that, since customers don't pick and choose which books they want, we have a guaranteed sale even before the book is published, and that allows us to be more imaginative in choosing short story collections to issue.

That's worth the 20% discount for us. Sign up now and start saving. Email us at orders@crippenlandru.com or visit our website at www.crippenlandru.com on our subscription page.

Catch up with Sid

www.ingramcontent.com/pod-product-compliance
Lightning Source LLC
Chambersburg PA
CBHW061923220726
48287CB00018B/839